There was no sign of Bitsy.

"Why don't I go back for Bitsy?" I suggested. "Maybe she's having trouble with the faucet or so...

M

th

a

T

B

to

th

g

sy

si

sc

he

rs.

d

th

d.

t.

e

ly

er

ie

t-

a

g

n

r.

Look for these and other books
in the Sleepover Friends Series:

SLEEPOVER FRIENDS

Lauren's New Friend

Susan Saunders

AN
APPLE
PAPERBACK

SCHOLASTIC INC.
New York Toronto London Auckland Sydney

ISBN 0-590-43194-3

Copyright © 1990 by Daniel Weiss Associates, Inc. All rights reserved. Published by Scholastic Inc. APPLE PAPERBACKS is a registered trademark of Scholastic Inc. SLEEPOVER FRIENDS is a registered trademark of Daniel Weiss Associates, Inc.

12 11 10 9 8 7 6 5 4 3   0 1 2 3 4 5/9

Printed in the U.S.A.   28

First Scholastic printing, May 1990

Chapter
1

"I sure don't need anybody to show *me* how to tie knots, or blaze a trail," Wayne Miller bragged from the back of the school bus. "Or start a camp fire in a rainstorm. I can start a camp fire with sticks, I can even start a camp fire with rocks!"

"How long can he keep this up?" Stephanie Green moaned under her breath.

Patti Jenkins looked at her watch. "We left town at about six-fifteen, and it's a quarter to seven now — about thirty minutes so far."

"Three buses going to Silver Maples Park, and we have to get the one with the dreaded Wayne Miller!" Kate Beekman muttered.

"He wasn't on it when we got on," I pointed out. I'm Lauren Hunter, and I'd noticed Wayne and

1

his best friend, Ronny Wallace, sort of hanging around the parking lot as the rest of the kids loaded up. They seemed to be watching us out of the corner of their eyes, as if they were waiting for us to choose our bus.

" . . . but when it comes to picking up papers and tin cans and garbage," Wayne rattled on, "no way! Cleaning is for women!"

"He'd change his mind if he got a look at your room, Lauren!" Stephanie said with a grin.

All four of us burst into giggles at the thought, because my room is usually a major disaster area.

Wayne Miller paused just long enough to scowl in our direction — I guess he thinks girls can be *seen*, but they're definitely not supposed to be heard. Then his mouth went into high gear again. "Cooking is for women, too. I mean, I'll catch the fish, all right — I've caught ten-pounders, easy. And I can clean 'em with my hunting knife. But cooking? Forget it! Real men don't cook!"

"Oh, yeah?" Kate said quietly. "My dad would be very surprised to hear that!" Dr. Beekman is a fabulous cook — even his *leftovers* are terrific!

"Wayne, would you ple-ease cut the yapping?" Mark Freedman said, adjusting the volume on his Walkman. "You're drowning out the game!" Mark's in 5B at Riverhurst Elementary with Kate, Stephanie, Patti, and me. Fortunately, Wayne Miller is normally in 5C.

"Those rocks you've started a fire with, Wayne?" Henry Larkin said innocently. "Where did you find them? In your head?"

"Let's get out of here," Mark said before Wayne could think up a smart answer. "This guy's starting to repeat himself."

And the two of them walked up the aisle to squeeze in next to Larry Jackson, who was dozing in a seat in front of us.

"Sure — go sit with the girls!" Wayne taunted.

"That will do, Wayne!" Mrs. Mead said firmly from her place just behind the driver. Mrs. Mead is the 5B teacher. Mrs. Milton is Wayne's teacher. I don't know how she takes him on a daily basis. Actually, I was beginning to wonder how we could stand him for two whole days.

All the fifth-graders at Riverhurst Elementary School were traveling to Silver Maples Park, along with the three fifth-grade teachers and a group of parents. The park would be closed to everybody else, just for the weekend. We'd be spending Saturday and Sunday helping the rangers pick up litter, plant new trees where there was a forest fire last year, and take

3

care of orphaned animals the rangers had rescued.

We were also going to have cookouts and go on nature walks. Stephanie planned to do some sketching, Kate and I had brought cameras along, and Patti would be collecting water samples for the Quarks, a science club for super-smart kids at school. We figured we'd have a great time — if Wayne and Ronny and a few others like David Degan would just cool it.

I swiveled around a little to check them out. David was leaning against the window on the long backseat. He's short and stocky, with sort of reddish-blond hair, and he's always wearing those green-and-brown splotched army shirts. Ronny was sitting next to him. He's a skinny kid with a crew cut, freckles, and a long nose that is usually runny. Ronny has lots of allergies.

Then there's Wayne. Wayne weighs about forty pounds more than anybody else in fifth grade. He has pale brown hair that always looks greased down with something. He has a perfectly round head, even rounder cheeks, shiny little brown eyes . . . Stephanie once said his eyes look like raisins stuck in an oatmeal cookie. And Wayne is a burper! He swallows a bunch of air, then slowly lets it out in the longest, loudest burps you ever heard. Gross.

"Just what are you looking at, twerp?" Wayne suddenly asked.

Twerp! I was ready to jump up and screech, "When you call me twerp, son, you'd better be sure you *smile!*" But Kate tugged at the back of my shirt. "Not you — Bitsy Barton."

Sure enough, Bitsy peeped nervously, "Uh . . . I wasn't looking at anything, Wayne. S-Sorry."

"Well — watch it!" Wayne growled.

"Tell about the bear, Wayne!" Ronny suggested eagerly.

Wayne launched into another wild story about camping with his dad in the mountains, and the ferocious bear he'd chased away from the tent all by himself, blah, blah, blah. . . .

"Can you believe she's his cousin?" Stephanie murmured, glancing over her shoulder at Bitsy, who was huddled in the corner of a bus seat behind a gray canvas tote. She looked as though she were trying to get smaller and smaller until she disappeared altogether.

Kate, Patti, and I shook our heads. Bitsy Barton is half Wayne's size, with a small, triangular face, and lots of curly dark-brown hair. She hardly ever opens her mouth, except to apologize for something completely unnecessarily.

"Poor thing. Has she always been this way —
so timid?" Patti asked in a low voice to Kate and me.
Kate and I have lived in Riverhurst forever, but Patti
and Stephanie are more or less newcomers.

Kate nodded. "Bitsy, Lauren, and I were in the
same kindergarten class together. Bitsy sat in a corner
and sobbed for the first two months."

"Then she made sort of a hideout for herself in
a big cardboard box, and we didn't see her again
until May," I added.

"She hid under the table at my seventh-birthday
party," Kate remembered. "She doesn't really have
any friends, and she never invites anyone over to her
house."

"Of course, growing up next door to Wayne
Miller could definitely do that to you," I said. "Can
you think of anything more embarrassing than having
old Wayne across the fence, burping his head off?
Plus Bitsy has two older brothers just like him — Biff
and Bob, on the high school wrestling team. And
two younger brothers, too. She's probably never had
a chance to get a word in edgewise."

"Barry Barton's in Horace's class — he's a real
bully," Patti said. Horace is Patti's little brother, and
an okay kid for a six-year-old genius.

6

" . . . girls can't handle the great outdoors!"
Wayne's voice drowned us out again. "Scares 'em
to death! Snakes, lizards, even your basic bugs send
'em screaming. . . ."

"On the other hand, girls aren't so bad at *some*
things," Henry Larkin interrupted slyly. "What about
the Bike-a-thon, Wayne?" He was talking about the
time Stephanie, Kate, and I beat Wayne in a bike
race around Riverhurst.

"Just luck! One of my tires went flat, and . . ."
Wayne mumbled, his round cheeks shading into a
dark red.

"Maybe these girls can't start a campfire with
rocks" — Henry waved his hand at the four of us —
"but I'll bet they can beat you at practically anything
else!" Henry has always been pretty good about
sticking up for us. Maybe it's because he and Patti
seem to be sort of interested in each other. He's a
great guy, but he wasn't helping matters. His comments just egged Wayne on.

"Dream on!" Wayne roared, an awful smile on
his face. "Hunting? Fishing?"

"Let's stick to the normal stuff." Mark Freedman
had turned off his Walkman to peer over the seat at
Wayne, Ronny, and David. "Like a baseball game."

"Give me a break!" Wayne snickered. "Girls are going to beat boys at baseball?"

"Instead of *us* giving *you* a break, how about *you* giving *us* a *game*?" I snapped. Kate looked at me with her "I-can't-believe-you-said-that" expression, but I'd had about enough of Wayne's attitude.

"Way to go, Lauren!" Mark said approvingly.

"When?" asked Wayne.

"Tomorrow afternoon!" Henry answered. "Lauren can be the captain of one team, and you can be the captain of the other, Wayne. Lauren, I'll catch for you."

"I'll play shortstop," Mark offered.

"No boys!" Wayne said, shaking his head. "What'll that prove?"

"No problem," I said. "Sally Mason is a great catcher, and Jane Sykes can be shortstop." Plus Robin Becker in 5C is a terrific fielder, and Patti can knock balls clear out of the playground at Riverhurst Elementary. Even Stephanie has a pretty good pitching arm; she could back me up. Kate, of course, would rather chill out on the sidelines, but I was pretty sure I could come up with an excellent team by Saturday afternoon.

"If we can't play, Mark and I will cheer you on," Henry said with a grin.

8

"Two, four, six, eight, who do we appreciate?" Mark chanted. "Girls, girls, girls!"

Even Mrs. Mead smiled at that one. I wasn't sure whether it was because the boys were such big fans, or because they wanted to irk Wayne, but it was nice all the same.

But Wayne was frowning — maybe he'd remembered seeing Sally and Jane and me playing on the Blaney Realty Little League team a couple of years ago.

"I didn't bring a ball with me," he said, starting to waffle. "And there's not enough space at the park. Too many trees. I guess we'll have to postpone it."

"I brought a ball," Mark said. "I even have a couple of gloves in my backpack — there's a field right behind the administration building, and the rangers have some baseball equipment, remember?" Mark's such a baseball freak, he'd take a ball and a glove along on a trip to the South Pole.

"Heads up!" Mr. Kreski the bus driver announced, interrupting our conversation. "Silver Maples Park, next stop!"

"Yay!" Everyone yelled and clapped as we turned off the highway onto a narrow gravel road.

The bus clattered around a curve, startling a bunch of noisy blue jays. It rolled past a family of fat cottontails, having their evening snack of weeds, and swung through a gate. It braked to a stop next to a tiny log hut, where you check into the park.

A ranger stepped out of the hut, straightening his hat. He smiled up at us and boomed, "Welcome to Silver Maples. I'm Ranger Richard Dalton."

Chapter 2

"Wow! I'll bet he can catch a *twenty*-pound fish *with his bare hands!*" Stephanie exclaimed, staring out the window at Ranger Dalton. He was tanned, dark-haired, and about the size of your average professional football player.

"And chase off a bear at the same time!" I added.

Wayne Miller let loose with a burp, to show *he* wasn't in the least impressed. Thank heavens it wasn't a loud one.

Mrs. Mead and Mr. Kreski leaned out their windows to say a few words to Ranger Dalton. Then he motioned the bus on.

"Children, please remain in your seats until we've stopped in the parking lot," Mrs. Mead called out over the uproar. Hardly anyone heard her. Everybody was too busy shouting, "There are the picnic tables!" "And a playground!" "And a stream!" as we bumped down the road.

"The Pond Trail," Patti said, thinking of her water samples when we passed the signpost.

"See the baseball field?" Mark Freedman stuck in for Wayne's benefit.

Then we turned into the parking lot. The other two buses were already unloading, with crowds of kids milling around them. A bunch of frazzled parents were huddled together to one side, studying sheets of yellow paper.

As soon as our bus lurched to a stop and the doors were cranked open, Kate, Stephanie, Patti, and I shot out of our seats and scooted down the aisle.

"I know Mark means well, but I wish he hadn't started this," Kate muttered. "Or you, either, Lauren — if Wayne beats us tomorrow, we'll never live it down!"

"He won't beat us," I said, sounding as convincing as I could.

" . . . unless he gets Pete Stone and Kyle Hubbard and — " Patti began.

"Kyle wouldn't play on Wayne's team!" Kate declared. She and Kyle were in the same fourth-grade

12

class last year, so they know each other pretty well.

"Pete Stone wouldn't, either," I said. Pete and I have had our differences, but I didn't think he'd stoop so low.

"What about Charlie Garner? And Bobby Krieger?" Stephanie asked. "They're both excellent hitters."

We didn't have any more time to worry about the boys' team, though, because Sally Mason yelled, "Kate, Lauren, hey, guys! Over here!" as soon as we dashed down the steps.

Sally's in our class, too. She was standing next to her mom, who was looking even more worried than usual. Mrs. Mason is a small woman with bright blue eyes that blink a lot when she's nervous, which is most of the time. But she's very nice, and she was going to be in charge of our cabin for the weekend.

"Good, good." Mrs. Mason glanced up from her yellow sheet of paper long enough to nod a quick greeting when we hurried over. "Kate, Lauren, Stephanie, Patti . . ." She checked off our names. "And Sally, of course." Another check. "Six girls and one adult per cabin. But where is number six?" She peered anxiously around.

"Who *is* number six, Mom? Judy Fisher, right?" Sally said. Judy's in 5C. She's funny, always telling jokes, and she's not a bad baseball player, either.

"No, Judy came down with the flu at the last minute, and some of the girls got shifted around. Our number six is little Bitsy Barton," Mrs. Mason answered, her eyes searching the clumps of kids in the parking area.

"I never thought I'd be having a Friday night sleepover with Bitsy Barton," Kate murmured to me.

Neither did I. Of course, up until last year, it would have been hard for me to imagine having a Friday night sleepover with anybody but Kate.

Kate and I live practically next door to each other on Pine Street in Riverhurst. We started playing together while we were still in diapers. By kindergarten we were best friends, and that's when the sleepovers started.

Every Friday night, Kate and I would take turns sleeping at each other's house. It got to be such a regular thing that Dr. Beekman named us the Sleepover Twins.

Not that there's anything twinlike about Kate and me. We don't look alike: Kate's small and blonde, I'm tall and dark. And we sure don't *act* alike. Kate's as neat as I am messy. She's always sensible; I have a pretty active imagination. I'm kind of a jock, Kate hates to get sweaty.

But in spite of our differences — or maybe because of them — we've spent thousands of hours together without a single major disagreement. We graduated from kid games of Dress-up and School to Truth or Dare, from cherry Kool-Pops to Kate's super-fudge and my special dip, from dopey fifties reruns on Channel 3 to film festivals on Channel 24. In all that time we never had a real fight.

Then, the summer before last, Stephanie moved to Riverhurst from the city. The Greens bought a house at the other end of Pine Street, and Stephanie and I got to be friends because we were both in 4A, Mr. Civello's class.

Stephanie was lots of fun. She told great stories about her life back in the city, and she had terrific ideas about hairstyles and clothes. By fourth grade, she already had her own personal look, like almost always wearing red, black, and white, which goes great with her black hair. I thought Stephanie was really special, and I wanted Kate to get to know her, too, so I invited her to a sleepover at my house.

Total bummer! Kate wrote off Stephanie as a complete airhead who could only talk about shopping. Stephanie thought Kate was a stuffy know-it-all. My older brother, Roger, said the problem was obvious: "They're too much alike, both bossy!"

But I can be pretty stubborn myself. Since all three of us live on Pine Street, I arranged it so that we ended up riding our bikes to school at the same time. Then Kate and I just happened to run into Stephanie at the mall a few Saturdays in a row, and we hung out together for an hour or so. Finally, when Stephanie invited me to spend a Friday night at her house, I said only if I could bring Kate. And I made Kate go with me.

She had to admit it wasn't so bad. We ate a platterful of Mrs. Green's peanut-butter chocolate-chip cookies. Plus we watched three movies in a row on Stephanie's private TV, and Kate's crazy about movies. The next time it was Kate's turn to have the sleepover, she asked Stephanie to come, too. Little by little, the Sleepover Twins became a threesome.

Not that Stephanie and Kate agreed about everything. Half the time I'd find myself caught in the middle of a pretty lively argument. That's just one of the reasons I was glad when Patti Jenkins showed up this year in Mrs. Mead's class.

Patti's from the city, too, although she's as low-key and quiet as Stephanie is bubbly and outgoing.

Patti's also one of the smartest kids in fifth grade, plus one of the nicest. And she's even taller than I am, which is a welcome change, since I tower over Stephanie and Kate.

Kate and I liked Patti a lot. Who wouldn't? When Stephanie wanted to have her be a part of our gang, Kate and I both agreed. Now there were *four* Sleepover Friends!

The four of us have had a sleepover together practically every Friday night since then, but this was our first at Silver Maples Park. And it was definitely our first with Bitsy Barton!

"There she is . . . I think." Stephanie pointed toward the rear of one of the buses, at what looked like a big gray canvas tote on skinny little legs.

"That's her," I said. "I recognize her feet." When Bitsy is really working at disappearing, her toes start to turn in. And the toes of the sneakers at the bottom of the legs were definitely facing each other.

"I'll get her, Mom," Sally Mason said, wading through the mob toward the gray tote.

"Kyle Hubbard! Bobby Krieger! Wayne Miller!" Mr. Jackson, Larry's dad, was yelling from one corner of the parking lot.

Robin Becker's mother was calling out, "Angela

Kemp! Barbara Paulsen! Karen Sims!'' from another corner.

The crowd of kids was slowly organizing itself into fifteen or so groups of six kids and one adult each.

Then Sally was back, with Bitsy lagging behind her. "Bitsy . . . how nice." Mrs. Mason smiled vaguely and glanced down at her yellow paper again. "Let me see . . . boys' cabins on the north side of the parking lot, girls' cabins on the south side. . . . But which is south?" She wrinkled her forehead, truly puzzled.

I wasn't any help — my sense of direction is rotten. I can get turned around in Riverhurst, where I've lived all of my life.

But Bitsy mumbled, "I think south is to the right."

"Fine! We'll find our luggage." The drivers had pulled everything out of the buses already, and lined it up beside them. "And then we'll look for our cabin. It's called . . . um" — yellow paper again — "Cardinal."

We trailed along after Mrs. Mason and Sally to pick up their stuff. Then the four of us and Bitsy collected our sleeping bags and backpacks from the pile next to our bus.

"Can I give you a hand with something, Bitsy?" Patti asked helpfully as Bitsy tried to hang on to her tote while she slung two or three bundles over her arms as well.

"I'll carry your tote for you," I said, reaching for it.

"No!" Bitsy said sharply, swinging it away from me.

"Well, excu-u-use us!" Kate murmured, raising an eyebrow.

"S-Sorry . . . I can manage," Bitsy fumbled, and smiled apologetically.

"Onward, girls," Mrs. Mason said, squaring her narrow shoulders. We headed up the dirt path that wove through the trees to the right of the parking lot.

Chapter
3

The cabins strung out along the path were square little boxes with two windows on each side and a small front porch. The sun had almost set, but we could just make out the names painted on the doors of each cabin: Blue Jay, Whippoorwill, Chickadee. . . .

"Here we are," Mrs. Mason said, stopping in front of the fourth cabin. "Cardinal."

We marched up the creaky wooden steps. Mrs. Mason pushed open the door and switched on the bare bulb overhead.

"Ick!" Stephanie said as we looked around. "This isn't exactly a luxury hotel, is it?"

The cabin *was* kind of gloomy. It was divided into two rooms: The front room was barely big enough for six canvas cots set side by side. The back room was even smaller, and it was divided again. A little more than half held Mrs. Mason's cot. The rest of it was a tiny bathroom, with just enough space for a sink and a toilet.

"A whole weekend with no showers?" Kate sounded horrified.

Mrs. Mason blinked nervously a few times. She scanned her sheet of yellow paper before replying brightly, "We're in luck. The showers are in a separate building on Indian Trail, which is just past our cabin. Now — why don't you girls decide where you want to sleep? Then we'll head over to the social hall — that's where we'll be having dinner tonight."

The fifth-graders' parents had prepared the food for that Friday night, since we knew we'd be getting to the park too late to do a real cookout. My mom had sent her curried chicken salad, Mrs. Green had made six dozen peanut-butter chocolate-chip cookies, and Dr. Beekman had broiled up a big pan of honey-dipped spareribs. I wanted us to get to dinner early so we wouldn't miss out on anything. Kate and Stephanie call me the Endless Stomach, but I think I just have a healthy appetite. All that clean outdoor air made me twice as hungry.

I plopped my backpack down on the nearest cot, which happened to be the fourth from the left. Sally chose the one to the right of mine. Kate, Patti, and Stephanie just naturally took the three to the left of mine.

Bitsy hung back until we'd all staked our claims. Then she dropped her bundles on the cot pushed against the far wall, leaning the gray tote carefully against them. She sat down beside the tote, resting her hand on it as though she were afraid it might try to get away from her.

"What's in that tote?" Kate murmured. "The Hope Diamond?"

"Maybe it's her security blanket," Stephanie whispered.

"I'd like to know who we're sharing this cabin with!" Sally exclaimed, pointing at a corner of the raftered ceiling. "Mutant spiders?!"

Zigzagging from one side of the corner to the other was a huge nest of spiderwebs that looked strong enough to trap a small animal.

"Not to worry," Stephanie said breezily. She unzipped her backpack and dragged out a king-size can of Bug-Off. "This'll take care of any creepy-crawlies."

Stephanie snapped off the top, walked over to

22

the webs, aimed, and got ready to fire, but Bitsy suddenly shot off her cot like a rocket. "Don't do that!" she yelped. "They're not hurting you!"

"Maybe not, but if anything waltzed out of that mess, I might hurt *myself*, trying to get away from it," Stephanie replied sensibly.

"I'll take it outside," Bitsy said. While Sally and the four of us exchanged looks, she dashed out the door. She was back in a flash with a large dead branch.

Bitsy might have been timid about people, but she sure wasn't timid about spiders. She used the branch to scoop the webs right out of the corner, and then paraded the whole nasty blob outside.

"Weird," Sally whispered.

Stephanie shrugged, and put her Bug-Off away for the moment. "I guess we'd better get ready. How often do we get to eat dinner with fifty or sixty boys?"

Everyone but Bitsy changed clothes two or three times. We took turns washing our hands and combing our hair and looking at ourselves in the mirror over the sink. Still sitting on her bed, Bitsy ran a comb through her hair.

"At least she's not *under* her bed," Patti whispered.

Mrs. Mason finally insisted, "That's enough

beautifying — we're supposed to be at the social hall by seven-thirty, and it's already seven twenty-five."

"Coming, Mom," Sally said, giving her long brown hair a last swipe.

"Would you mind starting without me?" Bitsy asked. "I want to wash my hands. . . ."

"Spider juice . . ." Stephanie mumbled.

"I'll catch up in a second," Bitsy promised.

"Well — " Mrs. Mason looked at her watch and frowned — "all right, but please hurry. We're supposed to head back to the parking lot, and turn north on Willow Way, then left at the fork . . ." She sighed and folded up her sheet of yellow paper.

"Just follow the crowds, Bitsy," Sally said.

"We'll walk very slowly, until you catch up with us," Mrs. Mason added.

There was no way Bitsy could have gotten lost. There were at least a hundred kids all making their way through the twilight to the social hall. But once we'd reached the parking lot, Mrs. Mason insisted that we hang around for several minutes, waiting for Bitsy.

I was starting to get seriously hungry, and plenty annoyed. I could just imagine Larry Jackson and Mark and the other guys, not to mention Wayne Miller, grabbing all the tastiest food, leaving us with Mrs. Mason's zucchini bread, or Mrs. Becker's bean-sprout salad ring.

"Why don't I go back for Bitsy?" I suggested. "Maybe she's having trouble with the faucet or something."

"I'll go with you," said Stephanie, before Mrs. Mason could think of reasons for us not to.

We hurried back up the path, past Blue Jay and the other cabins. There was no sign of Bitsy.

"Maybe she got freaked out about eating with all those people, and she's hiding," Stephanie said.

"She eats in the school cafeteria," I pointed out. Then I remembered Bitsy hunched down under the Beekmans' table.

I bounded up the steps of Cardinal cabin, ready to shove open the door and drag her out from under the bed, or wherever she was, when Stephanie grabbed my arm. "Ssssh!" she barely breathed. "Bitsy's talking to somebody in there! Come on!"

We crept down the steps again to peek into a side window of the cabin. Bitsy was definitely saying *something*, but to whom? She was sitting all alone on her cot. There was nobody else in the room with her.

"You know what?" Stephanie murmured in my ear.

I shook my head.

"I think she's talking to her tote!"

Chapter
4

Talk about *weird*! Bitsy was sitting cross-legged on her cot. She had both arms around her big gray tote, and her head practically stuffed inside it. She seemed to be carrying on a long, involved conversation.

One-sided, though — as far as I could tell, the tote wasn't very chatty. I couldn't make out exactly what Bitsy was saying, either. But whatever it was, it was a lot more than I'd heard her say to any living, breathing human being.

"Can you hear her?" I whispered to Stephanie, who was closer to the window than I was.

Stephanie shook her head. "If we wait a second, maybe she'll talk louder."

But I didn't want to wait a second. I figured

whatever Bitsy was telling her tote, it couldn't be nearly as interesting as Dr. Beekman's spareribs. I could just imagine them disappearing off the table in the social hall at a rate of one rib every ten seconds.

"I'm going in," I told Stephanie.

I'd barely reached the steps, though, when Mrs. Mason, Sally, Kate, and Patti came chugging up the path.

"Did you find her? Is she all right?" Mrs. Mason asked.

"Bitsy's fine, Mrs. Mason." I calmed her down. "She's in the cabin."

"I was afraid she'd taken a wrong turn and was wandering around in the dark." As Mrs. Mason clattered up the steps and through the door, I remembered how Bitsy had known right off which way was south earlier that evening. It was unlikely she'd take a wrong turn.

Still, a wrong turn I could have accepted. I've taken them myself. But a serious discussion with her tote bag? No way!

However, by the time we'd all crowded into the cabin, the tote bag was zipped up tight and leaning against the wall at the head of Bitsy's cot. She was standing on one foot, tying her sneaker.

28

"Oh — hi," she said. "Sorry, really sorry — I broke a shoelace, and I had to change both of them."

"As long as you're okay," Mrs. Mason said, patting Bitsy on the shoulder.

Stephanie and I didn't say a word. What could we say — "Hear any good gossip from your tote bag lately?" But I was afraid Bitsy caught me raising an eyebrow at Stephanie.

Finally, we made it to the social hall, but it was too late for the spareribs. I saw David Degan grab the last two just as we barreled through a side door. Not that there wasn't plenty of other good stuff to eat, such as a baked ham with brown sugar and pineapple slices on it from Patti's mom. "I helped her with it," Patti assured us, because Mrs. Jenkins has had a few major failures in the kitchen. She's a professor at the university in Riverhurst and when she's busy grading papers she sometimes loses her place in the recipe.

Mrs. Freedman had sent fried chicken and deviled eggs; Henry Larkin's granddad had made his special potato salad with bacon and pimentos; Mrs. Mead had mixed up a huge bowl of yummy fruit salad, with blueberries, apples, bananas, oranges, and those tiny marshmallows in it.

The desserts were great: double fudge brownies,

and German chocolate cake, and butterscotch pudding, and cherry pie, just for starters. There were even plenty of Mrs. Green's peanut-butter chocolate-chip cookies left, although some of the guys, like Mark and Henry, got a jump on us by having their desserts first.

I wish I could have enjoyed it all more, but we'd barely filled our paper plates when I noticed Kyle Hubbard in a mumbled conference with Kate.

"Wayne's bribing people," Kate reported back to us. "He offered Kyle a copy of the latest Heat tape" — Heat's one of our favorite rock groups — "and some fishing gear if Kyle would play first base on his team tomorrow. Can you believe it?!"

I could believe it all right. Hadn't Wayne rolled his bike through a bramble thicket in the Bike-a-thon, instead of going around the curve the way he was supposed to? Luckily, the cheater got a bunch of thorns in his tire and it went flat, or he might actually have beaten us.

"Is Kyle going to do it?" Patti asked.

"Kyle's not like that," Kate said.

"*Some* people can be bought, though," Stephanie said. "Check this out." She nodded toward the bowl of punch at one end of a wide table. A grinning

30

Pete Stone had a paper cup of punch in one hand, and with the other he was pumping Wayne's fist up and down.

"I guess Wayne's got his shortstop," I said glumly, my heart sinking. And Pete looked so cute that night, too. He was wearing his striped sweatshirt that I've always liked.

Of course, a lot of girls came up to us and volunteered for our team. Henry and Mark had been spreading the word.

Jane Sykes said Wayne made her gag, and she'd love to be shortstop.

Robin Becker said she was dying to show up David Degan, who lives down the street from her and is always chasing her cat with his dog. "Sign me up for fielder," she said.

Sally would catch, Patti would play first base. Stephanie would play second and help me out with pitching if I needed her.

You'd never guess by looking at Stephanie that she has a mean pitching arm. That evening she wore a long black sweater with little red bows all over it, and had her hair in banana curls. It was hard to imagine her knocking Mr. Civello into the water in the dunking booth at the school fair so many times that he'd advised her to sign with the Mets as soon as possible.

Karen Sims, Tracy Osner . . . even Karla Stamos, who hates sports, said she'd play if I could use her, just to prove "boys aren't necessarily better than girls."

But Wayne had Pete Stone, who is a star of the Riverhurst Elementary School baseball team, and David, who isn't bad, either, and probably Charlie Garner, and Bobby Krieger, and a bunch of other boys who think they *are* naturally better than girls at sports. It kind of took my appetite away.

Before I could get totally dismal thinking about it, Ranger Dalton appeared at the far end of the social hall, carrying a rolled-up movie screen. "Arr-humm!" He cleared his throat loudly for attention. "Hi, boys and girls," he spoke into the silence that followed. "I'm Ranger Richard Dalton, and this is Ranger Annabelle Meyers."

Ranger Meyers was pretty and sporty-looking with short blonde hair.

Stephanie nudged me. "She looks great in khaki, and that's not easy."

"We've put together a slide program for you, to show you a few of the terrific things about Silver

Maples Park, and also to give you an idea about how you'll be helping us out tomorrow and Sunday," Ranger Dalton went on. "So if you'll all face this way, make yourselves comfortable on the wooden benches, or on the floor, we'll turn off the lights and get started."

Sally Mason and the four of us squeezed onto a wooden bench. "Where's Bitsy?" Patti asked.

"I haven't seen her since we got here," I replied. I started thinking how she'd acted in the cabin, talking to her tote. Weird! Then I remembered that Bitsy was Wayne Miller's first cousin. Wasn't that sort of like having a spy in our midst?! Maybe there was a tape recorder in that gray bag, and Bitsy was telling it everything we'd said or done!

Ranger Dalton hit a switch, the overhead lights went out, and the first slide flashed onto the screen at the end of the social hall.

Most of the kids said, "Aaaah!" because it was a really sweet picture of a deer family: a father with antlers, a mother without, and two spotted babies, all drinking from a pond at sunset.

Wayne Miller was slouched on the floor almost twenty feet away from us, but I heard him bellow to David and Ronny, "That buck would make great eating!" I wanted to throttle him. Then Henry Larkin said, "How do you think you'd look to a mountain lion, Wayne? Mighty tasty!" Which shut him up nicely.

We saw pictures of gray owls floating through the woods on huge wings, a red fox bringing home a tasty mouse to its family, a nest of squirrels in a hollow tree, lots of different kinds of birds, even a grinning bobcat, although Ranger Meyers said bobcats are rare at Silver Maples.

Then there was a shot of a big, fat raccoon, caught in the act of turning over a garbage can. He looked so surprised, and at the same time so innocent, that everyone laughed.

"How did you take that picture?" somebody in the audience asked.

"We'd been having a lot of trouble with this particular garbage can — it's at campsite twenty-two," Ranger Meyers explained. "We'd often find it lying on its side, with trash scattered all around it, but we never managed to catch a glimpse of the culprit. So we tied one end of a string to the top of the can, and one end to the shutter of a camera we'd hidden in a tree. And bingo! Our litterer!"

"But raccoons are not our biggest garbage problem in the park — humans are," Ranger Dalton said.

The next group of slides showed a pile of litter at a campsite, a winding stream with three old tires thrown into it, a pond with rusty tin cans lining the banks. "Just a few thoughtless people can ruin the park for the animals who live here, and for everybody who visits," Ranger Meyers added.

"And you boys and girls have been nice enough to volunteer to help us clean up," said Ranger Dalton.

"I'd like to see Wayne argue with him!" Kate murmured, and we all giggled. Standing next to the slide projector, Ranger Dalton looked about seven feet tall.

The rangers showed us some shots of the acres destroyed by fire the year before.

"Not all forest fires are started by careless campers," Rangers Meyers continued. "This one was the result of a bolt of lightning striking a tree during a thunderstorm. We've begun to replant, and you'll be helping us with that, too. Now we'll look at the steps we'll follow to get each of the new little trees off to a good start."

For each plant, Ranger Meyers explained, "You

dig a hole about twice the size of its roots. You fill in some of the hole with damp peat moss, pop in the new plant, and fill in the rest of the hole with the dirt you dug out. Then you firm it all down, and water it.''

"Easy," Sally said. The Masons have a big garden in their backyard.

"Dirty," said Stephanie, wrinkling her nose. "Luckily, I packed some rubber gloves." Stephanie was definitely prepared for The Great Outdoors.

"That's it for tonight," Ranger Dalton announced, switching the lights back on. "We'll be waking you up bright and early tomorrow morning, at six-thirty on the dot."

"Six-thirty!" The social hall echoed with groans.

"Children!" Mrs. Milton, who teaches 5A, stood up and raised her hands for quiet. Everybody says she's the strictest teacher at Riverhurst Elementary. She looked down at the index cards she was holding. "The other teachers, the parents, and I have worked out our schedules. The girls will shower in the evening before bed . . ."

"Wooo-ooo!" Wayne and David and some of the dopier boys hooted and whistled.

Mrs. Milton withered them with a frown. "The boys will shower in the morning, which means they'll have to get up a little before six-thirty," she went on.

"Nyah, nyah!" we said under our breaths.

"Breakfast at seven o'clock tomorrow. At eight, we'll join the rangers in planting new trees. At eleven-thirty we'll break for lunch. The girls will start the camp fires, and prepare the meal."

"See? Girls will be doing the cooking!" Wayne Miller broke in.

"In the early afternoon we'll visit the area where orphaned or wounded birds and animals are housed, and learn how to take care of them. Then, from four to six, you'll have some free time . . . I understand a baseball game is planned?"

Wow! Even old Mrs. Milton knew about the game! My stomach did a flip-flop. If we lost, we lost in front of practically the whole world!

"Tomorrow evening, the boys will prepare our meal," Mrs. Milton said, with a glance in Wayne's direction. He's in her class, so she must have heard all of his routines a million times.

"On Sunday, the rangers will take us on an early nature walk. Then we'll spend the greater part of the morning picking up litter. The parents will provide lunch, we'll have a free hour or two in the afternoon to explore, sticking close to the cabins and the ranger station, of course, and then we'll get on the buses for the ride back to Riverhurst. Any questions?"

Who would have dared to question Mrs. Milton?

"That's all for tonight, then. Let's give Rangers Dalton and Meyers a big round of applause for their slide show, then file out in an orderly fashion," Mrs. Milton told us.

Everyone clapped for the rangers. As soon as we stood up, Mrs. Mason hurried over to collect us. "Where's Bitsy?" she asked anxiously.

"I think she's sitting with Mr. Patterson, Mom," Sally said.

If Mrs. Milton is the strictest teacher at Riverhurst Elementary, Mr. Patterson is the most easygoing. He's the kind of teacher who tells you ahead of time the exact questions you'll be having on a test. He's never sent a single kid to the principal's office, not in the six years he's been in Riverhurst.

Not even Bitsy Barton could be nervous around Mr. Patterson, plus he's her teacher. Which I guess is why she was sticking to him like glue, unless she just wanted to avoid us.

Mrs. Mason pried her loose. "Our cabin is second in line for the showers tonight," she announced after she'd herded the five of us over to Mr. Patterson and Bitsy. "We don't want to be late and lose our places."

"A clean student is a keen student," Mr. Patterson said with a grin. He has a wide, friendly face, and a curly brown mustache.

Bitsy ducked her head, and followed us out.

Chapter 5

As soon as we got back to our cabin, we pulled everything out of our backpacks that we'd need for the showers. I grabbed my soap, shampoo, towel, comb, clean underwear and sweats, and flashlight. On the cot next to mine, Stephanie gathered together more or less the same stuff, plus her Bug-Off. "Spiders, beware," she warned, with an eye on Bitsy.

"I've never seen you get organized in such a hurry," I told her.

"If this place is like the camp I went to a couple of years ago," Stephanie said, "they'll run out of hot water pretty quickly. And I absolutely hate cold showers!"

Mrs. Mason let us go ahead. "Turn left on Indian

Trail. The showers are in a new, shingled building with swinging doors," she told us. "We'll be right behind you."

Stephanie and I hurried down the steps. We switched on our flashlights and started up the dirt path, past a cabin called Mockingbird in which I could see Karla Stamos through the window, reading a book about baseball. Where does she find these things?!

We found the signpost for Indian Trail and had just turned left, as Mrs. Mason had told us to, when I thought I heard something rustling in the bushes. My imagination runs away with me sometimes, so at first I tried to ignore it. I told myself it was just the wind in the trees, but as Stephanie and I walked along, our eyes on the beams of our flashlights, the rustling grew louder.

Stephanie was talking about Bitsy, and how she was basically sort of a cute-looking girl, and all she needed was a different kind of haircut. Stephanie's into makeovers for everybody. I interrupted her to whisper, "Stephanie? Don't you hear something?"

Stephanie shrugged. "Our sneakers on the gravel?" Indian Trail is paved with pebbles.

"No — listen!" I stopped dead, and so did she

a few paces ahead of me. The rustling continued, and now I thought I heard some snuffling, too! It got closer . . . and closer . . . and . . .

Sometimes Stephanie does things that are so unexpected, she totally knocks me out. She whirled around toward the noise, her eyes narrowing. Raising her can of Bug-Off, she pointed it . . . and fired!

Now she's done it! A furious bobcat with bug spray up his snoot is going to jump out of those bushes, right on top of us. The best we can hope for is that the Bug-Off makes his eyes water for a few seconds, and we can climb a tree before his vision clears . . . No, bobcats can climb trees! . . . Run! whirled through my head in about two seconds flat.

But before I could move, the sneezing started, one muffled sneeze after another, until it sounded like a little mechanical train I had inherited from Roger. *Ka-chik-ka-chik-ka-chik-ka-chik!*

"That's not a bobcat!" I said. "That's a . . ."

Stephanie aimed her flashlight into the nearest shrub. "A Ronny Wallace. And . . ."

"Wayne Miller, you creep!" I yelled, shining my light right at his round pink face. "You thought it would be neat to scare some girls half to death on their way to the showers, and laugh your dumb head off about it!"

Only Wayne wasn't laughing. "Chemical weapons!" he complained, wiping his streaming eyes. "Cool it, okay?" he added in a half whisper.

Cool it? "Wayne Miller!" I yelled again, just in case anyone had missed it the first time.

Not fifteen seconds later, Mr. Patterson came thundering up the trail.

"Miller! Wallace! Just what in blazes do you think you're doing out here?!"

"Trying to frighten us, Mr. Patterson," I said in a trembly voice. You think girls are sissies, Wayne? I'll give you girls who are sissies!

"I don't like this — I don't like this one bit!" Mr. Patterson was actually *scowling*. "And Mrs. Wainwright isn't going to like it one bit, either, when I tell her about it on Monday!"

Mrs. Wainwright is the principal at Riverhurst Elementary. For the first time in six years, Mr. Patterson was going to report someone to the principal. Who could possibly be a better candidate than Wayne Miller?

"Do you girls want me to walk you the rest of the way to the shower building?" Mr. Patterson asked.

"No, thank you, Mr. Patterson," Stephanie answered sweetly. "We'll be all right *now*. . . . History in the making!'' she added in a whisper to me. ''A Patterson *first*!''

Mr. Patterson barked, ''March!'' at Wayne and Ronny Wallace, who were still sneezing like crazy.

''Bug-Off certainly took care of *those* worms,'' I said with a giggle as they disappeared down the trail.

We didn't want to talk about Wayne in front of Bitsy, so Stephanie and I had to save our stories. We hadn't had a chance to tell Patti and Kate about the tote, either. Plus Mrs. Mason insisted we all go to bed early that night.

Just before she announced, ''Lights out!'' I had an appetite emergency — I was suddenly *starving*. Stephanie dug through her backpack again and came up with a big bag of chocolate-covered almonds from Sweet Stuff, our favorite candy store in Riverhurst. Stephanie sure had thought of everything.

Sally took a few almonds, so did Patti, and I snagged a handful. Kate and Stephanie were too stuffed from dinner to want any, and Bitsy whispered, ''No, thank you.'' She was scrunched down in her sleeping bag until just the top of her head showed. The mysterious gray tote was on the far side of her cot, jammed between Bitsy and the wall.

After Sally, Patti, and I had helped ourselves to the chocolate almonds, there was still way over half a bag left. Stephanie pushed it into her backpack again, and we all crawled into our own sleeping bags.

"Good night!" Mrs. Mason called from her little room.

That was almost the last thing I heard until morning, except . . . was that the sound of a zipper unzipping, on Bitsy's side of the room, just before I dozed off?

The next morning, at six-thirty on the dot, Ranger Meyers rapped on our door and sang out, "Rise and shine!"

"Unfortunately, there's nothing shining out there!" Kate grumbled, sitting up to peer sleepily out her window. The sun was hidden behind thick clouds. It looked gray and damp outside, the kind of day I like to sleep late. Instead we were going to plant trees, cook lunch . . . not to mention play baseball.

We fell out of bed, moaning and groaning, got dressed, and trudged gloomily toward the picnic area. But Mr. Jackson, Mrs. Becker, and five or six other parents had already started campfires in the round, stone barbecue pits at one side of the clearing.

The smell of sausages and pancakes cooking improved my mood before we even got there.

Mrs. Mason veered off to sit with Mrs. Mead and Mrs. Milton. Bitsy disappeared into the crowd of drowsy kids lining up for food.

Sally and the four of us found a table, and eventually grabbed our food. I had two helpings of whole wheat pancakes, a slice of hoecake with maple syrup, a big paper cup of orange juice, and another of milk.

"I can just feel my face plumping up!" Stephanie said, sucking in her cheeks.

Sally shook her head. "You need lots of carbohydrates for outdoor work."

That was good news. Stephanie and I both shared one of Mr. Jackson's buttermilk biscuits when he passed them around.

"Hey, look — I think Wayne's giving Bitsy a hard time," Kate said. The two of them were standing by themselves, past the last barbecue pit. Wayne was leaning forward and waving his finger under Bitsy's nose.

"I think *she's* giving *him* information," I said.

Finally, Stephanie and I had the chance to tell the story of Bitsy and the gray tote bag. We threw in the episode with Wayne and Ronny in the woods for a little comedy. Then I mentioned my idea about maybe Bitsy keeping a tape recorder in her tote, to spy for Wayne.

"A tape recorder?" Kate raised an eyebrow, which meant, "Lauren — your imagination!" But she admitted, "There is something strange about that tote."

"I wish we could get a peek inside it," Sally said.

"We can't!" Patti was shocked. "It's Bitsy's, and it's private."

"I know, I know," Sally said. "Still . . ."

I knew exactly how she felt.

After we'd finished eating, we dumped our plates and cups and forks into trash cans and hurried back to our cabin to get ready for planting. That's when we discovered that considerably more than Bitsy's tote was weird.

Stephanie was reaching into her backpack for the gloves she'd brought to keep her hands from getting dirty. "Lauren!" she exclaimed, "I know you have a hollow leg, but did you have to eat the paper bag, too? I do have more candy in here somewhere."

I was pulling on my warmest sweater, but I stopped midway to reply, "What are you talking about?!"

Stephanie was holding the green-and-white bag from Sweet Stuff, the one the chocolate-covered almonds had been in. The bag was completely empty but the top was still closed tight. Not only that, there was a sizable hole in the side of it.

"I didn't do it!" I said. "The only almonds I've eaten were the ones you gave us last night."

"Me, too," Sally and Patti said.

"Don't look at me," said Kate. "Mutant spiders?"

There was a loud thud in the far corner of the room. All five of us turned around to stare at Bitsy.

Chapter
6

"S-Sorry. I dropped my hiking boot . . . ," Bitsy
said. She was quick to add, "I didn't eat your candy.
I can't eat sugar at all — I have problems with my
teeth."

So why was she blushing?

Stephanie shrugged, and all of us turned around
to check out the Sweet Stuff bag again.

"Mice?" Patti suggested, poking her finger in the
hole in the side.

"Where?" Stephanie shrieked. I think she would
have jumped up onto her canvas cot if it hadn't been
so flimsy. Kate didn't look very happy, either. She
glanced uneasily into the darker corners of the cabin.

"Not *now*," Patti told them. "Mice sleep in the

49

daytime. Maybe there was one roaming around last night."

"Yuck!" Stephanie shuddered. "Tonight I'll bring my luggage to bed with me. And the next time we come to Silver Maples, I'll be sure to pack a mousetrap, too!"

There was a loud, irritated sigh from the back of the room.

"Insect sprays, mousetraps — what next?!" Bitsy muttered as she stamped past us in her hiking boots and out the door.

"I just don't know," said Sally, shaking her head.

All the fifth-graders, the three teachers, and some of the parents met the rangers outside the old social hall.

"I'm sure you remember the slides we saw last night that showed us how to plant," Ranger Meyers said from the front steps. "The section of Silver Maples Park that was destroyed by fire is just a short distance away, and the new seedlings have already been trucked there. So if everybody's ready . . ."

"Ready!" we all sang out.

"Great! Let's hit the trail!" said Ranger Dalton. We started off at a brisk pace. Once we'd left the campgrounds behind, we hiked for a while next to a clear, fast-running stream. Patti scooped out a water sample for the Quarks to look at back in Riverhurst.

"Where does the stream begin?" she asked Ranger Dalton, who was answering questions up and down the line of hikers.

"At a spring named Napateague by the Indians," he said, "farther back in the hills. The stream bubbles out of the spring, tumbles down a cliff in a pretty little waterfall, and races through some rapids. It levels out and widens into a pond we'll be passing, narrows again along here, and finally flows into the Pequontic." The Pequontic is the *river* in *River*hurst.

We walked past the pond — another water sample for Patti — and Kate snapped a picture of a red-shouldered hawk that was sitting on a dead branch, hunting for frogs. She had the small camera her uncle Paul had given her. I hadn't brought my dad's Polaroid along that day because I wasn't sure what I'd do with it while we planted.

We turned away from the pond, and the land started to slope uphill. Suddenly, it was as though we'd crossed an invisible line. On one side was the lush, green forest. On the other was a desert as gray as the clouds overhead, where nothing was living.

Oh, there might have been a few blades of grass popping up, and some mosses, and a twig here and there with a couple of leaves. But basically the forest fire had wiped out everything living. It was scary, like the end of the world or something.

The rangers led us over to a long, flat trailer hitched to a park truck. The trailer was absolutely crammed with little plants in tan paper containers.

"These are our seedlings," Ranger Meyers said. "I think you'll notice that there are lots of different kinds of plants here. That's because there are so many different kinds of plants in the forest, and we want to restore this burned area so that it looks as natural as possible."

"If we planted one evergreen after another, we'd end up with a Christmas tree farm," Ranger Dalton added with a smile. "The wildlife wouldn't be comfortable with it. Instead we'll plant oaks and maples, of course, some evergreens, like pines and firs, and even low bushes, like wild blueberries, which will give the birds and animals food as well as shelter."

In the back of the truck was a large water tank, plus little buckets of peat moss, trowels, and watering cans. "I think we'll divide into teams of three each," Ranger Meyers said. "A peat moss person, a planter, and a waterer."

"If you'll just number off, all the number ones will do the peat moss, twos will plant, and threes water. One, two, three, one, two, three," said Ranger Dalton starting us off.

I ended up a planter, and so did Sally. She got Patti for peat moss and Stephanie for a waterer. Kate joined Kyle and Mark, and I was just about to hook up with Jane Sykes and Tracy Osner, when a burp practically broke my eardrum!

"Planter? Meet your peat moss man!" Wayne Miller said importantly. "And waterer." He reached out and pulled Ronny Wallace over, too.

Words absolutely failed me. Before I could regain my speech, the rangers called out, "All you number ones, please come over to the truck! Twos, the back of the trailer . . ."

I guess I would have been stuck with Wayne and Ronny for the rest of the morning if Mr. Patterson hadn't been keeping an eye on them.

"Don't you guys ever give up?" he asked grimly, after he'd charged around a pile of blackened tree trunks to get to us. "Tommy Brown, you and Betsy Chalfin." He snagged two kids from his class. "You're with Lauren. I'll be the planter for you clowns," he said to Wayne and Ronny, fixing them with a steely glare.

A hundred kids can get a lot done in a morning. Our fifth-grade teams must have dug, peat-mossed, planted, and watered at least a thousand seedlings. Tired? *You* try bending down and digging and firming and straightening up and bending down again for two and a half hours without stopping!

And how were we going to be in any shape to play baseball that afternoon? Let alone, *win*. By the time we knocked off for lunch, though, Wayne and Ronny looked totally beat, too. Thank goodness, Mr. Patterson hadn't let them goof off for a second.

No one paused to admire the views on the way back. It was all we could do to drag ourselves to the social hall, where we washed up. Sally, Kate, Patti, Stephanie, and I perked up a little when Mr. Jackson showed us how to build a fire in one of the stone barbecue pits beside the picnic tables.

We collected a big bundle of thin twigs, not off the ground where they're damp, but from dead bushes. Then we looked for slightly thicker twigs, then small logs. We lit the smallest twigs with a match, placed them in the center of our pit, and slowly added on, first the thicker twigs, and, once they were flickering, the logs.

Cooking fires should be small, or you end up

burning the food *and* your fingers. Mr. Jackson told us there's a famous old saying about it: "The bigger the fire, the bigger the fool."

Sure enough, Wayne Miller slouched by about then, took one look into our pit, and said, "Give me a break! I can build a fire five times that size with one hand tied behind my back!"

Mr. Jackson just winked at us.

"The bigger the fire, the bigger . . ." Stephanie murmured. We all burst out laughing.

Once the flames had died down a little bit, we laid some baking potatoes right in the fire itself. Then we lifted the iron grill into place over the top of the pit and started slapping down hamburgers and hot dogs. We toasted the buns around the edges of the grill.

Lunch was great. Everybody said so, even Mrs. Milton, who is definitely hard to please. Plus a square meal gave me some of my energy back.

All the kids cleaned up. Then it was time to troop over to the animal hospital and orphanage, a green building near the park entrance. Outside it, in a large cage, there was a deer with a gash in its shoulder. "We think she crashed into something, trying to get away from the fire," Ranger Dalton explained. "But she's almost recovered — we'll be reintroducing her to the wild soon."

"That's important to remember," Ranger Meyers said. "These are wild animals, not pets." She led a group of twenty or so kids into the building where they house the smaller animals and birds. We turned a corner to find ourselves face to face with a cage of baby raccoons.

There were three of them. We admired their wiggly little noses, the black masks across their eyes like bandits, and their thick, striped tails. As soon as they saw us, they cried, gripping and rattling the bars of their cage with their long fingers.

"They're saying, 'Let us out, *please* let us out!'" Kate translated.

"Can't we?" Stephanie asked Ranger Meyers. "I'd love to hold one."

"That's exactly what I meant," Ranger Meyers said. "They look as cute and cuddly as stuffed toys. But they're not, they're wild animals. They might scratch you badly, or bite. Wild animals can carry dangerous diseases. Just as important, *you're* not good for *them*, either. We don't want them to get too used to people. These animals belong in the woods. It's not fair to make them into pets."

"What are they doing here?" Sally asked.

"Something must have happened to their mother. One of the other rangers heard them whimpering inside a hollow tree. They were practically starved," Ranger Meyers said. "We'll keep them here until they're old enough to hunt, fish, climb, and swim. Then we'll actually have to teach them how to do those things. Eventually we'll take them farther into the park, and set them free. Always remember, no matter how darling they look, these are wild animals."

Ranger Meyers stepped over to the next cage. "Now then, would anyone like to help me change the bandage on this gray squirrel?"

Before anyone else had a chance to answer, to our surprise, Bitsy actually spoke up. She'd been hanging back at the edge of the group, but now she raised her hand and said, "Yes, I would!" just like a regular person.

And she was good at it, too. One of the squirrel's hind legs had a deep, infected sore on it, probably due to "a dog bite, or a fox," as Ranger Meyers said. The rangers had trapped him and brought him into the hospital just a few days earlier. They were afraid he'd be killed if they didn't, since a crippled squirrel that couldn't climb was pretty defenseless.

The squirrel was really wild. I guess his wound hurt, too. He wriggled and kicked and struggled and whipped his head around, trying to bite. With Ranger Meyers showing her how, Bitsy managed to wrap a small towel around the top half of the squirrel and hold him still. Ranger Meyers pulled off the dirty bandage, cleaned the sore, squirted more medicine onto it, and bandaged him again with clean gauze.

"Excellent work!" she said to Bitsy when he was safely back in his cage, chattering angrily. "I can tell you really care about animals."

"We can personally vouch for spiders, rats, and . . ." Stephanie murmured.

"Mice," Patti corrected softly.

"You were calm and firm with him. I'll bet you've had experience with lots of pets, haven't you?" Ranger Meyers smiled encouragingly at Bitsy.

"Some," Bitsy admitted, beaming at Ranger Meyers.

"You're not kidding. Her house is practically a zoo!" Wayne Miller had just walked into the building with another group of kids.

Bitsy caught us watching her then. Staring down at the dirt, she turned and slowly walked to the back of the crowd without saying another word.

"I've never seen anyone so shy," Patti said to me.

"Maybe it isn't shyness," I said. "Perhaps she feels guilty about spying on her cabin mates."

Chapter
7

We couldn't worry about Bitsy Barton that afternoon. We had the game to worry about.

Ranger Dalton had come up with more gloves and a couple of old bats from the rangers' office. At least we didn't have to bother with uniforms. If you were a girl, you were on one team. If you were a boy, you were on the other team. Pretty simple.

There were a few crossovers in the cheering section. Mark and Henry insisted on leading the cheers for us. And Jenny Carlin, Christy Soames, and Ginger Kinkaid would naturally cheer for the boys — they're just like that. We'd barely gotten to the field, and they were already tuning up: "Give us a B! Give us an O! Give us a Y!" Clap, clap. "Give us an S!"

60

Clap, clap! "Boys . . . boys . . . BOYS!" Wouldn't you be *embarrassed*?

The girls' team tried to psyche itself up, bouncing up and down, and running in place, tying and retying sneakers, and glaring at the boys' team on the opposite side of the diamond.

"Michael Pastore is playing for Wayne?!" Stephanie exclaimed. "That rat! And to think I actually *liked* him a few months ago!"

"Wayne's giving him a videotape of the Boodles concert as soon as we get back home," Karen Sims told her. "I heard Michael say so."

"And what's Charlie Garner's excuse?" Kate said disapprovingly. She and Charlie are in the school Video Club together.

"Wayne promised him ten of his best baseball cards," Robin Becker said.

"And Bobby Krieger?" Patti asked.

"He just thinks boys should stick together," Tracy Osner answered. Tracy is Bobby's first cousin, once removed.

Steven Gitten, Donny McElroy, Pete Stone . . . Wayne had definitely gotten together a pretty good team. "But our team is great!" I said out loud for everyone's benefit, and I really meant it. Karen, Tracy, Robin, Sally . . . I was putting Karla in right field, behind Patti at first base, where she could do the least damage.

Kate and Robert Ellwanger — he's in 5B, too — would be the scorekeepers, because they're both really dependable and serious. Mr. Patterson was going to be the umpire.

Wayne and I walked over to the batter's box, where Mr. Patterson flipped a coin to see who would bat first.

"Heads!" Wayne yelled as the quarter turned in the air.

Mr. Patterson caught it and smacked it down on his wrist. "Heads it is," he said. "Batter up!"

The girls took their places in the field: Sally catching, Patti at first, Stephanie at second, Tracy Osner at third. Jane Sykes was our shortshop, and Robin, Karla, and Karen were fielders. I stepped up to the pitcher's mound.

The baseball field at Silver Maples seemed larger than the one at Riverhurst Elementary. It looked like a mile, at least, from the pitcher's mound to home plate. Since David Degan was catching for the boys' team, he was the first at bat. He's shorter than I am, and when he hunched over the plate, he looked about two feet tall.

Oh, well. I took a deep breath . . . wound up,

the way my brother, Roger, had taught me . . . and let fly!

"Ball one!" Mr. Patterson yelled. "High and outside!"

High and outside! Why did David have to be so short? I wound up and threw again.

"Ball two!" Mr. Patterson called out. "Low and inside."

Doing great, Lauren, I scolded myself. I threw the third time, David swung, and hit a pop fly straight to Patti — who caught it. We had our first out!

Wayne Miller was up next, pounding the plate with his bat and scuffing up dirt with his feet like an angry bull. I would have giggled if I hadn't been so keyed up. Sally made a sign for me to throw to the inside of the plate if I could.

I wound up and let it fly. "Steee-rike!" Mr. Patterson shouted.

"Hey — I stopped my swing!" Wayne complained.

"Not soon enough," Mr. Patterson told him. "Strike one, and play ball!"

The next time, I threw to the outside. I guess Wayne figured girls could only throw one way, so he wasn't expecting that. He swung again and missed.

"Strike two!" said Mr. Patterson, and I thought he sounded the tiniest bit pleased.

The third time I threw, Wayne hit a foul tip. It arched over his head and dropped right into Sally's glove. He was OUT!

"Two bits, four bits, six bits, a dollar! All for the girls, stand up and holler!" Mark Freedman and Henry Larkin yelled from the sidelines. I noticed even some of the guys on *Wayne*'s team clapped!

Getting Wayne out felt great, but it wasn't all going to be that easy. In fact, I walked the next batter, Ronny Wallace. And Charlie Garner hit a ground ball past Tracy on third. He made it to first base, and Ronny moved to second.

Then I got lucky again, or maybe Bobby Krieger's heart just wasn't in it (he sort of likes Karen Sims), because I managed to strike him out, one . . . two . . . three! Three outs, and it was our turn to bat!

I'll have to admit, Wayne's not a bad pitcher. He makes stupid faces, chews a big wad of gum, and shows off, but he *can* strike people out. He struck out Sally Mason, first thing. Then he must have gotten a little nervous when I came to the plate, because he ended up walking me.

I strolled casually to first, grinning like crazy.

Which must have freaked out Wayne even more, because he just lobbed a ball past Patti, nice and easy . . . and she knocked it practically to the other side of Silver Maples Park!

"Way to go!" "Home run!" "Patti hit a homer!" Everybody on our side was jumping up and down and yelling. Patti had batted me in, too, of course. It was only the first inning, and the girls already had two runs.

I'm sorry to say that Wayne pulled himself together and struck out Stephanie and Tracy, one right after the other. Then it was the boys' turn at bat again.

The first person up was Pete Stone. I couldn't help noticing that he was wearing a dark green sweater that went really well with his eyes, and when he smiled at me I kind of fell apart. Pete hit the first ball I threw, into left field, and made it to second base. Steven Gitten and Donny McElroy got hits as well. By the time the girls were at bat again, the boys had two runs, too.

And that's the way it went. They'd get a run or two, and then we would. We were pretty evenly matched. I don't know how long the game would have gone on, if nature hadn't taken over.

Wayne was just about to step into the batter's box again — score: girls, 5; boys, 5 — when those gray clouds that had been hanging around all day absolutely split open. *Cra-a-ack!* There was a tremendous bolt of lightning, practically right over the diamond, and instant thunder. Then the rain poured down, and Mr. Patterson yelled, "Game's called! Get yourselves into a shelter, fast!"

In five seconds, the field was totally soaked and so were we. All the kids, except Wayne Miller, scattered for their cabins. He was still standing at home plate, shaking his bat up at the sky and shouting. We could only make out a few words over the torrents of rain, such as, "going to win" and "not fair!"

"Poor Wayne," Patti said as the four of us and Sally raced across the field.

"Yeah — he can't believe we tied," Sally said.

"In a way, the girls won," Patti said. We were squishing up the trail toward Cardinal.

"How do you figure that?" Stephanie asked her.

"Mother Nature's a girl, isn't she? And she sure struck Wayne Miller out!" Patti answered with a grin.

Stephanie, Kate, Sally, and I burst out laughing.

Chapter
8

We made it back to our cabin, absolutely dripping, to find Bitsy Barton high and dry, sorting through her luggage.

"What has she been doing all afternoon?" Kate whispered as we changed into drier clothes.

"Getting to know her luggage better," Sally Mason answered with a giggle. The gray tote was zipped up tight and resting against Bitsy's rolled-up sleeping bag.

"I'm starving," I said, toweling some of the water out of my hair.

"Have some of this. It may be a long time before we eat tonight. The boys are cooking." Stephanie dug into her backpack for another large bag of candy from Sweet Stuff, this time malted milk balls, and passed it around. Everybody except Bitsy took some, but there was still quite a bit left in the bag.

"Did you buy out the store before we left Riverhurst?" Kate asked Stephanie, handing the bag back.

"Just two or three samples," Stephanie said, putting the candy away again. Then she exclaimed, "Wow! Can you believe this?! And they're my favorites!"

She dragged a red-and-black-checked sock out of her backpack to show us the hole chewed in its toe. "After stuffing himself with almonds and paper, he finished off my best sock for dessert! I'm going to kill that mouse!"

A little while later, Mrs. Mason burst through the door, looking wet and bedraggled. "The rain is stopping, and it's almost time for dinner, girls," she announced breathlessly.

We tumbled eagerly out of the cabin. Stephanie's candy hadn't done the trick. I was really hungry.

When we got to the picnic area we found Wayne still sulking. The boys were supposed to be cooking dinner that night, and even though the rain was over, every bit of wood within ten miles was damp.

"Hey, Wayne, having trouble? I thought you

could start a camp fire in a rainstorm," Mark yelled from the barbecue pit where he and Henry Larkin and Larry Jackson were working with Larry's dad.

"So funny I forgot to laugh," Wayne mumbled to himself through clenched teeth. He was hulking over a pit on the other side of the tables. His face was dark red, and even Ronny and David were keeping mum.

"Maybe it's time to take out those rocks you were talking about yesterday," Henry suggested to him helpfully, meanwhile grinning at us. "The wood sure isn't working."

The wood didn't work for anybody. Ranger Dalton came up with a big bag of charcoal chunks — enough for two of the barbecues but not enough to cook all of the chicken pieces we were supposed to be having for dinner. Some of us had to snack on leftovers from lunch that day, plus chips and stuff the parents had been saving for lunch on Sunday. Before we'd even finished with that, it started drizzling again. Everyone was too tired to hang around any longer, anyway, so we all headed back to our cabins.

"More candy, anybody?" Stephanie asked as we got together our stuff for the showers.

"Sure." I took three or four chocolate-covered cherries. "Patti?"

"Don't eat them all, guys," Kate said in a low voice. "I want to try something."

"What?" said Stephanie.

"Sssh. Tell you in a minute." Kate nodded at Bitsy and Mrs. Mason, who were picking their way around luggage and cots to the front door.

"Coming, girls?" Mrs. Mason paused with her hand on the knob.

"Be right there, Mom," Sally said, and Mrs. Mason and Bitsy started down the steps. I noticed Bitsy actually had her gray canvas tote with her.

"What's up?" Sally asked Kate.

"Remember the way the rangers rigged that camera to photograph the littering raccoon?" Kate said.

"Sure . . . I know, you're going to try to snap a picture of Stephanie's visitor!" I guessed. Kate loves fooling around with cameras. Still cameras, video cameras, *hidden* cameras. She'd like to direct movies some day.

"With your Polaroid, Lauren," Kate said. "We'll know *instantly* what we're up against."

"If it's anything larger than a ladybug, I'm spending the night in the social hall," Stephanie said.

"Why didn't you want Bitsy and Mrs. Mason to hear?" Patti asked.

"Mrs. Mason, because she'd probably get awfully upset about furry prowlers," Kate said.

"Too true," said Mrs. Mason's daughter.

"And Bitsy would give us some kind of lecture about damaging the darling little whatever's eyesight with a flashbulb," Kate finished. "You guys go ahead," she told Stephanie, Patti, and Sally, "and distract them until we get there."

Kate and I got busy with my Polaroid, Kate's dental floss, and the rest of the chocolate-covered cherries. We rigged things so that a piece of dental floss was attached on one end to the shutter of my camera, which we'd hooked to the head of my cot and tilted toward the floor. The other end of the piece of dental floss was tied to the paper bag of candy, which we stuck inside another paper bag, just to make things a little more difficult for the mysterious visitor. We scattered a few bits of chocolate-covered cherries around the floor between my cot and Stephanie's. Then we stretched the floss out pretty tightly, and set the candy bag down on the floor in the middle of the cherry bits.

"Done!" said Kate. "Now all we have to do is wait."

The only problem was, all of us were completely

71

worn out. We'd gotten up at six-thirty that morning, hiked, planted, cooked, played baseball, gotten soaked. We tried to stay awake after Mrs. Mason turned off the lights. But Stephanie started to snore the minute her head hit the cot and Kate wasn't far behind her. Sally was already mumbling something in her sleep. And as soon as I closed my own eyes, I was *gone*.

I was dreaming about baseball. I was a major league pitcher and I'd just thrown a no-hitter. My fans were clapping, cameras were clicking, flashbulbs were going off in my face. . . .

Flashbulbs were going off in my face! I heard the whir of the Polaroid next to my head, which meant somebody's portrait was about to roll out!

"Stephanie. Stephanie!" I nudged her awake. "We've got something!"

"Grab a flashlight," Sally whispered sleepily on my other side, scrabbling through her backpack. She shone the light on the floor between my bed and Stephanie's. Nothing. But the candy bag had been moved an inch or so.

I grabbed the photograph before it fell out of the camera. Kate, Sally, Patti, and Stephanie gathered around, waiting breathlessly for it to lighten.

"Here it comes," I said.

The photograph suddenly flicked into focus under the beam of Sally's flashlight.

"Eeeuu!" Stephanie squealed. "What kind of grotesque rodent is that?!"

"Sssh. You'll wake up my mom," Sally warned. "Let me see it."

But before any of us could really get a good look at it, a hand reached over my shoulder and snatched the photo away.

"Give that back, Bitsy!" Kate said sternly.

"It's mine!" Bitsy yelled.

"Yours? How can it be yours?" Kate was flabbergasted.

"I think there's something scurrying along the rafters," Patti said, shining her flashlight up at the ceiling.

"Eeeuuu!" Stephanie dived under her sleeping bag and covered up her head. All the rest of us pointed our flashlights up at the ceiling. The beams crisscrossed the rafters like searchlights in one of those old black-and-white war movies, until they locked onto something small and gray, racing across a board high above our heads.

"What is it?"

73

"It's not a rat, it has a fluffy tail."

"Not really fluffy enough for a squirrel — "

"He's a flying squirrel!" Bitsy interrupted. "Please turn off the lights. *Please?* You're scaring him half to death!"

Chapter
9

What's a flying squirrel doing in our cabin, eating my candy and socks?'' Stephanie's voice was muffled because her head was still covered with her sleeping bag.

"I'll tell you, if you'll just turn off your flashlights," Bitsy pleaded.

Now the story came out. Bitsy had found the squirrel in a vacant lot near her house a few months before, its front leg broken. She'd carried it home, managed to set its leg in a splint of toothpicks, and nursed it back to health.

Now that it was well, "Kevin" — the squirrel was named for a TV star all of us liked — had started getting into trouble. He'd knocked dishes off of shelves, turned over bags of flour and sugar, chewed holes in Mrs. Barton's best curtains.

"Now my mom wants me to get rid of him," Bitsy explained.

"I know the feeling," Stephanie said.

"I was afraid she'd kick him out of the house while I was away this weekend," Bitsy went on. "Which is why I put his cage in my tote and brought him with me. I let him out last night to get some exercise, and I guess he smelled the candy."

She'd been talking to the squirrel all along, not her tote!

"But, Bitsy," Patti said quietly. "Didn't you hear what the rangers said? This is a wild animal, not a pet. He should be living outdoors. . . ."

"So that a dog can kill him, or he gets run over by a car?" Bitsy replied. "No way!"

Nobody said anything for a few seconds. We just sat there in the dark, listening to Kevin scrambling around overhead.

"Are you going to tell anybody?" Bitsy asked at last.

"No." Kate answered for all of us.

I don't think Bitsy believed her. She insisted that she'd rather catch the squirrel on her own, which she could manage if we'd just go back to sleep.

"How can I sleep when there's a rat doing a trapeze act over my head?" Stephanie grumbled. But she started snoring just as quickly *under* her sleeping bag as she had inside it.

Bitsy must have caught Kevin, because he didn't leave any more pictures behind that night. Or holes in anyone's socks.

When we woke up the next morning, there was no sign of Kevin or Bitsy. We figured she'd gotten up really early and left the cabin. The tote was gone, too.

"I'll bet she's hidden it somewhere," Sally said. "She didn't trust us."

I saw Bitsy from a distance during breakfast, toteless. Then we got busy picking up bushels of litter in the park, and I didn't think about her at all, not even at lunch, which was fabulous. The parents had driven to the nearest town to get double-cheese pizzas with sausage and pepperoni for everybody.

After lunch Mrs. Milton announced, "You have three free hours to explore the area close to the campground, children. At four o'clock sharp we'll board the buses for our trip back."

Sally and the four of us were standing near the

side steps of the social hall, trying to decide what to do with our free time, when an all-too-disgusting burp sounded in my ear.

"Going to get in a little more cooking and cleaning?" Wayne Miller asked with a smirk. Ronny Wallace snickered.

"Sure, as soon as you bring in a bear for us to grill," Kate shot back.

Wayne scowled. "We're going to do some serious exploring," he boasted. "We're going to check out the Napateague, that spring where the stream starts."

"Isn't it too far away?" Patti said. I knew she was interested, because of her water samples for the Quarks.

"All of Silver Maples Park isn't *that* big," Wayne said scornfully. "But it's probably too rough a hike for you *ladies*," he added.

"Oh, yeah? I can keep up with you any day, Wayne Miller!" There I went again!

"You're on!" he said.

"Lauren," Kate said cautiously, "Mrs. Milton told us . . ."

"You guys don't have to come." I was practically stepping on Wayne's heels as he marched across the baseball field.

Kate, Patti, Stephanie, Sally Mason, and Ronny Wallace fell into line behind us.

I'll have to admit, it wasn't much of a nature walk. It was more of an endurance race. We didn't stop to admire birds, animals, or views. Or pay much attention to where we were going. It was just one foot in front of the other, down one hill, up another. At one point, Patti said, "Why aren't we following the stream?"

"Short cut," Wayne replied, plowing on through the forest.

"I have to sit down for a second," Stephanie said at last. "I'm pooped." Her face was flushed and she was really out of breath.

"Me, too," said Sally. "I have a blister on my heel. I can't go another step until I've taken my shoe off and looked at my foot."

"Okay, we'll rest for a minute," I said, collapsing on a log. "Wayne? Wayne?" I called. He and Ronny had disappeared.

"Oh, they're probably hiding not ten feet away, waiting for us to panic," Kate said. "*So* childish!"

"Right," I agreed. "It's Wayne's idea of a great joke. If we don't act scared, they'll get bored and come back for us."

Kate, Stephanie, Patti, Sally, and I started carrying on as cheerful a conversation as we could under the circumstances. We weren't at all sure we knew the way back and were furious at the boys for leaving us. We tried to talk about how much fun we'd been having at Silver Maples, and how great Ranger Meyers and Ranger Dalton were.

"And he'll eat you alive, Wayne Miller, if you leave us out here!" Stephanie added in case Wayne was listening from his hiding place.

I said something about how much trouble they'd be in with Mrs. Milton if we were late, because I thought that might shake Wayne up more.

But when we stopped talking, we didn't hear Wayne's big feet thumping back toward us, or even Ronny's icky giggle. The only sound was the wind whistling through the pines.

"Wayne Miller, you get back here or you'll be sorry!" Kate tried the direct approach.

No answer. We all sat down on the log and waited. The hands on Kate's watch crept from two o'clock to two-twenty to two-forty. Our only visitors were a couple of crows.

"We're doomed!" Stephanie said dramatically.

"Don't be dumb!" Kate said. "Mrs. Mason will

send the rangers to find us, won't she, Sally?"

"She won't realize we're missing until four o'clock," Stephanie pointed out. "By the time they organize a search party, the sun will be setting. And they sure won't find us in the dark!"

"In the dark," Sally repeated, her eyes opening wide at the thought. "Are there . . . uh . . . bears around here?"

"I suppose there *could* be," Patti said slowly.

"In the dark, we wouldn't be able to see them coming," I said.

"They'd just burst out of the trees on top of us, and rip us to — " Sally began, when suddenly something did burst out of the bushes practically at our feet!

"Aaagh!" all five of us screamed, and jumped onto the log, afraid to look.

Kate was the first to turn around and check out the intruder.

"A rabbit!" she exclaimed. "Let's get a grip on ourselves, okay? I think we'd better consider trying to make our way back to the campgrounds on our own."

"How?" I asked.

"Maybe we should climb one of these trees and

try to spot the campgrounds from higher up,'' Patti suggested.

"What if we fell? A broken leg out here — '' Stephanie shook her head, leaving the rest to our imaginations.

"I'll do it,'' I said. After all, I'd gotten us into this fix.

There was a pine just behind us with branches like the rungs of a ladder. I shinned up the trunk to the first branch and started to climb. I wasn't a third of the way to the top when I glimpsed something moving at the edge of a little clearing below us.

Kate spotted it at the same time. Before I could call down, she exclaimed, "Hey — over there!''

"I never thought she could look so good!'' Stephanie said, relieved.

It was Bitsy Barton. She was carrying a small cage and appeared to be lost in thought.

I scrambled down the pine and joined the other girls. "If she *got* here, she can *get back*,'' I said. Just as I was about to yell to her, Kate shushed me with a finger to her lips.

As we watched, Bitsy set the cage down on a stump, leaned over, and spoke for a minute or two. Then she straightened up and wiped her eyes with her hand. Squaring her shoulders, she opened the cage door.

A little gray animal darted out of the cage. He climbed onto the top of it and sat there for a second, as though he were saying good-bye. Then he flicked his tail once, dashed down the stump, and up the trunk of the nearest oak. Bitsy stared up at the tree and so did we, just in time to see the squirrel leap into the air, and glide to a maple at least fifty feet away.

"Good for her!" Patti said softly before I yelled out, "Bitsy!"

Bitsy jumped and turned around. Then she began to walk slowly toward us.

"What are you doing here?" she asked suspiciously when she got close enough. Maybe she thought *we* were spying on *her*.

"Wayne Miller and Ronny . . ." Sally began.

"Oh, no! Wayne ditched you?!" Bitsy said.

Stephanie nodded. "Are *we* glad to see *you*!"

"It must have been hard to let Kevin go," Patti said.

Bitsy looked at the ground and shuffled her feet. "You were right," she finally said to Patti. "He was a wild animal, and I was trying to turn him into a pet, like my cats and dogs. Riverhurst was too dangerous for him, but I think he'll be happy in the park."

It was the longest speech I'd ever heard her make.

"Wayne ditched me a couple of times when our families went camping together," she went on shyly. "Only I have a kind of a built-in compass in my head."

"Then you're just the person we need," Kate said. "Can you get us back to the campgrounds?"

"No problem. It's right this way." She was dead certain, even though it all looked alike to me.

"Bitsy, I know Wayne doesn't have much use for girls in general," I said. "But is it my imagination, or does he have something against *me* in particular?"

Then I heard one of the most embarrassing things I've ever heard in my life. Bitsy shook her head and replied, "Wayne really *likes* you, Lauren. He just doesn't know how to show it. He talks about you all the time!"

Have you ever heard anything so weird? I didn't say another word all the way back to the cabins. Bitsy got us there with almost an hour to spare. She's a lot better outdoor person than her cousin Wayne is, that's for sure. Do you know why he and Ronny didn't come back for us after they'd tried to scare us? They'd gotten lost themselves. Smart, huh?

The teachers had to hold the buses while the rangers tracked them down. About an hour later, they finally showed up in the parking lot, wrinkled, dirty, and red-faced.

Henry Larkin stuck his head out of a bus window and yelled, "Hey, guys, next time you take a hike, you'd better stick with the girls if you want to get home!"

Everyone made fun of Wayne and Ronny as they climbed sheepishly into the last bus.

Bitsy sat with us all the way back to Riverhurst. She talked to us, too. About all kinds of stuff. And we laughed all over again at the expressions on Wayne and Ronny's faces when they'd finally made it to the parking lot.

Back at Riverhurst Elementary we stood around and waited while Bitsy got her luggage, and waved good-bye when she got into the Barton station wagon and drove off. Then we loaded our stuff into Mr. Jenkins's van for the ride to our houses.

"Well, guys," Patti said as the van bumped over the road, "what would you think about inviting — "

"Bitsy Barton to one of our sleepovers?" Kate finished. "Okay by me."

"Me, too," Stephanie said.

"I agree!" I chimed in. "Definitely!"

Bitsy wasn't weird at all. In fact, she was pretty special.

#25 Stephanie and the Wedding

"We'll just have to be patient," Patti advised. "Wait until Stephanie makes up her mind to tell us what's bothering her."

"And you know she can't keep a secret for more than a few hours," said Kate. "I'm sure we'll hear about it this afternoon."

"I hope so." I said. I was getting kind of worried. I'd seen Stephanie get mad before and I'd definitely seen her sulk before, but I'd never seen her look quite so glum.

As soon as school was over, though, Stephanie rushed out the door.

"Why are you in such a hurry?" Kate asked her, cutting her off at the bike rack.

"I have lots of errands to do," she replied, unlocking her bike. "See you tomorrow." Then Stephanie jumped on her bike and pedaled away.

"She's avoiding us!" Kate said.

"She's avoiding *someone* . . . ," Patti said.

Pack your bags for fun and adventure with

SLEEPOVER FRIENDS™

by Susan Saunders

THE BABY-SITTERS CLUB

by Ann M. Martin

Collect Them All!

The seven girls at Stoneybrook Middle School get into all kinds of adventures...with school, boys, and, of course, baby-sitting!

NI43388-1	#1	Kristy's Great Idea	$2.95
NI43513-2	#2	Claudia and the Phantom Phone Calls	$2.95
NI43511-6	#3	The Truth About Stacey	$2.95
NI42498-X	#30	Mary Anne and the Great Romance	$2.95
NI42497-1	#31	Dawn's Wicked Stepsister	$2.95
NI42496-3	#32	Kristy and the Secret of Susan	$2.95
NI42495-5	#33	Claudia and the Great Search	$2.95
NI42494-7	#34	Mary Anne and Too Many Boys	$2.95
NI42508-0	#35	Stacey and the Mystery of Stoneybrook	$2.95
NI43565-5	#36	Jessi's Baby-sitter	$2.95
NI43566-3	#37	Dawn and the Older Boy	$2.95
NI43567-1	#38	Kristy's Mystery Admirer	$2.95
NI43568-X	#39	Poor Mallory!	$2.95
NI44082-9	#40	Claudia and the Middle School Mystery	$2.95
NI43570-1	#41	Mary Anne Versus Logan (Feb. '91)	$2.95
NI44083-7	#42	Jessi and the Dance School Phantom (Mar. '91)	$2.95
NI43571-X	#43	Stacey's Revenge (Apr. '91)	$2.95
NI44240-6		Baby-sitters on Board! Super Special #1	$3.50
NI44239-2		Baby-sitters' Summer Vacation Super Special #2	$3.50
NI43973-1		Baby-sitters' Winter Vacation Super Special #3	$3.50
NI42493-9		Baby-sitters' Island Adventure Super Special #4	$3.50
NI43575-2		California Girls! Super Special #5	$3.50

For a complete listing of all the Baby-sitter Club titles write to:
Customer Service at the address below.

Available wherever you buy books...or use this order form.

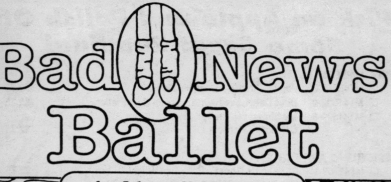

APPLE*PAPERBACKS

Pick an Apple and Polish Off Some Great Reading!

NEW APPLE TITLES

☐ MT43356-3	Family Picture Dean Hughes	$2.75
☐ MT41682-0	Dear Dad, Love Laurie Susan Beth Pfeffer	$2.75
☐ MT41529-8	My Sister, the Creep	
	Candice F. Ransom	$2.75

BESTSELLING APPLE TITLES

☐ MT42709-1	Christina's Ghost Betty Ren Wright	$2.75
☐ MT43461-6	The Dollhouse Murders Betty Ren Wright	$2.75
☐ MT42319-3	The Friendship Pact Susan Beth Pfeffer	$2.75
☐ MT43444-6	Ghosts Beneath Our Feet Betty Ren Wright	$2.75
☐ MT40605-1	Help! I'm a Prisoner in the Library Eth Clifford	$2.50
☐ MT42193-X	Leah's Song Eth Clifford	$2.50
☐ MT43618-X	Me and Katie (The Pest) Ann M. Martin	$2.75
☐ MT42883-7	Sixth Grade Can Really Kill You Barthe DeClements	$2.75
☐ MT40409-1	Sixth Grade Secrets Louis Sachar	$2.75
☐ MT42882-9	Sixth Grade Sleepover Eve Bunting	$2.75
☐ MT41732-0	Too Many Murphys	
	Colleen O'Shaughnessy McKenna	$2.75
☐ MT41118-7	Tough-Luck Karen Johanna Hurwitz	$2.50
☐ MT42326-6	Veronica the Show-off Nancy K. Robinson	$2.75

Available wherever you buy books...or use the coupon below.

Scholastic Inc., P.O. Box 7502, 2932 East McCarty Street, Jefferson City, MO 65102

Please send me the books I have checked above. I am enclosing $_____ (please add $2.00 to cover shipping and handling). Send check or money order — no cash or C.O.D. s please.

Name_____

Address_____

City _____ State/Zip _____

Please allow four to six weeks for delivery. Offer good in the U.S.A. only.
Sorry, mail orders are not available to residents of Canada. Prices subject to change.

APP1089

W9-COE-332

by Ellen Finkelstein

IDG Books Worldwide, Inc.
An International Data Group Company

Foster City, CA ♦ Chicago, IL ♦ Indianapolis, IN ♦ Braintree, MA ♦ Dallas, TX

AutoCAD® For Dummies® Quick Reference

Published by
IDG Books Worldwide, Inc.
An International Data Group Company
919 E. Hillsdale Blvd.
Suite 400
Foster City, CA 94404

Library of Congress Catalog Card No.: 94-079877

ISBN: 1-56884-198-1

Printed in the United States of America

10 9 8 7 6 5 4 3 2 1

1A/RQ/QU/ZV

Distributed in the United States by IDG Books Worldwide, Inc.

Distributed by Macmillan Canada for Canada; by Computer and Technical Books for the Caribbean Basin; by Contemporantea de Ediciones for Venezuela; by Distribuidora Cuspide for Argentina; by CITFC for Brazil; by Ediciones ZETA S.C.R. Ltda. for Peru; by Editorial Limusa SA for Mexico; by Transworld Publishers Limited in the United Kingdom and Europe; by Al-Maiman Publishers & Distributors for Saudi Arabia; by Simron Pty. Ltd. for South Africa; by IDG Communications (IIK) Ltd. for Hong Kong; by Toppan Company Ltd. for Japan; by Addison Wesley Publishing Company for Korea; by Longman Singapore Publisher Ltd. for Singapore, Malaysia, Thailand, and Indonesia; by Unalis Corporation for Taiwan; by WS Computer Publishing Company, Inc. for the Philippines; by WoodsLane Enterprises Ltd. for New Zealand.

For general information on IDG Books in the U.S., including information on discounts and premiums, contact IDG Books at 800-434-3422 or 415-655-3000.

For information on where to purchase IDG Books outside the U.S., contact IDG Books International at 415-655-3021 or fax 415-655-3295.

For information on translations, contact Marc Jeffrey Mikulich, Director, Foreign and Subsidiary Rights, at IDG Books Worldwide, 415-655-3018 or fax 415-655-3295.

For sales inquiries and special prices for bulk quantities, write to the address above or call IDG Books Worldwide at 415-655-3000.

For information on using IDG Books in the classroom, or for ordering examination copies, contact Jim Kelly at 800-434-2086.

About the Author

Ellen Finkelstein learned AutoCAD in Israel, where she was always the one sent to pore over the manual because it was in English. After drafting and then teaching AutoCAD there, she returned to the United States and started consulting and training in AutoCAD and other computer programs. Recently, she has been the technical editor for several books from IDG Books Worldwide.

Dedication

To MMY, who taught me how to find my inner intelligence so I could write clearly — and my inner creativity so I could be funny.

Acknowledgments

First, I would like to thank my husband for his incredible support while I was writing this book, which included washing innumerable clothes and dishes and putting the kids to bed every night. And my friends (and moms of my kids' friends) who helped out when I needed it. Thanks, too, to my parents for their support all my life and their belief that I could do anything (even write a book about AutoCAD, of all things). My kids didn't know they were helping, but their love, sweetness, and snugliness helped, too.

Thanks to George Swanson of Swanson Associates and Frazer Jones of CADD America for their support and the use of great computer facilities at all hours, even nights and Sundays. Frazer, a computer wizard, magically resurrected a floppy diskette that was unreadable on my computer, saving me from redoing 56 screen captures on my final due date for this book. Thanks to Jim Meade who gave me my first technical writing assignment and introduced me to IDG Books. And who was always fun to talk to when I needed advice. Thanks to the folks at Kibbutz Yahad, where I first learned AutoCAD. It was a great time! Randy Bush, the all-knowing technical editor from Autodesk, had the inside story on bugs (would you believe there are a couple?) and added many helpful hints and comments. Finally, thanks to all the people at IDG Books, including Megg Bonar, Bill Barton, Mike Kelly, Kathy Simpson, and the folks in Production who put it all together.

(The publisher would like to thank Patrick J. McGovern, without whom this book would not have been possible.)

Credits

Contents at a Glance

Introduction

Hi! I'm Nobody! Who are you?
Are you nobody, too?
Then there's a pair of us — don't tell!
They'd banish us, you know.
            Emily Dickinson

This book is for us nobodies (or us Dummies) — normal people who want or need to use AutoCAD without having to be an engineer or a programmer. (Even those engineers and programmers among you must have a normal side!) Sure, AutoCAD is complex, but it doesn't have to be scary. This book organizes a vast amount of information about AutoCAD for you, so you can read only the parts that you need. You can stay blissfully unaware of the rest and still get your job done.

Who Needs This Book

This book is useful for beginning and advanced AutoCAD users, as well as for most of you who fall somewhere in the middle. The book covers almost every command in Release 13, including how to use each command and what those obscure AutoCAD terms mean. The book is loaded with icons that tell you how useful or safe a command is, tips that help you get more out of AutoCAD, and warnings that tell you when to be careful. Part I, "The Basics," will get you started even before you get into the commands.

AutoCAD For Dummies Quick Reference is, as the name implies, a reference book. You probably should know just a little about AutoCAD first. A great place to start is with Bud Smith's *AutoCAD For Dummies,* from IDG Books Worldwide; it's informative, chock-full of good advice, easy to read, and (most important) funny!

After you start using AutoCAD, this book is the one to keep by your computer all the time. No one can know everything about AutoCAD, so you'll always need to look things up. That's OK. Really! (Now that you know the secret — that even advanced users continue to look up things about AutoCAD — you won't feel so self-conscious when you do it.) And if you have this book next to your computer, you'll find that all your fellow AutoCAD users will be stopping by regularly to use the book (probably a good way to meet someone, as long as the boss doesn't mind this new substitute for the usual gatherings around the water cooler.)

How I Stuffed All of AutoCAD into This Tiny Book

I actually included the vast majority of AutoCAD commands, including all the regular 2D, 3D, and rendering commands. What did I leave out? Because this book is a Quick Reference, I felt that I couldn't do justice to some subjects in a short format. Those subjects are the commands related to LISP (AutoCAD's programming language), importing and exporting other types of files, customizing AutoCAD (such as writing script files or customizing menus), and the AutoCAD SQL Environment (ASE) commands. There's no point doing a bad job of describing something, so I left those subjects out, as well as a few more that are very rarely used.

Also, I covered each command only briefly (remember, this book is a reference, not a long-winded technical explanation). I tell you *how* to use the command, walking you through the options, suboptions, and sometimes sub-suboptions.

The Marriage of DOS and Windows

This book is for users of both AutoCAD for DOS and for Windows. Right now, about 80 percent of AutoCAD users have the DOS version, but watch out — those Windows fans are increasing (taking over the world, some people might say). To tell you the truth, covering both DOS and Windows wasn't that hard; Autodesk pretty much cloned the DOS version when it created AutoCAD for Windows. True, the Windows version has toolbars and icons, and its dialog boxes are prettier. But when it comes down to the nitty-gritty, Autodesk always reverts to the command line — and that, dear reader, is the same for both versions. DOS users can, therefore, switch to Windows quite comfortably.

Even UNIX users can use this book, because the UNIX commands are pretty much the same as the DOS commands.

Those Little Icons

Here are the icons I use in the book. These icons can give you an instant impression of a command, helping you decide whether the command is the one that you want.

This command is used by almost all AutoCAD users.

 Generally, this command is not used by beginners.

 This command is usually for advanced users or special purposes (includes 3D commands).

 This command is safe to use.

 Generally, this command is safe unless you really don't follow instructions.

 This command is potentially dangerous; be careful!

 Whenever a command or comment applies to DOS users only, I use this icon.

 Whenever a command or comment applies to Windows users only, I use this icon.

 This icon warns you of problem areas that can mess up your work.

 This icon points out clever AutoCAD tricks to help you along the way.

 This icon directs you to other commands in this book.

 This icon directs you to more information in *AutoCAD For Dummies* from IDG Books Worldwide.

How This Book Is Organized

Because this is a reference book, the material is organized for easy look-up. The headings will help you find what you need to know quickly. And although your sixth-grade teacher probably told you not to do this, I give you permission to fold down the corners of any pages you wish.

Part I: The Basics

This part gives you the basics that you can't find under any command. The part includes sections on getting started, using commands, setting up a drawing, specifying points, moving around the drawing, selecting objects, using Help, and getting in and out of drawings safely and efficiently.

Part II: The Commands

This part is an alphabetical listing of all (well, almost all) the commands. I don't expect you to read this part through from beginning to end — this is a reference book — although it's okay if you want to; you'd probably learn a lot if you did. Part II is the main reference section; just look up the command that you need.

Part III: The System Variables

This part lists the system variables not controlled using any command. As AutoCAD slowly improves its interface, more of the system variables are handled in dialog boxes, but you still may want to type some of them in the command line. I organized these variables by function so that you can find them easily.

Part IV: The Menus and Toolbars

If you know that you want to change something but don't know the command name, you can look in this part, because the menus are organized by type of task (Draw, Modify, and so on).

Part V: Glossary

You've heard of Newspeak (from George Orwell's *1984*)? Well, AutoCAD has AutoSpeak. Actually, I have to thank Autodesk, because some of my best jokes in this book came from the absurdity of the terminology used in AutoCAD. In the glossary, I include words that have unique meanings in the AutoCAD world — usually meanings quite different from what their names suggest.

Part I

The Basics

If you're a new AutoCAD user, be sure to read this part; it tells you how to get started and reviews the basics you need to know to understand the unique world of AutoCAD. If you're already familiar with AutoCAD, you may want to skim through; you'll know most of this stuff, but you're sure to find something new.

Throughout this part, I refer as necessary to commands listed in Part II of this book.

Getting Started

It's good to start at the beginning, and you start by opening a drawing — a new one or one you've already created.

Opening a new or existing drawing

When you start AutoCAD, either by using a batch file from the DOS prompt (created for you by the installation process) or by double-clicking the AutoCAD icon in the Windows Program Manager, you find yourself magically transported into a new drawing. You can click your heels to get home or just start drawing. Or you can open an existing drawing by choosing File⇨Open. In Windows, you also can click the Open icon in the Standard toolbar. (See the OPEN command in Part II; also see the NEW command for some special ways to open new drawings.)

The DOS and Windows screens

The following figure shows the DOS screen with the status bar displayed at the top of the screen.

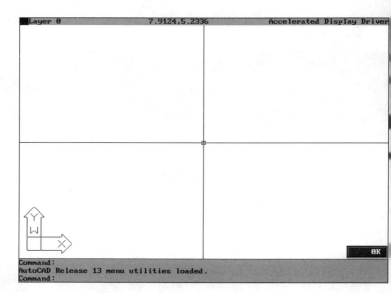

The status bar shows your current layer; your current coordinates; and snap, grid, and ortho modes. When you enter paper space, a *P* appears. At the bottom of the screen is the famous (or infamous, depending on your opinion) command line, where you can type commands, blissfully ignoring those wimpy menus. On the right would be the original screen menu, but because this book ignores it, I configured AutoCAD not to show it. (More drawing space for me!) That big space in the middle, of course, is where you draw.

The menu bar is hidden behind the status bar. The trick is simply to move your mouse until the pointer is on the status bar. Then — poof! — the menu bar appears, as in the following figure.

File   Assist   View   Draw   Construct   Modify   Data   Options   Tools   Help

See Chapter 4 of *AutoCAD For Dummies* for the procedure for getting rid of the screen menu.

Here's the Windows screen.

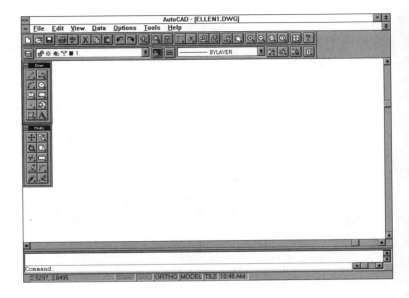

The status bar is at the bottom. The snap, grid, and ortho indicators double as buttons; double-click to turn them on and off. The same goes for the model button (to toggle between model and paper space) and the tile button (to turn tilemode on and off). That's cool. (It would have been even cooler if you only had to click once.) The menu bar at the top never disappears. (Generous of AutoCAD, isn't it?) Of course, you also have all those toolbars filled with icons. In their default positions, you'll find the Standard and Object Properties toolbars near the top of the screen and the Draw and Modify toolbars at the side. You, the magician, can make many more toolbars appear by using the TOOLBAR command. Many toolbars have secondary menus called *flyouts*; you find them by clicking any icon that has a little black arrow in the corner. Again, the big space in the middle is where you draw.

Save me, save me!

It may seem funny for me to talk about saving before I've talked about drawing anything, but you can't learn this procedure too soon. Use the QSAVE command frequently to save your drawing. Furthermore, I recommend setting AutoCAD to save your drawing automatically at regular intervals. That way, the only time you forget is when your computer crashes.

If you have Windows, choose Options⇨Preferences and click the System tab of the Preferences dialog box. In the Automatic Save section, make sure that the check box contains a little *x* and type the time interval you want. The default is a ridiculous 120 minutes. Whoever thought you wouldn't mind redoing two hours of work if AutoCAD crashes is just a little nuts. Change the setting to 15 or 30 minutes — max.

If you have DOS, choose Options⇨Auto Save Time, type the time interval you want between saves, and press Enter.

Ordering AutoCAD Around

I don't know what AutoCAD's menus do at night when we're not looking, but they do seem to multiply. AutoCAD has the screen menu, the menu bar, the tablet menu, the button menu, the cursor menu, and (in Windows) the toolbars. And, of course, there's the ever-present command line if you hate menus.

Pointing devices: mouse or digitizer

Most people use a mouse with AutoCAD. Some people use a digitizing tablet, which has something that is officially called a *puck* or *stylus* but that everyone calls a *digitizer*. Technically, *digitizing* means copying a paper drawing with the stylus on the tablet, point by point. People sometimes use this method to convert paper drawings to computerized ones. You can use the digitizing tablet as a menu as well; in fact, AutoCAD comes with a sample tablet template.

The left button on your mouse is the *pick* button, which means that you pick things with it — a menu item, an icon, or an object that you've drawn. The right button is the *Return* button, which means that clicking it is the same thing as pressing the Enter key on your keyboard. If your mouse has more than two buttons, try them out to see what they do. You may like what you find.

The command line

You can enter all commands at the command line just by typing them. So even though Part II tells you how to access each command by using a menu or toolbar, you can always type the command name in the command line. Try as you might, you can't get away from the command line completely. Often, a command that starts with a dialog box or an icon reverts to the command line for you to input coordinates, values, or command options.

Options are listed along the command line, separated by slashes (/). One or more letters of the option are capitalized. You need type only the capitalized letter or letters to choose the option. (But you can type in uppercase or lowercase letters.) The command's default, if any, appears in angled brackets (< >). Press Enter to choose the default.

Every time you need to type something at the command line — such as the name of a command, an option, coordinates, or values — you must press Enter afterward.

Transparent commands are commands that you can type at the command line while you're in the middle of another command. These commands appear in Part II preceded by an apostrophe (') because that's how you type them if you want to use them transparently. Suppose that you have snap on, and you select an object to move. When you need to specify where to move the object, however, you need to turn the snap off. Type **'snap** at the command line, press Enter, type **off**, and press Enter again. Then your MOVE command continues, and you can complete the command.

After you use a command, you can repeat it by pressing Enter. If you start a command and change your mind, press the Esc key.

You can use the F1 key (if you have DOS) or the F2 key (if you have Windows) to open the text screen and see more of the command-line history. Pressing F1 or F2 also gets you back to the drawing screen.

All the pretty little menus and toolbars

Using the mouse to start commands in AutoCAD is convenient. You're looking at the screen as you draw, and you don't need to look down at the keyboard or anywhere else. The commands are right there, where you're drawing. In this book, I ignore the hallowed screen menu (AutoCAD's first menu) and direct you to the menu bar (and, for Windows, to the toolbars).

The pull-down menus are easy to use. An ellipsis (. . .) after an item means that the item opens a dialog box. An arrow means that suboptions pop out from the item.

In Windows, you can use the keyboard to access a pull-down menu. Hold down the Alt key and press whichever letter is underlined in the menu. Most people, though, use the mouse.

AutoCAD also has a cursor menu, which you get to by pressing the Shift key and clicking the Return (right) button of your mouse. The menu is called a cursor menu because it pops up at the cursor. By default, the menu offers you object snaps and filters. If you're into that sort of stuff, you can customize this menu.

A word about toolbars: You can't use AutoCAD for Windows efficiently without knowing how to use the toolbars. Most toolbars are hidden until you command them to show themselves (by using the TOOLBAR command, which is covered in Part II).

Part IV provides a complete list of menus and toolbars in both AutoCAD for Windows and AutoCAD for DOS.

Dialog boxes

Some commands open dialog boxes. Usually, these dialog boxes are fairly simple to understand; almost always, they're easier to understand than the same operation in the command line. Some dialog boxes offer image tiles that enable you to see the results of your choices. When I have the choice of using a dialog box or the command line, I go with the dialog box.

If you like to use the keyboard, dialog boxes have underlined letters that you can use to get to an option. Most people find using the mouse to be easier. Don't forget the Help button, which explains each dialog-box option (although not always very completely).

It's a Setup!

This section explains how to set up a drawing. AutoCAD is famous for the extent of its customizability — this is just one example. Before you draw, you'll need to make some preparations for the most efficient drawing, and that's what this section is all about.

The prototype drawing

When you open a new drawing, AutoCAD bases it on a *prototype* (standard) drawing called ACAD.DWG. You can change this drawing the way you do any other to give it the settings you want. For example, you can create layers (see the DDLMODES command), set drawing limits (see the LIMITS command), and create text and dimension styles (see the STYLE and DDIM commands). This is a great time-saver, because you don't have to create these settings every time you start a new drawing.

You can create several prototypes. You may want to insert a title block and border for each size of drawing that you use. That way, when you start a new drawing, everything is set up for you. When you start a new drawing (see the NEW command), type in the Create New Drawing dialog box the name of the prototype drawing that you want to use. You can choose No Prototype if you really want to start from scratch.

Units

When you set up a drawing, one of the first things that you want to use is the DDUNITS command. With this command, you decide such basics as whether your measurements will be in plain inches, or in feet and inches, and how precise the measurements will be.

Drawing, Ltd.

Another basic setup item is the drawing limits that set the basic size of your drawing. Usually, you draw life-size and then scale your drawing when you plot. See the LIMITS command.

Layer upon layer

If you created a prototype drawing, you may have several layers to choose among. If not, you should create layers before you draw, using the DDLMODES command. Layers are *very* important. If you use AutoCAD at work, your office probably has standards for layers. These standards help ensure that all drawings use the same layers for the same types of objects. These standards should be written down and made available to everyone to prevent confusion.

After you define your layers, you need to make a layer current by using the DDLMODES or DDEMODES command. (Don't those names just sing to you?)

Stylish writing

When the time comes to annotate your drawing, you need to get into text styles. Your prototype drawing may have some text styles defined, and your office should have some standards regarding text styles — it would look funny for some drawings to use a script font and for others to use a boxy font.

Create text styles with the STYLE command. When you create a style, it becomes the current style. If you haven't just created a style, the DTEXT and MTEXT commands have a Style option that allows you to specify the style before you type your text.

Cool dimensions

Dimension styles are very complex. You're lucky if someone else has gone through all those dialog boxes and created a dimension style for you. If not, look up the DDIM command. Then use any of the dimension commands (all of them start with DIM . . .) to start creating dimensions.

Creating a User Coordinate System (UCS)

If you're into 3D, you can set up your coordinates anywhere and in any direction you want. (You can do so for a 2D drawing, but it's not as necessary.) If you're drawing an angled roof for a house, you can set the origin to the bottom-left corner of the roof and angle the X,Y coordinates so that they match the edges and angle of the roof. That procedure would make drawing a skylight in the roof a lot easier. See the UCS command in Part II.

After you create a UCS, you can save it for later use. (Or you can use one of AutoCAD's preset UCSes; see DDUCSP.) After you have your UCS, all coordinates are based on the origin and axes that you defined in your UCS.

Getting Picky: Specifying Points

You're going to spend a lot of time specifying X,Y coordinates of the objects that you draw. You can specify coordinates in several ways. The simplest way is to pick a point on-screen with your mouse. But that method may not be the most accurate. Often, you need to type coordinates to get the precision that you need.

Displaying coordinates

Before you start typing coordinates, knowing where you are helps. AutoCAD helpfully displays coordinates in the status bar (at the bottom of the screen, if you have Windows; at the top of the screen, if you have DOS). AutoCAD has three types of coordinate display: *static,* which shows only points that you specify; *dynamic,* which moves as the cursor moves; and *distance<angle,* which also moves as the cursor moves. You toggle among these displays by pressing the F6 key or Ctrl+D. Get into the habit of looking at those coordinates so that you don't get lost!

Oodles of coordinates

There are five types of coordinates; as you get used to them, you'll know which is the right one to use in your particular situation. Coordinates are based on a Cartesian coordinate system, with X and Y (and Z, for 3D) axes. Positive numbers go in one direction from the origin (0,0,0); negative numbers go in the other direction. Two types of coordinates are used only for 3D.

Absolute coordinates

This type of coordinate is called *absolute* because it is based on the X,Y coordinate system. The point is (no pun intended — well, maybe I did intend a little. . .) that absolute coordinates are relative to the 0,0 point of your X and Y axes. If drawing in 3D, add the Z axis coordinate.

Relative coordinates

Relative coordinates are relative to the last point that you drew. You tell AutoCAD that you are using a relative coordinate by typing the @ symbol in front of the coordinates. (You'll find that symbol on the 2 key on your keyboard, and you need to press the Shift key to get it. Why the creators of AutoCAD picked something that's so hard to type, I'll never know.)

Very often, you know how long your line is supposed to be and in what direction it should go, but not its absolute coordinate. If you are drawing in 3D, all you do is add the Z-axis coordinate.

Polar coordinates

Polar coordinates can be both relative and absolute. These coordinates define a point in terms of a distance (the length of your line, for example) and an angle.

The format for polar coordinates is *length<angle*. The angle of absolute polar coordinates is measured relative to the origin (usually 0,0). Relative polar coordinates are measured relative to the last point that you drew and require the @ symbol.

Zero degrees runs along the positive X axis, and angles are measured counterclockwise from there. (If you're into weird angle measurements, you can change how they're measured by using the DDUNITS command.) You can type negative angles to move clockwise, so that –90 degrees is the same as 270 degrees.

Cylindrical coordinates

If drawing in 3D makes you run in the opposite direction, just skip this section. Cylindrical coordinates are the 3D version of polar coordinates. They can also be absolute or relative. They can also be confusing. That's because the lengths don't indicate the length of the line (or whatever you're drawing), as polar coordinates do, but the number of units in a certain direction.

The format for cylindrical coordinates is *distance<angle,distance*. The first distance is the number of units in the XY plane. The angle is the number of degrees from the X axis in the XY plane. With these two points, you have defined a point on the XY plane. Now comes the last distance, the number of units along the Z axis, which defines the point in three dimensions. (Don't forget to use the @ symbol if you're specifying the coordinate relative to the last point that you entered.)

Spherical coordinates

Spherical coordinates are like cylindrical ones, except that instead of a second distance, you use a second angle. Got it?

The format for spherical coordinates is *distance<angle<angle*. The distance is the number of units from the origin or your last point. The first angle is the angle from the X axis in the XY plane. So far, these coordinates are just like cylindrical coordinates. The second angle is the angle up from the XY plane (in the Z direction).

Object snaps

If the coordinate that you want is on an object, you often can use *object snaps,* which are geometric points on objects. For example, you can move the endpoint of one line to the midpoint of another using object snaps. Anytime AutoCAD asks you for a point, you can use an object snap. You can use an object snap for one object, or you can set running object snaps that continue until you turn them off. See the DDOSNAP command (that's object snaps in AutoSpeak) for details on setting running snaps.

You can snap to a single object in several ways. Probably the best way is to use the Cursor menu (press Shift and click the Return button). In Windows, the Standard toolbar has an Object Snap flyout that contains icons for each object snap type. In DOS, choose Assist⇔Object Snap. If you're typing coordinates anyway, you can type the object-snap abbreviation. (Try typing the first three letters; that method usually works.)

The objects snaps are *endpoint, midpoint, intersection, apparent intersection, center, quadrant, node, insertion, perpendicular, tangent, nearest, quick,* and *none*. Obviously, some objects snaps are appropriate only for certain objects. Only circles, arcs, and ellipses have a center, for example. *Insertion* means the insertion point in text and blocks.

Filters

Point filters, which are used mostly for 3D drawing, allow you to extract all or part of a coordinate from an object. This capability helps when the coordinate that you need isn't obvious. The format is a period (.) and one or two axis letters. Whichever filter you use, AutoCAD prompts you for the *other* axis value(s).

Say that you want to draw an antenna on top of a boom box. You know the X,Y coordinates but not the Z coordinate. Start the LINE command. At the From point: prompt, type **.z**; AutoCAD displays the prompt of, which means that it wants to know the Z coordinate of what object. Select the top of the box, because that's where the antenna starts. Then AutoCAD displays need XY. Type the X,Y coordinates. AutoCAD starts the line at the X,Y coordinates that you specify, using the Z coordinate of the boom box. At the To point: prompt, you could type **@0,0,2** to make your antenna go straight up.

Often, you can get the same result by drawing temporary construction lines and using the ID or LIST commands. But the filters are quicker and slicker — if you can figure out how to use them!

SNAP to it!

This section gets back to 2D drawing. (Whew!) When you turn on snap, you can set it to a certain distance. If you turn on snap at .5, for example, the cursor jumps to points every half-unit apart; anything in between is off-limits.

If your drawing has lots of complex coordinates, such as (3.165,4.2798), snap won't help you. But if you use simpler coordinates, such as (3.25,6.5), snap is for you. Turning on snap allows you to draw without typing coordinates. You just watch those coordinates in the status bar and, when you have the coordinates that you need, click. This method is fast and accurate. See the SNAP and DDRMODES commands in Part II for details.

The itsy-bitsy, teeny-weeny, yellow polka-dot grid

OK, so it's not yellow; it's grayish. (Or off-white. Whatever.) The grid is a rectangular array of dots you can turn on to help you get your bearings. Usually, you want to set the grid equal to the snap. See GRID and DDRMODES in Part II for further information.

The military meal: drawing at right angles

Many things in life are at right angles. Walls and doors are at right angles from the floor (otherwise, the house comes tumbling down). ORTHO allows you to draw at right angles only. Like snap, ortho (in the right situation) can increase drawing speed and accuracy. See ORTHO and DDRMODES in Part II.

Here's Looking at You, Kid

After you draw something, you often need to zoom in closer to see the fine detail of your masterpiece and then zoom out again to see the drawing as a whole. The ZOOM command has many helpful options. This command is indispensable, so be sure to look it up in Part II. See also DSVIEWER.

When you zoom in, you may find that you want to move a little to the right (or left, or whatever). Panning allows you to move from place to place in your drawing. Look up the PAN command in Part II. If you have Windows, you also can use the scroll bars to pan.

The REDRAW and REGEN commands refresh the drawing screen. The REGEN command also recomputes coordinates, reindexes the database, and so on. You may want to redraw to get rid of those pesky blips (but see the BLIPMODE command for a tip on that).

If you're drawing in 3D, you want to view your drawing from different angles. You can look at your 3D drawing from any angle, even from below (I call that the gopher view). Use the DDVPOINT or VPOINT commands, which both set the viewing angle but in different ways. Pick the method that's most meaningful for you.

Obviously, part of looking at your drawing involves plotting it. Look up the PLOT command for details. You also may want to check out the concept of *paper space,* which is a way of setting up a drawing for plotting. Paper space is most useful for 3D drawings, because it allows you to create floating viewports, each with a different view of your objects. But even 2D drawings can benefit from paper space. The procedure is a bit complex, but — hey! — this is AutoCAD. Look up the following commands: PSPACE, MSPACE, and MVIEW.

Be Choosy: Selecting Objects for Editing

No one ever drew a drawing without making any mistakes, so you always need to edit. Even the basic drawing process will often involve copying or mirroring objects. Along with the editing process comes the need to select which objects to edit.

Which came first: object or command?

When you want to make changes, you need to know two things: which command to use and which objects to change. By default, AutoCAD requires you to enter a command first and then select the objects. The DDSELECT command allows you to customize the way you select objects.

AutoCAD, in true AutoSpeak, calls the concept of selecting the objects first and the command second *Noun/Verb Selection.* You see, the object that you're selecting is a thing, which is a *noun.* (You never thought of your circles as being nouns?) The command carries out an action, so it's a *verb.* The only good thing about all this nonsense is that if you choose Noun/Verb Selection (which you can do with the DDSELECT command), you get the best of two worlds: AutoCAD accepts object selection first or second, whichever you want. So choosing the option pays.

As an exercise in AutoSpeak, try turning your editing operations into little sentences, according to whether you select objects first or second. *I move a circle. A circle I move.* (I don't advise you to do this out loud if other people are around.)

You also can use the SELECT command, which simply selects objects. Then you start a command and, at the `Select objects` prompt, type **p**, which stands for *previous*. All the objects that you choose during the SELECT command will be highlighted and ready for action.

Pick and click

When you see the `Select objects` prompt, the crosshairs turn into a *pickbox,* which is a little box for picking objects. Move that box over the object that you want to pick and then click.

Selection options

You can select objects in other ways, too. For example, you can create windows (or fences or polygons) around objects and then select everything inside the window. These methods are especially good for selecting many objects at the same time. See the SELECT command for details.

Get a grip on yourself

Grips are little handles (no, not love handles) that you can use to select objects and choose a base point for an editing command. Use the DDGRIPS command to turn grips on and to play around with their color and size. Then, when you select an object, all the little handles appear, generally at strategic places such as endpoints and midpoints. Before you get too excited, you should know that the only tasks you can do with grips are stretch, move, rotate, scale, or mirror.

Here's how to use grips. Select the object, using any selection method. Do *not* start a command. Then click the grip that you want to use as the base point for the operation. Press Enter until you see the editing command that you want to use. If you need to specify a new point (for example, a new location for your grip), do so. In some operations, you can drag the grip. Each operation is slightly different, but the procedure is supposed to be intuitive, so play around. Command line prompts appear, but the point is to manipulate the object using only the mouse. Press Ctrl+C once to remove an object from the selection set. Press Ctrl+C twice to make the grips disappear.

Help!

Every once in a while using AutoCAD makes you feel like you've been underwater for too long (you forgot to breathe), and you need someone to come rescue you. Sometimes, using Help really helps. Other times, well...

Help comes in two species: regular and context-sensitive. You get to regular help by choosing Help⇨Help (if you have DOS) or Help⇨Contents (if you have Windows). The command teleports you to the Help Contents screen, in which you can choose the topic that you need. If you don't find the contents screen very helpful (I wondered myself what something so puny was doing in a place called Help), click the Search button. You move to something like an index with a long list of topics. Try typing a topic to see what you get. If you don't get anything, you can scroll through the list and try to find what you want. When you find the topic, double-click it. Related topics appear in the Select a Topic box. Double-click again to finally get the help that you want.

Context-sensitive help displays help on the command that you are using. Start a command and press F1 (or type **help** in the command line). The help screen for that command appears. Dialog boxes also contain a Help button that provides help information for the dialog box.

Get Me out of Here!

If you don't want to stay in AutoCAD forever (you could always draw some apples and try to eat them, and then draw a bed, too), here's how to get out.

The END command saves your drawing and exits AutoCAD. This command is quick and safe, but it's not the best method. The best method is to use the QSAVE command to save your drawing and then the QUIT command to exit. This technique deletes from the database all the stuff you don't need anymore, such as objects you erased and the former locations of objects you moved. The procedure means that you have smaller drawings, which means that you save hard-drive storage space — and I don't know anybody who doesn't need to save hard-drive storage space.

Part II

The Commands

Folks, here's the meat and potatoes of the book — a radical statement for a vegetarian like me! Each command tells you how to find it using menus and, for Windows, using toolbars.

A note about those toolbars. First of all, when you first open AutoCAD, you'll probably see only four toolbars: the Standard toolbar along the top, the Object Properties toolbar underneath it, and the Draw and Modify toolbars. But there are lots more, and it could be a mite bit mystifying when I tell you to use the Solids toolbar, and it's nowhere in sight. I humbly refer you to my explanation under the TOOLBAR command, which explains how to pull toolbars out of a top hat.

Some toolbars have flyouts, which are just visual submenus. You click on a toolbar icon, and out flies a bunch more icons. The problem is that when you use a flyout icon, that icon pops to the top of the flyout (on the assumption that you'll want to use it again soon). This makes it nigh unto impossible for me to show you where to find an icon hidden in a flyout — I have no idea what will appear on top on your toolbar! The flyouts have names, such as the Resize flyout, but guess what: The names don't appear anywhere. Nooooo!

So here's how I solved the problem. I used the flyout names; I had to say *something*. But if you can't figure out which flyout is which, go straight to Part IV. Each and every toolbar, with each and every flyout, is shown there *with its name* so you can find it.

Moving along, under the "How to Use It" sections that follow each command, I tell you how to use the command, walking you through the prompts or dialog box options. Then there's usually a section called "More Stuff" that includes more advanced or unusual information as well as warnings, tips, and references.

Draws 3D polygon surfaces that look like wire frames.

Windows: From the Surfaces toolbar, click the icon of the shape you want to draw.

DOS: Choose Draw⇨Surfaces⇨3D Objects.

How to Use It

If you use the menu, you get the 3D dialog box. If you type on the command line, you get a command line prompt. In either case, you have the following options:

⬚	Box	First, specify one corner of the box, then a length and a width. Specify an angle for the rotation around the Z axis. If you use the Cube option, you only specify the length because the width is the same.
△	Cone	Specify the center of the base, then its radius or diameter. Then type in the radius or diameter of the top. If you type **0,** you get a true cone; a bigger number results in a cone with its top chopped off. Now you type in a height and the number of segments. The number is how many facets or surfaces the cone has.
◉	Dish	This is just the bottom half of a sphere. Specify the center, which is the center of the imaginary circle covering the top of the sphere. Then type in a radius or diameter. Now type in the number of *longitudinal segments* around the sides of the bowl. Then type in the number of *latitudinal segments* from the bottom of the bowl to its rim.
◉	DOme	This is an upside down dish. It works the same way.
◈	Mesh	What is a mesh? You'll see when you draw one. (I'm so helpful, aren't I?) It's easy. Just specify four corners. Then type in a *Mesh M* size between 2 and 256, which in AutoCAD jargon means the number of row vertices, and a similar *Mesh N* size to specify the number of column vertices.

Pyramid This command creates regular and truncated pyramids, ridges (like a pup tent), and tetrahedrons. Specify three base points. You can branch off into tetrahedron making (tetrahedrons have only three base points) and finish it with the apex, or continue bravely on and specify a fourth base point. Now, if you're making a pyramid, all you do is define the apex and you're done. If you want a pup tent, specify the two top ridge points. Finally, if making truncated shapes, you'll need to specify three or four top points, depending on the shape. Never fear, AutoCAD prompts you as you go.

 Sphere Specify a center and radius or diameter and type in a number of longitudinal and latitudinal segments as in Dish.

 Torus This is a 3D donut. Specify the center and then the radius or diameter of the torus. Then define the radius or diameter of the tube, which is the width or fatness of the donut. Finally, type in a number of segments around the tube circumference (the inside) and around the torus circumference (the outside).

 Wedge This is the shape of a triangular doorstop. It has one right angle. Specify the corner at the right angle, and type in a length, width, and height. Finally, specify a rotation angle about the Z axis.

 ## More Stuff

Because these shapes have surfaces, they can be shaded or rendered (see SHADE and RENDER).

3DARRAY

Creates 3D arrays.

 Windows: From the Modify toolbar, click the Copy flyout and then one of the 3D Array icons (rectangular or polar).

DOS: Choose Construct⇨3D Array.

How to Use It

Before you use this command, be sure you know how to make plain-Jane 2D arrays. See the ARRAY command.

Select the objects to array. Pick either the Rectangular or Polar option. If you're making a rectangular array, type in the number of rows, columns, and levels (levels is the third dimension). Finally, specify distances between the rows, columns, and levels.

To make a polar array, type in the number of copies you want and the angle to fill, up to 360 degrees. Decide whether you want to rotate objects as they are copied (press **y** or **n**). Now specify a center point for the array. The last prompt is a second point on the axis of rotation. These last two points create a line that is an imaginary axis which the objects are arrayed about.

3DFACE

Draws a 3D surface.

Windows: From the Surfaces toolbar, click the 3D Face icon.

DOS: Choose Draw⇨Surfaces⇨3D Face.

How to Use It

3DFACE creates surfaces in 3D space. You simply specify X,Y,Z coordinates for each point, moving clockwise or counterclockwise. AutoCAD prompts you for the first through fourth points and then repeats the third and fourth point prompts so you can continue to create adjacent faces. Press Enter to end the command.

This is not an easy way to create surfaces since you have to know the coordinates of each point, but it can be very useful for creating odd-looking surfaces.

More Stuff

Before you specify any point, you can type **i** at the command line to make the edge created by that point and the next point invisible. This creates realistic-looking models because it hides edges that are in back.

DDMODIFY allows you to edit edge visibility.

3DPOLY

Draws a polyline in 3D space — lines only, no arcs.

Windows: From the Draw toolbar, click the Polyline flyout and then the 3D Polyline icon.

DOS: Choose Draw⇨3D Polyline.

How to Use It

AutoCAD starts with the From point: prompt. When you specify the point (using X,Y,Z coordinates), AutoCAD asks you for the Endpoint. AutoCAD continues to ask you for the endpoint of segments, and you keep on providing coordinates until you press Enter to complete the command.

The only other options are Undo (for those few of us who might make a mistake specifying those 3D points) and Close, which draws a line from the last endpoint to the first point.

More Stuff

The PEDIT command edits 3D polylines.

ALIGN

Aligns objects with other objects.

Windows: From the Modify toolbar, click the Rotate flyout and then the Align icon.

DOS: Choose Modify⇨Align.

How to Use It

AutoCAD prompts you to select the objects that you want to move. These objects are called *source objects.* You can specify one, two, or three pairs of points.

Aligning using one pair of points is just like using the MOVE command. AutoCAD prompts you for the 1st source point and the 1st destination point. Your first source point might be a corner of the rectangle you want to move. Your first destination point might be the centerpoint of a line. The corner of the rectangle will move to the centerpoint of the line. When AutoCAD prompts you for the second source point, press Enter to complete the command.

When you use two pairs of points, you can both move and rotate the first object to match the position and angle of the second object. Start in the same way as you do for one-point alignment but then pick a second source point and a second destination point. Press Enter when prompted for a third source point. Now choose either 2d or 3d. Use 2d when you want the alignment to remain in the current XY plane, *even if the objects you're aligning are 3D objects.* Use 3d when the first object needs to move in three dimensions. Either way, AutoCAD moves the first object and rotates it so that the line created by your two source points matches up with the line created by your two destination points.

Using three pairs of points allows a second rotation of the object in a different direction. It's used only for 3D objects. Specify three pairs of source and destination points. AutoCAD not only moves and rotates the first object to match up the first two pairs of points but also tumbles it so the third pair of points is aligned.

APERTURE

 See the DDOSNAP command to do the same thing (that is, change the size of the object snap target box — that's the aperture) using a dialog box.

ARC

Draws an arc.

 Windows: From the Draw toolbar, click the Arc flyout and select one of the icons.

DOS: Choose Draw⇨Arc.

How to Use It

AutoCAD gives you a dizzying array of options, but the concept is simple. First, choose Start point or Center and specify that point. (You can also press Enter to start your arc at a point that is tangent to the last line or arc you drew.)

AutoCAD then shows you your next options and guides you through the creation of your arc. You decide which points you want to specify and in what order. The elements of the arc (depending on your choices) are: Start point, End point, Second Point, Center, included Angle, Length of chord, and Radius.

More Stuff

See the section, "Arcs (the 'erald angels sing . . .)," in Chapter 7 of *AutoCAD For Dummies* for more on arcs.

AREA

Calculates area and perimeter of an object or an area you specify.

Windows: From the Object Properties toolbar, click the Inquiry flyout and then the Area icon.

DOS: Choose Assist⇨Inquiry⇨Area.

How to Use It

Your options are: First point, Object, Add, and Subtract. If you want the area and perimeter of an object, choose Object and then select the object. Choose First point to define an area by selecting points. AutoCAD prompts you for additional points. Add and Subtract allow you to add objects or points until you have the shape you want. Press Enter to complete the command.

ARRAY

Creates copies of an object in a rectangular or polar (that is, circular) pattern.

Windows: From the Modify toolbar, click the Copy flyout and then one of the Array icons (rectangular or polar).

DOS: Choose Construct⇨Array.

How to Use It

Select the object or objects you want to copy. Rectangular gives you copies in rows and columns. Tell AutoCAD how many rows and columns you want. Then type in the distance between the rows and columns. (You can also point to diagonal corners of an imaginary rectangle. The rectangle's width and height define the distance between the columns and rows, respectively.) Positive distances build the array up and to the right. Negative distances build it down and to the left.

Select Polar to array copies around a center point. AutoCAD prompts you for the Center point, number of items, and angle to fill (360 degrees fills a circle). You have to specify only two of the three prompts. Press Enter to pass by the prompt you don't want. Finally, tell AutoCAD whether you want to rotate the objects as they are copied.

More Stuff

If you make a mistake you can wind up with endless copies all over your drawing! The U command undoes your array.

ATTDEF

See the DDATTDEF command.

ATTDISP

Sets the visibility of attributes. An attribute is explanatory text attached to a block.

Windows and DOS: Choose Options⇨Display⇨Attribute Display.

How to Use It

When you create an attribute, you decide whether it will be visible or not. This command overrides that decision. AutoCAD gives you three options:

Normal (does nothing), ON (makes all attributes visible), and OFF (makes all attributes invisible).

More Stuff

Because this command overrides attribute visibility modes, think twice before using it.

Changes attribute information and definitions.

Windows: From the Attribute toolbar, click the Edit Attribute Globally icon.

DOS: Choose Modify⇨Attribute⇨Edit Globally.

How to Use It

This command allows you to edit attributes individually, one by one, or to make global changes to all of them at once. At the prompt Edit attributes one at a time? <Y>, type **n** to edit globally. Then AutoCAD prompts you for the name of the block and the attribute tag so that you can edit all copies of it.

Then you select an attribute and get the following options:

Value | Changes or replaces the value of the attribute. Use Change to change a string of characters instead of replacing the entire value.

Position | Changes the text insertion point.

Height | Changes the text height.

Angle | Changes the rotation angle of the text.

Style | Changes the text style.

Layer | Changes the layer.

Color | Changes the color.

More Stuff

You can use DDEDIT's dialog box to change the attribute's tag, prompt, and default. DDATTDEF creates an attribute.

ATTEXT

See DDATTEXT.

ATTREDEF

Redefines a block with attached attributes and updates the attributes according to the new definition.

Windows: From the Attributes toolbar, click the Redefine Attribute icon.

DOS: Choose Modify⇨Attribute⇨Redefine.

How to Use It

First, explode one copy of the block if you want to change its parts. ATTREDEF prompts you for the name of the block you want to redefine. Then you select the objects for the block, including the attributes. When AutoCAD prompts you for an insertion base point, pick a point. AutoCAD updates the block and its attributes wherever the block has been inserted.

More Stuff

When redefining the block, select the attribute text in the same order you want AutoCAD to prompt you for the attribute information when you insert the block.

AUDIT

Finds errors in the drawing caused by data storage malfunctions.

Windows and DOS: Choose File⇨Management⇨Audit.

How to Use It

AutoCAD asks permission to fix any errors detected. You answer **y** or **n.**

More Stuff

The RECOVER command tries to retrieve those *really* messed up drawings that AUDIT can't fix.

BASE

Sets the insertion base point for your drawing.

Windows and DOS: Type **base** at the command line.

How to Use It

If you want to change the base point, simply specify the point using absolute coordinates.

More Stuff

Use this command to insert the drawing into another drawing and want the base point to be relative to the other drawing. Otherwise, the base point should generally be (0,0,0).

BHATCH

Creates a hatch pattern inside an enclosed area. A hatch pattern isn't an instinct of baby birds, it's just a bunch of parallel lines that fill in an object or enclosed area. This command allows you to create an *associative* hatch pattern; the hatch pattern is adjusted automatically if you change the enclosed area.

Windows: From the Draw toolbar, click the Hatch flyout and then the Hatch icon.

DOS: Choose Draw⇨Hatch⇨Hatch. (Take my word for it, it's easier to type **bhatch** on the command line.)

How to Use It

The Boundary Hatch dialog box opens; it has three sections:

- **Pattern Type:** You can use a Predefined hatch pattern — the ones that AutoCAD gives you — a User-defined pattern that creates a hatch out of the current linetype, or a custom hatch pattern that you have created (not Dummies material).

- **Pattern Properties:** Offers the following options:

Pattern	Selects your hatch pattern from AutoCAD's predefined list (or a custom pattern if that's the type you selected).
Scale	Increases or decreases the size of a hatch pattern.
Angle	Rotates the pattern relative to the X axis (but some patterns are created at an angle, so specifying an angle can create unintended results).
Spacing	Defines how wide apart the lines are; only for a user-defined hatch.
Double	Creates a second set of lines 90 degrees from the first set; for user-defined hatches.
Exploded	Creates a hatch pattern of individual lines instead of a block.

- **Boundary:** You can either pick points or select objects. If there are objects inside your objects — called islands — you can click Remove Islands to avoid hatching them.

Before you complete the command, you can preview your hatch — a wise idea. The dialog box disappears, and you see what damage you've done. Continue gets you back to the dialog box.

To make things easier, you can specify a hatch you've already created and copy its Pattern Type and Pattern Properties to your new hatch. Click Inherit Properties (don't expect to find your rich uncle has left you a major hotel chain), and AutoCAD prompts you to select the original hatch.

Select the Associative radio button to create an associative hatch.

When you're all done, click Apply to create the hatch.

More Stuff

Click Advanced, if you're the daring type, for the Advanced Options dialog box. Style defines how objects within objects are hatched. As you select each type, an image tile shows you an example. Another useful option is Retain Boundaries. If not selected, you get just the hatch without boundaries around it.

 See Chapter 12 in *AutoCAD For Dummies* for more on hatching.

'BLIPMODE

Turns on and off those pesky little blips that appear whenever you pick a point.

Command line: Type **blipmode.**

How to Use It

Choose On to show blips; Off if you don't ever want to see them.

More Stuff

Even with blipmode on, every time you use REDRAW, REGEN, ZOOM, or PAN, and the drawing is redrawn or regenerated, the blips disappear.

BLOCK

Creates one defined object from a group of objects. The block can then be inserted elsewhere using DDINSERT.

Windows: From the Draw toolbar, click the Block flyout and then the Block icon.

DOS: Choose Construct⇨Block.

How to Use It

When AutoCAD prompts you for a name, type a name for your block at the command line. AutoCAD then asks you for the Insertion base point. This is the base point that will be used when you insert the block somewhere else.

 Use an object snap to create an exact insertion base point. The lower-left corner or center of your block are good choices.

AutoCAD asks you to select objects. Once you finish the selection process, your block is created. But your objects disappear! Uh oh! Just type OOPS on the command line to bring them back.

More Stuff

If you type **?** instead of a name, AutoCAD lists previously created blocks.

See DDINSERT, EXPLODE, and WBLOCK for more on blocks.

You can also check out Chapter 15, "Playing with Blocks," in *AutoCAD For Dummies*.

BOUNDARY

Creates separate, non-overlapping regions or polylines from overlapping objects that form an enclosed area.

Windows: From the Draw toolbar, click the Polygon flyout and then the Boundary icon.

DOS: Choose Construct⇨Boundary.

How to Use It

The Boundary Creation dialog box appears with the following options:

Object Type	Choose either Region or Polyline.
Define Boundary Set	Leave unchecked if you want to do nothing (the easiest option!), and let AutoCAD analyze everything, or check to define a narrower boundary set for quicker results.
Ray Casting	Leave it at Nearest unless you're not getting the results you want. Then you may want to experiment.
Island Detection	Islands are objects inside your objects. Click this only if you want AutoCAD to pay attention to them.
Pick Points	This creates the boundary. You pick a point or points *inside* objects to define the boundary. Press Enter to end the selection of points and complete the command.

BOX 35

More Stuff

See the PLINE and REGION commands for more information.

BOX

Draws a 3D solid box.

Windows: From the Surfaces toolbar, click the Box icon.

DOS: Choose Draw⇨Solids⇨Box.

How to Use It

The first prompt offers you the choice of defining the box from its center or from a corner. If you choose the corner method (the default), specify a point on the bottom of the box. Now you have three options:

Other corner	Specify the diagonally opposite corner of the *bottom* of the box. AutoCAD then prompts you for a height. A positive number makes the box rise along the positive Z axis. (A negative number makes the box descend into — oops — in the direction of the negative Z axis.)
Length	Type **l** to use this option. AutoCAD prompts you for a length, a width, and then a height. Positive numbers expand the box along positive axes. (Negative numbers expand the box in the direction of the negative Z axis.)
Cube	Type **c** to draw a cube. Of course, all you have to do is specify a length, and AutoCAD figures out that the rest of the sides are the same and draws your cube.

The center option just lets you specify the center of the box instead of the first corner. All the other prompts are the same.

More Stuff

Boxes cannot be stretched or otherwise changed in size. You can also draw a rectangle and use EXTRUDE to create a solid box.

BREAK

Creates a break in an object.

Windows: From the Modify toolbar, click the Break flyout and select one of the icons.

DOS: Choose Modify⇨Break.

How to Use It

You can do this command in two ways:

1. First, select the object to break by clicking on it any old place. Then type **f** (for first point) on the command line and select your first point. Then select your second point. AutoCAD erases the object between the two points. If you have Windows, you can use the 2 Points Select icon on the Break flyout of the Modify toolbar. If the second point is beyond the end of your object, AutoCAD erases the object from your first point to its end.

2. If you are the precise type, you can select the object in a location that is also the first point you want to select. Then just select the second break point, and you are done. If you have Windows, you can use the 2 Points icon on the Break flyout of the Modify toolbar.

More Stuff

You can break lines, arcs, polylines, circles, ellipses, donuts, and so on. The 1 Point and 1 Point Select icons allow you to break an object into two parts with no gap. The object still looks like it's one object but if you try to move it, you'll see it's actually two objects.

'CAL

An on-line geometry calculator for evaluating expressions as you draw.

Windows: From the Standard toolbar, click the Object Snap flyout and then the Calculator icon.

DOS: Choose Tools⇨Calculator.

How to Use It

This calculator is loaded with features not easily explained in a Quick Reference book. It can calculate regular numeric expressions, as well as work with vectors (collections of points), measurements (feet and inches), angles, and more. You can use snap modes in your expressions.

Here are two simple examples:

- Start the **CAL** command. When AutoCAD prompts you for an expression, type in something like (575+72.2154) * (2^5) – (6 * PI). In other words, something you would never figure out yourself in a million years. (I got 20692.0, did you?)

- Say you want to move a circle so that its center is halfway between the midpoint of two lines. Type **move** on the command line and select the circle. When AutoCAD prompts you for a base point, type **cen** and select the circle. At the Second point of displacement prompt, type **'cal** (to use it as a transparent command). AutoCAD will ask for an expression. Type **(mid+mid)/2.** AutoCAD then wants to know which midpoints you're talking about and prompts you to select an object for each midpoint snap. Select one line, then the other. AutoCAD moves the circle. Cool!

CHAMFER

Bevels (cuts at an angle) two intersecting lines (or almost-intersecting lines).

 Windows: From the Modify toolbar, click the Feature flyout and then the Chamfer icon.

DOS: Choose Construct⇨Chamfer.

How to Use It

At the prompt, select the first line, then the second line, and—presto!—AutoCAD creates a new line at an angle to the original lines. Here are the other options:

Polyline   Chamfers an entire polyline (every angle).

Distances   Specifies how far from the selected line the chamfer starts.

Angle	Defines the chamfer by a distance from the first line and an angle to the second line.
Trim	Usually, AutoCAD trims the two selected lines so that they meet the chamfer, but you can nix that.
Method	Tells AutoCAD whether to use the Distances or Angle method of defining a chamfer.

More Stuff

When you define Distances, the command ends, so if you want to chamfer something, press Enter to get the command again. You can also chamfer a 3D solid.

See also the FILLET command.

CHANGE

Changes certain properties of existing objects.

Windows: From the Modify toolbar, click the Resize flyout and then the Change icon.

DOS: Type **change** at the command line.

How to Use It

First, select the objects.

The first option is Change point. For a line, you pick a new endpoint, and AutoCAD changes the line. For a circle, you specify a point that becomes the new radius. For text, the point you select becomes the new text insertion point. For blocks, the point becomes the new insertion base point.

The second option is Properties. See the DDCHPROP command.

More Stuff

This command may give you unpredictable results if you select lines with other types of objects, so do them separately.

CHPROP

See the DDCHPROP command.

CIRCLE

Draws a circle.

Windows: From the Draw toolbar, click the Circle flyout and select one of the icons.

DOS: Choose Draw⇨Circle.

How to Use It

There are four ways to define a circle:

Center Point	Pick the center point. Then pick a radius or type in a length. Or type **d** (for diameter) and pick the diameter or type in its length.
3P	This isn't the beginning of 3PO's name. (Remember *Star Wars*?) It stands for 3 point. Specify three points on the circumference of the circle.
2P	You specify two opposing points on the circumference of the circle.
TTR	That means Tangent, Tangent, Radius. You need two other objects nearby for the circle to be tangent to. Select the two objects and then type in a radius length. This sometimes gives unexpected results because more than one circle can meet your definition.

More Stuff

See the "(Will he go round in) circles . . ." section in Chapter 7 of *AutoCAD For Dummies*.

COLOR

 See the DDCOLOR command.

CONE

Draws a solid cone.

 Windows: From the Solids toolbar, click the Cone flyout and select one of the icons.

DOS: Choose Draw⇨Solids⇨Cone.

How to Use It

The default is to create a cone with a circular base. Specify the center point of the base. Then you have a choice of specifying the radius or the diameter. Type **d** to specify the diameter. At the next prompt, type in a height. (A negative height will draw an upside-down cone, like an ice cream cone.) Or you can type **a** for apex and specify a point for the apex. Use the apex option if you want a cone that rises at an angle (the Leaning Tower of Pisa look).

If you type **e** for elliptical at the first prompt or use the Elliptical cone icon, you define an ellipse just as for the ELLIPSE command, using either the axis or the center method. The rest of the prompts are the same.

More Stuff

See the ELLIPSE command.

CONFIG

Configures AutoCAD to tell it what video monitor, digitizer/ mouse, printer/plotter you have.

Windows and DOS: Choose Options⇨Configure.

How to Use It

AutoCAD shows you your current configuration. Press Enter and type the number of the menu item you want to change. AutoCAD prompts you through the process.

More Stuff

You have to configure the first time you use AutoCAD. Afterwards, use this command only when you change equipment.

COPY

Copies objects.

Windows: From the Modify toolbar, click the Copy flyout and then the Copy icon.

DOS: Choose Construct⇨Copy.

How to Use It

First, select the object or objects you want to copy and press Enter to complete the selection process.

Select a point as the location to copy from. It doesn't have to be on the object(s) you are copying. AutoCAD then prompts you for a second point that shows the distance and location from the base point for the copy. Press Enter to complete the command.

More Stuff

You can type **m** for multiple, and AutoCAD continues to prompt you for second points so that you can make as many copies as you wish. Press Enter to complete the command.

CYLINDER

Draws a solid cylinder.

Windows: From the Solids toolbar, click the Cylinder flyout and select one of the icons.

DOS: Choose Draw⇨Solids⇨Cylinder.

How to Use It

If you want the base of your cylinder to be a circle, then the procedure is quite easy. Choose the Center option and specify the center point of the base circle. Type in the radius or the diameter. Radius is the default, but if you want specify the diameter, type **d.** Now AutoCAD prompts you to type in the height but gives you an option to specify the center of the other end of the cylinder. Either task completes the command.

If you want the base of your cylinder to be an ellipse, choose the Elliptical option or icon. AutoCAD prompts `<Axis endpoint>/ Center`. AutoCAD prompts to define the ellipse. The rest is the same as the circular cylinder, defining either the height or the center of the other end.

More Stuff

You can also draw a circle or ellipse and EXTRUDE it.

DBLIST

Lists information for every object in the drawing.

Windows and DOS: Type **dblist** on the command line.

How to Use It

AutoCAD displays information about every object in the drawing — lots of it. Press Enter to continue from page to page. Press Esc to cancel.

DDATTDEF

Defines an attribute, which is text attached to a block.

Windows: From the Attribute toolbar, click the Define Attribute icon.

DOS: Choose Construct⇨Attribute.

How to Use It

Attributes can be used just to facilitate the entry of text labels related to blocks, but they also allow you to extract a database of all the information contained in them. The steps are:

1. Create the object. You will make it into a block later.

2. Define the attribute using DDATTDEF. You will probably want to put it next to the block. You can define more than one attribute for a block.

3. Back in your drawing, you will find the attribute text. Create the block and include in it both the object(s) and the attribute(s).

4. Insert the block. AutoCAD will prompt you for the attribute information.

When you enter this command, AutoCAD opens the Attribute Definition dialog box, which has four sections for you to complete: Mode, Attribute, Insertion Point, and Text Options.

Here are the Mode options:

Invisible	If you click Invisible, the attribute will not show up in your drawing, but you can still extract the information it contains for use in a database.
Constant	You can give an attribute a constant value, and then AutoCAD will not prompt you for a value when you insert the block, but just put the constant value in automatically.
Verify	If you click this option, you will have to verify that the attribute is correct each time you insert the block.
Preset	Creates a default value that you can change.

The Attribute section:

Tag	This is the name of the attribute. Use something meaningful. It can't have any spaces.
Prompt	This is what AutoCAD will use when it prompts you to type in the attribute. It may be the same as the tag or something more helpful. It can have spaces. (But don't get too spacey.)
Value	Use this if you checked Preset to enter the default value.

For the Insertion Point section, you can type in X,Y,Z coordinates or click the Pick Point button to pick a point in the drawing. As soon as you do, the dialog box magically returns.

In the Text Options section, you specify the justification, style, height, and rotation of the text as with the text commands.

If you are creating more than one attribute, you can click the Align below previous attribute button to put the attribute directly below the previous one. Click OK to complete the command.

More Stuff

If you make a mistake defining your attribute and catch it before you've defined the block, use DDEDIT. Once you've inserted the block and typed in the specific attribute data, use DDATTE to change the data.

See the DTEXT and STYLE commands for information on setting the text options. See the BLOCK and DDINSERT commands for information on creating and inserting blocks.

DDATTE

Edits the data that has been input for the attribute.

Windows: From the Attribute toolbar, click the Edit Attribute icon.

DOS: Choose Modify⇨Attribute⇨Edit.

How to Use It

You inserted the block and input the attribute data, but now the data's been changed. Here's how you change it.

AutoCAD prompts you to select a block, meaning the one with the attributes you want to edit, and then opens the Edit Attributes dialog box. Just type in the new or corrected data and click OK.

More Stuff

Use DDEDIT to change attribute definitions such as the tag, prompt, and default value.

DDATTEXT

Extracts attribute data to a file for use as a database.

Windows: Type **ddattext** at the command line.

DOS: Choose File⇨Export⇨Attributes.

How to Use It

Now comes the fun stuff, extracting your attribute data into a file for use in a database program. But it ain't easy. Oh well! Remember, this is the feared and awesome AutoCAD.

First, you have to make a template file. This is a plain text file that AutoCAD uses to design the database.

If you are using Windows, press Alt+Esc to get to the Program Manager. In the Accessories Group, choose Notepad.

If you are using DOS, type **shell** on the command line, press Enter twice, and type **edit**.

Translation: Get to any text editor that saves files in plain text (ASCII) format.

Say you have a block named DESK. You want to extract the block name, its X and Y coordinates, and two tags: name and phone number. Your kid's teacher may use this to make up a class layout of which student sits where and wants to extract the information to make up a phone tree list of each student's name and phone number.

The attribute file you create in the text editor should look something like the following figure.

AutoCAD is very finicky about this. (Oh, for a Template File wizard!) As you type, end each line, including the last, by pressing Enter. Use spaces only, no tabs.

When you've created the template file, save it and remember its name. (Better yet, write it down.) Then go into the DDATTEXT command, which opens up the Attribute Extraction dialog box.

```
 ═                    Notepad - CLASS-DB.TXT              ▼ ▲
 File   Edit   Search   Help
 BL:NAME            C010000                                  ↑
 BL:X               N006000
 BL:Y               N006000
 SPACESAVER         C002000
 NAME               C015000
 PHONE              C008000
                                                            ↓
 ←                                                          →
```

First, select the format you want for the file you will create. Usually, you will use a comma delimited file, which means there will be commas between the fields of each record, or a space delimited file (you can guess what that means). The fields of space-delimited files have a fixed width. Which to use? That depends on the database application you are going to use. The secret is to go to the documentation of that program and find out what types of files it can import.

Now click Select Objects. This returns you to your drawing so that you can select the blocks with the attributes that you want in the database. When you're done, the Attribute Extraction dialog box returns.

Next to the Template File button, type in the name of your template file. (You wrote it down, remember?) If you click Template File, you get a dialog box similar to a File⇨Open box that allows you to select the file from a list.

Next to Output File, type a name for the database file you want to create. AutoCAD will automatically give it a .TXT file extension.

Finally, click OK to extract the attribute information and create the database file. Here are the results.

In the earlier example, the name of the block (DESK) and the X and Y coordinates are a bit useless, but they're the standard options available with DDATTEXT. (If your kid's teacher needs X,Y coordinates to find your kid, you'd better consider switching schools!)

Notepad - CLASLIST.TXT				
File Edit Search Help				
DESK	3	2	Camille	472-1234
DESK	6	2	Eliyah	469-5432
DESK	3	5	Yeshayah	472-0987
DESK	6	5	Paul	472-6789

More Stuff

AutoCAD has several commands (which I've left out — they're a book in themselves) that use the AutoCAD SQL Environment (ASE) to help you work with external database management applications.

DDCHPROP

Uses a dialog box to change the following properties of an object: color, layer, linetype, and thickness.

Windows and DOS: Type **ddchprop** at the command line.

How to Use It

First, select the objects you want to change.

Color	See the DDCOLOR command to change color.
Layer	See the DDLMODES command to change layers.
Linetype	See the DDLTYPE command to change linetype.
Linetype Scale	Type in the scale you want for the linetype.
Thickness	Type in the thickness you want.

Click OK to close the Change Properties dialog box.

More Stuff

See the DDMODIFY, DDCOLOR, DDLMODES, DDLTYPE, LINETYPE, and ELEV commands.

DDCOLOR

Sets the color for new objects.

Windows: Choose Data⇨Color; or from the Object Properties toolbar, click the Color Control icon.

DOS: Choose Data⇨Color.

How to Use It

This command opens the Select Color dialog box, opening a whole vista of color possibilities. You can select one of the standard colors or select from the full color palette. You can also select BYLAYER, which gives new objects the color assigned to their layer (the default), or BYBLOCK, which draws new objects in the default color until they are grouped into a block. The inserted block takes on the block's color setting.

More Stuff

When you define a layer, you include a color. Generally, the best way to use color is to simply change the layer. Think twice before changing the color of objects using DDCOLOR or COLOR because this overrides the layer color definition. If objects are on the same layer but have different colors, expect to be confused!

See the DDLMODES command.

DDEDIT

Edits text and attributes.

Windows: From the Modify toolbar, click the Special Edit flyout and then the Edit Text icon.

DOS: Choose Modify⇨Edit Text.

How to Use It

Select the text to edit. What happens next depends on how you created the text. If you used TEXT or DTEXT, AutoCAD opens the Edit Text dialog box. If you used MTEXT to create paragraph text, AutoCAD opens the EDIT text editor on DOS systems and the Edit Mtext dialog box on Windows systems. From then on, editing the text is fairly straightforward. Click OK to close the dialog box or text editor and then press Enter to end the command.

More Stuff

You can edit attributes with this command, too, but you have to explode the block first. AutoCAD opens the Edit Attribute Definition dialog box, allowing you to change the tag, prompt, and default value.

'DDEMODES

Opens a dialog box to set color, layer, linetype, text style, linetype scale, elevation, and thickness for new objects.

Windows: Choose Data⇨Object Creation; or from the Object Properties toolbar, click the Object Creation icon, Color icon, Layer icon, or Linetype icon.

DOS: Choose Data⇨Object Creation.

How to Use It

Color	Opens the Select Color dialog box.
Layer	Opens the Layer Control dialog box.
Linetype	Opens the Select Linetype dialog box.
Text Style	Opens the Select Text Style dialog box. Select a style from the list or type an existing style name in the Style Name text box. You can type a few letters in the Sample Text box and see them in the preview box. Click OK.

Linetype Scale	Type in a number.
Elevation	Type in a number. Sets elevation (height above the "ground" XY plane).
Thickness	Type in a number. Sets the thickness, which is the height of the object in the Z direction.

More Stuff

DDEMODES is a catch-all dialog box that allows you to change the properties for new objects you will create. There is a separate command for each of the individual properties. The STYLE command creates and defines new styles.

See the DDCOLOR, DDLMODES, DDLTYPE, ELEV, LINETYPE, and STYLE commands.

You can also review the "Objective creation" section in Chapter 6 of *AutoCAD For Dummies*.

'DDGRIPS

Turns on grip display.

Windows and DOS: Choose Options⇨Grips.

How to Use It

The Grips dialog box opens. Click Enable Grips to display them. Click Enable Grips Within Blocks to show grips for each object within the block. If your blocks have many original objects, this might be a bit overwhelming.

Then choose the color of selected and unselected grips, using the Select Color dialog box. (Refer to the DDCOLOR command.) You also get to choose the size of your grips using the slider bar. To the right makes your muscles bigger; to the left — oh, well.

More Stuff

See Chapter 4 and Chapter 8 of *AutoCAD For Dummies* for a thorough discussion on using grips.

DDIM

Defines dimension settings into groups called dimension styles.

Windows and DOS: Choose Data⇨Dimension Style.

How to Use It

AutoCAD opens the Dimension Styles dialog box, which allows you to control every aspect of the appearance of dimensions. In the Dimension Style section, you can select the style name you want to be current from the drop-down list box. To create a new style, define settings using the rest of the dialog box and then type a name in the Name text box. Then click Save to save your style. You can also click Rename to rename a dimension style.

The Family section is where you create families — I'd better be careful what I say here! The default is the Parent — this is the basic style. Once you have the default style, you can create variations of the parent — sort of like children, except they have strange names for kids, like Linear, Radial, Diameter, and so on. Unless you're creating a variation of a parent style, leave the Parent button blackened.

Now go on to the three main dialog boxes — Geometry, Format, and Annotation.

Geometry   Make your choices for the dimension line, arrowheads, extension line, and center marks. You also get to choose the scale and whether or not you want to scale to paper space. Click OK.

Format   Here you choose the location of dimension text, arrowheads, leaders, and dimension line. Click OK.

Annotation   Set the definitions for your dimension text. Click OK.

More Stuff

See all the commands starting with DIM.

See the section, "Doing Dimensions with Style(s)," in Chapter 11 of *AutoCAD For Dummies* for the latest and greatest on dimensioning.

DDINSERT

Inserts a block or drawing.

Windows: From the Draw toolbar, click the Block flyout and then the Insert icon.

DOS: Choose Draw⇨Insert⇨Block.

How to Use It

AutoCAD opens the Insert dialog box. Type in the name of the block or drawing to insert or click <u>B</u>lock or <u>F</u>ile to select from a list. Click <u>E</u>xplode if you want the block to be inserted as individual objects.

Click <u>S</u>pecify Parameters on Screen if you want to pick the insertion point, scale, and rotation angle on-screen or type in your Insertion Point, Scale, and Rotation. Choose OK to insert.

More Stuff

If you click <u>E</u>xplode and make a mistake, you may have dozens of itty-bitty objects all over your drawing. You can use U to undo the command, but you can also insert the block unexploded first, to see the results, and then explode it.

See the EXPLODE and XPLODE commands for information on exploding blocks.

You find out more in the "Inserting blocks" section in Chapter 15 of *AutoCAD For Dummies*.

'DDLMODES

Everything you ever wanted to know about layers.

Windows: Choose <u>D</u>ata⇨<u>L</u>ayers; or from the Object Properties toolbar, click the Layers icon.

DOS: Choose Data⇨Layers.

How to Use It

The Layer Control dialog box gives you full control over — you guessed it — layers. At the top, the current layer appears. To simply set a new current layer, select one from the Layer Name list and click Current. Click OK to close the dialog box. Note that the Layer Name listing allows you to select more than one layer at a time. Select a layer name again to deselect it.

You can type in a layer name in the text box up to 31 characters long and click New, Current, or Rename.

If you select New, you have created a new layer. Then select it on the Layer Name listing and click Set Color to define its color and Set Ltype to define its linetype. The defaults are white color and continuous linetype. Choose Current if you want your new layer to be the current layer.

There are three things you can do to layers:

Turn Off and On	On is the normal state for a layer. If you turn it off, it becomes invisible, but still regenerates when the drawing regenerates.
Freeze and Thaw	Thawed is the normal state for a layer. If you freeze it, it becomes invisible and is not regenerated.
Lock and Unlock	If you lock a layer, it's visible but cannot be edited. This can make it easier to edit overlapping objects on other, unlocked layers.

More Stuff

The Cur VP box stands for current viewport and allows you to freeze or thaw layers by viewport, if you're in model space, or for all of paper space, if that's where you are. New VP freezes or thaws layers for new viewport objects.

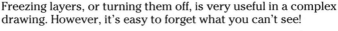

Freezing layers, or turning them off, is very useful in a complex drawing. However, it's easy to forget what you can't see!

Other related commands are DDCOLOR, DDLTYPE, PSPACE, and VPORT.

See "Getting the layered look" in Chapter 4 and "Using that layered look" in Chapter 6 of *AutoCAD For Dummies*.

'DDLTYPE

Sets current linetype, loads new ones, and defines scale and pen width.

Windows and DOS: Choose Data⇨Linetype.

How to Use It

The Select Linetype dialog box pops open with a list of loaded linetypes. Select one and choose OK to make it current.

You can also specify an ISO pen width and linetype scale.

If you click Load, you go to the Load or Reload Linetypes dialog box. The default file, ACAD.LIN, has the standard linetypes, but you can load another file that you have created. You can then select any or all linetypes to load and use in your drawing. Click OK to return to the Select Linetype dialog box. Then select a linetype from the Loaded Linetypes list and click OK.

More Stuff

When you define a layer, you include a linetype. Generally, the best way to use a new linetype is to simply change the layer. Think twice before changing the linetype of objects using DDLTYPE because this command overrides the layer linetype definition.

See the DDLMODES command for information on creating layers.

See "Loading up linetypes" in Chapter 4 of *AutoCAD For Dummies* for the low-down on linetypes.

DDMODIFY

Changes properties of existing objects.

Windows: Choose Edit⇨Properties; or from the Object Properties toolbar, click the Properties icon.

DOS: Choose Modify⇨Properties.

How to Use It

Select the object you want to modify. The dialog box that appears depends on the object you select. Each box has a Properties section allowing you to change color, layer, linetype, linetype scale, and thickness. For example, if you select a circle, you get the Modify Circle dialog box. I like the Modify Body dialog box — it saves me from having to go to the health spa!

More Stuff

Other related commands: DDCHPROP, DDCOLOR, DDLMODES, DDLTYPE, ELEV, and STYLE.

'DDOSNAP

Sets object snap modes that continue in effect until you turn them off. These are called Running Object Snap modes.

Windows and DOS: Options⊃Running Object Snap.

How to Use It

AutoCAD opens the Running Object Snap dialog box, a warning that if you run into an object too hard, something may go snap.

In the Select Settings section, click the object snaps you want. Or click Clear All to turn off all the object snaps. You can also set the size of the target box (*aperture*) that you use to select objects using the slider bar.

More Stuff

See "Turning on running object snaps" in Chapter 4 of *AutoCAD For Dummies.*

'DDPTYPE

Defines how points are shown.

Windows and DOS: Choose Options⊃Display⊃Point Style.

How to Use It

The Point Style dialog box opens. Click on the picture of the style you want. Type in the point size. If you want the points to look the same on your screen no matter how much you zoom in or out, click Set Size Relative to Screen.

DDRENAME

Changes names of objects, like blocks, layers, styles, and views.

Windows and DOS: Choose Data⇨Rename.

How to Use It

Select the type of object you want to rename from the Named Objects list. The Items box then lists your objects by name. Select the one you named AuntMelda and type her new name in the Rename To text box. Click OK.

More Stuff

You can't rename certain standard objects such as layer 0, style STANDARD, and so on.

'DDRMODES

Sets 'ORTHO, SNAP, 'GRID, FILL, 'BLIPMODE, and other drawing aids.

Windows and DOS: Choose Options⇨Drawing Aids.

How to Use It

In the Modes section, you turn on or off Ortho, Solid Fill, Quick Text, Blips, highlighting, and groups. Most of these controls are all available under their own commands.

The Snap section allows you to turn snap on and off and specify its spacing, angle, and base point.

The <u>G</u>rid section allows you to turn the grid on and off and specify its spacing.

The Isometric section turns isometric on and off and sets a plane to the left, top, or right.

On the status bar, you can double-click the SNAP, GRIP, and ORTHO buttons to turn them off and on.

More Stuff

For more information on these drawing aids, see BLIPMODE, FILL, GRID, ISOPLANE, ORTHO, QTEXT, and SNAP.

See "Making Your Screen Smart" in Chapter 5 of *AutoCAD For Dummies*.

'DDSELECT

Controls how objects are selected.

Windows and DOS: Choose Options⇨Selection.

How to Use It

DDSELECT opens the Object Selection Settings dialog box. The Selection Modes section controls the selection of objects.

<u>N</u>oun/Verb Selection	This allows you to select objects before starting a command. The cursor includes a pickbox to select objects. You can then give a command that applies to the selected objects. Even with this option on, you can still do it the old-fashioned AutoCAD way — command first.
<u>U</u>se Shift to Add	Requires you to hold down the Shift key to add more objects.
<u>P</u>ress and Drag	Requires you to hold down the pick button of your mouse when creating a selection window.
<u>I</u>mplied Windowing	The default is on; when you click on an empty spot on your screen, AutoCAD assumes you want to create a window.
Object <u>G</u>rouping	You place objects in named groups.

The next section of the Object Selection Settings dialog box allows you to adjust the Pickbox Size using the slider bar.

The Object Sort Method button opens the Object Sort Method dialog box. This simply forces various procedures (such as object selection by window, redraws, regens, and plotting) to process objects in the order in which you created them.

More Stuff

See the GROUP command for information on creating groups.

See "The Selective Service" in Chapter 8 of *AutoCAD For Dummies* for a thorough discussion of this command.

 Makes a new User Coordinate System current.

Windows: From the Standard toolbar, click the UCS flyout and then the Named UCS icon.

DOS: Choose Draw⇨Named UCS.

How to Use It

AutoCAD opens the UCS Control dialog box, which lists coordinate systems that you have defined. (You define a UCS using the UCS command.) Click the name of the UCS you want and click Current. Then click OK to return to your drawing. You can also delete, list, and rename coordinate systems.

More Stuff

DDUCSP selects one of the coordinate systems that come preset with AutoCAD. That's for the rest of us folks who aren't into making up our own.

DDUCSP

Allows you to change to one of several standard, preset 3D views by changing the User Coordinate System (UCS).

Windows and DOS: Choose View⇨Preset UCS.

How to Use It

Click the image tile that shows the view you want. Click OK.

More Stuff

The WCS is the World Coordinate System, which is the default view. The dialog box makes more sense if you click <u>A</u>bsolute to WCS, but you can also change the view relative to the current UCS.

 The VPOINT and DDVPOINT commands set your viewpoint. The UCS command manages the User Coordinate System.

'DDUNITS

Specifies how coordinates and angles are shown, including their precision (the number of places after the decimal point).

Windows and DOS: Choose Data⇨Units.

How to Use It

AutoCAD opens the Units Control dialog box. First, select the type of units you want to use. De<u>c</u>imal is the default. <u>E</u>ngineering and <u>A</u>rchitectural units show feet and inches, using inches for the drawing unit. Otherwise, a unit can be any measurement you want it to be. Then set the precision you want shown.

In the Angles section, you can choose how you want angle degrees shown and their precision.

 For more, see the section, "Choosing your units," in Chapter 5 of *AutoCAD For Dummies.*

DDVIEW

Creates and restores named views.

 Windows: From the Standard toolbar, click the View flyout and then the Named Views icon; or Choose <u>V</u>iew⇨<u>N</u>amed Views.

DOS: Choose View⇨Named Views.

How to Use It

This command opens the View Control dialog box, which lists the views you've defined and named. A view can be a small, zoomed-in section of your drawing or the whole thing. Naming views helps you get from place to place quickly in a large drawing.

To see a named view, select it from the list and click Restore.

To create a new view, click New to open the Define New View dialog box. Here you name your view (no spaces allowed in the name) and click Current Display (here it helps if you have set up your display the way you want it before you entered the command) or Define Window. You can either type in the coordinates of two corners or click Window, which returns you to your drawing momentarily to pick the corners of your view. When you're done, click Save View to return to the previous dialog box.

Click Delete in the View Control dialog box to delete a view. Try clicking Description to get information describing your view.

More Stuff

Views can be in model or paper space, but you have to be in the same type of space where the view was created to restore it. A named view can be used to create a scene that is used in rendering. See the SCENE and RENDER commands for more information.

DDVPOINT

Controls the 3D angle from which you view your drawing.

Windows and DOS: Choose View⇨3D Viewpoint⇨Rotate.

How to Use It

AutoCAD opens the Viewpoint Presets dialog box. First, click Absolute to WCS, which calculates relative to plan view and is easiest to comprehend. However, if you like to get esoteric, and are already in some other UCS, go ahead and click Relative to UCS.

If this is your first time using this command, you will probably have to play around with it and see the results in your drawing before it becomes clear.

Imagine that you're Superman, flying in outer space around the Earth. In an instant, you can see the Earth from any viewpoint you choose. Pick a longitude, say at Greenwich, to be your left/right dividing line. Of course, the equator is the top/bottom dividing line. The Earth is equivalent to the 3D object you have drawn, and you choose to look at it from top or bottom and left or right. With your X-ray vision, you don't even have to use the center of the Earth for your base point (called *Origin point*) but can start anywhere. Now fly back down to Earth and create a viewpoint.

On the left is a square with angles marked about a circle where you define your viewing angle relative to the X axis. Click inside the circle to specify any degree or outside the circle to specify degrees in the implements shown. Or type in the degrees you want in the X Axis text box.

If you choose a 45-degree angle, you will be looking at your 3D object from halfway between its right side and its back side.

Now go to the right side of the dialog box to define your viewing angle relative to the XY plane, which means going up or down in the Z direction. Again you can click on the inside for an exact angle, on the outside for the increments shown, or you can type the degree you want in the XY Plane text box.

If you choose a 30-degree angle, you'll be looking at your 3D object from 30 degrees above your object.

Click OK to return to your drawing and see the results. Try it with many different angles until you get the hang of it.

The great thing about this dialog box is the panic button in the middle called Set to Plan View. When you get totally befuddled, click this button to return to 2D space. Ahh, that looks familiar!

More Stuff

VPOINT accomplishes the same thing on the command line using a different system, called the compass-and-axis tripod. You can also enter X,Y,Z coordinates.

See Chapter 16, "3D for Me, See?" of *AutoCAD For Dummies*.

DIM

Puts AutoCAD into dimensioning mode to use the dimensioning subcommands from earlier releases of AutoCAD. This provides compatibility with earlier releases, but all the dimensioning commands are separately available. Refer to the commands that follow, all starting with DIM, except for LEADER which somehow got lost among the Ls.

DIMALIGNED

Draws an aligned linear dimension. When a line is at an angle, an aligned dimension is drawn parallel to the line.

Windows: From the Dimensioning toolbar, click the Aligned Dimension icon.

DOS: Choose Draw⇨Dimensioning⇨Aligned.

How to Use It

You can press Enter and just select an object to dimension. Then AutoCAD automatically creates the extension lines that extend from the object to the dimension line. If you don't like AutoCAD's way of doing things, you can instead pick an origin for the first extension line, and AutoCAD prompts you for the second point.

Next, AutoCAD asks you to specify where you want the dimension line with Text and Angle options. If you specify the location for the dimension command, AutoCAD creates the dimension and ends the command.

Text allows you to customize the text, either on the command line (DOS) or in the Edit Mtext dialog box (Windows).

Angle changes the angle of the dimension text.

If you choose the Text or Angle options, AutoCAD prompts you again for the dimension line location, which you specify to complete the command.

More Stuff

Remember that the appearance of your dimension is controlled by the DDIM command.

Chapter 11 in *AutoCAD For Dummies* has more on dimensioning.

DIMANGULAR

Draws an angular dimension that measures an angle.

Windows: From the Dimensioning toolbar, click the Angular Dimension icon.

DOS: Choose Draw⇨Dimensioning⇨Angular.

How to Use It

AutoCAD prompts you to select an arc, a circle, a line, or you can press Return (same as Enter).

If you press Enter, AutoCAD prompts you for three points that define a vertex and two endpoints. This prompt is for measuring an angle that you create "on the fly."

If you select an arc, AutoCAD creates the dimension.

If you select a circle, you need to tell AutoCAD what part of the circle you want to dimension. The point with which you selected the circle is used as the start of the dimension, so watch where you're pointing! AutoCAD prompts you for a second point.

You can even select a line, and AutoCAD asks for a second line that should be at an angle to the first.

Once you've finished telling AutoCAD what to dimension, the dimension line location prompt appears with the Text/Angle options. If you specify the location for the dimension command, AutoCAD creates the dimension and ends the command.

Text allows you to customize the text, either on the command line (DOS) or in the Edit Mtext dialog box (Windows).

Angle changes the angle of the dimension text.

If you choose the Text or Angle options, AutoCAD prompts you again for the dimension line location, which you specify to complete the command.

More Stuff

Remember that the appearance of your dimension is controlled by the DDIM command.

Chapter 11 in *AutoCAD For Dummies* has more on dimensioning.

DIMBASELINE

Draws a linear, angular, or ordinate dimension that continues from the beginning of the previous (or a selected) dimension. This means that the second dimension includes the first and the second measurements, the third includes all three measurements, and so on.

Windows: From the Dimensioning toolbar, click the Baseline Dimension icon.

DOS: Choose Draw⇨Dimensioning⇨Baseline.

How to Use It

If the previous dimension was linear, angular, or ordinate, AutoCAD assumes that you want to continue working from that dimension and allows you to simply specify the beginning of the second dimension's extension line. AutoCAD keeps asking the same question over and over, so you can continue to dimension, until you press Esc.

Or you can press Enter to select a dimension to start from and continue from there. To start from scratch, you first create a regular dimension. Then you can use this command.

More Stuff

Remember that the appearance of your dimension is controlled by the DDIM command.

Chapter 11 in *AutoCAD For Dummies* has more on dimensioning.

DIMCENTER

Draws a center mark or line through the center of a circle or arc.

Windows: From the Dimensioning toolbar, click the Center Mark icon.

DOS: Choose Draw⇨Dimensioning⇨Center Mark.

How to Use It

All you do is select a circle or an arc. That's it. Really.

More Stuff

Remember that the appearance of your dimension is controlled by the DDIM command. That determines what your center mark looks like.

Chapter 11 in *AutoCAD For Dummies* has more on dimensioning.

DIMCONTINUE

Draws a linear, angular, or ordinate dimension that continues from the end of the previous (or a selected) dimension. Unlike DIMBASELINE, the second dimension does not include the first.

Windows: From the Dimensioning toolbar, click the Continue Dimension icon.

DOS: Choose Draw⇨Dimensioning⇨Continue.

How to Use It

First, select the dimension you want to continue to next. Then point to the second extension line or select the object to dimension.

More Stuff

Remember that the appearance of your dimension is controlled by the DDIM command.

See Chapter 11 in *AutoCAD For Dummies* has more on dimensioning.

DIMDIAMETER

Draws a diameter dimension for a circle or an arc.

Windows: From the Dimensioning toolbar, click the Radial Dimension flyout and then the Diameter Dimension icon.

DOS: Choose Draw⇨Dimensioning⇨Radial⇨Diameter.

How to Use It

Select an arc or a circle. Move the cursor and watch the dimension move around. Click when you like what you see.

Text allows you to customize the text, either on the command line (DOS) or in the Edit Mtext dialog box (Windows).

The Angle option changes the angle of the dimension text.

More Stuff

Remember that the appearance of your dimension is controlled by the DDIM command.

Chapter 11 in *AutoCAD For Dummies* has more on dimensioning.

DIMEDIT

Edits dimensions. You can change the dimension text as well as its location. There's also an option for creating oblique extension lines, that is, extension lines that come out at some weird angle that happens to suit your needs.

Windows and DOS: Type **dimedit** at the command line.

How to Use It

This command provides several options:

Home   Moves the dimension text to its default position.

New   Changes dimension text.

- Windows: AutoCAD displays the Edit Mtext dialog box, allowing you to edit the text.

- DOS: You have to change the text the old-fashioned way, by retyping it at the command line. (If you don't remember the "good" old days, you're lucky.)

Rotate   Rotates the text. You tell AutoCAD the angle.

Oblique Creates oblique extension lines for linear dimensions. Use this when the regular extension lines interfere with the rest of your drawing. Type in an angle.

When you've selected your option, AutoCAD prompts you to select objects (you can select more than one dimension); this completes the command.

More Stuff

The DIMTEDIT command moves and rotates dimension text.

DIMLINEAR

Draws linear dimensions.

Windows: From the Dimensioning toolbar, click the Linear Dimension icon.

DOS: Choose Draw⇨Dimensioning⇨Linear.

How to Use It

If you want AutoCAD to automatically create the extension lines, just press Enter and select the object you want to dimension. Sometimes this isn't what you want, so you can specify the extension line origins instead.

Then AutoCAD prompts you for the dimension line location with several options.

Text allows you to customize the text, either on the command line (DOS) or in the Edit Mtext dialog box (Windows).

The Angle option changes the angle of the dimension text.

You can also draw Horizontal, Vertical, and Rotated dimension lines.

More Stuff

Remember that the appearance of your dimension is controlled by the DDIM command.

Chapter 11 in *AutoCAD For Dummies* has more on dimensioning.

DIMRADIUS

Draws radial dimensions for arcs and circles.

Windows: From the Dimensioning toolbar, click the Radial Dimension flyout and then the Radius Dimension icon.

DOS: Choose Draw⇨Dimensioning⇨Radial⇨Radius.

How to Use It

At the prompt, select an arc or a circle. As you move the cursor, the text moves with it. Click when you like what you see.

AutoCAD also offers Text and Angle options. Text allows you to customize the text, either on the command line (DOS) or in the Edit Mtext dialog box (Windows).

Angle changes the angle of the dimension text.

More Stuff

Remember that the appearance of your dimension is controlled by the DDIM command.

Chapter 11 in *AutoCAD For Dummies* has more on dimensioning.

DIMSTYLE

See the DDIM command.

DIMTEDIT

Moves and rotates dimension text.

Windows: From the Dimensioning toolbar, click the Align Dimension Text flyout and then the Rotate icon.

DOS: Choose Draw⇨Dimensioning⇨Align Text.

How to Use It

AutoCAD prompts you to select a dimension. Then you can pick a point for new text location or select one of the options:

Left Left-justifies the text along the dimension line.

Right Right-justifies the text along the dimension line.

Home Returns the text to its default location.

Angle Changes the angle of the text.

'DIST

Measures the distance between two points.

Windows: From the Object Properties toolbar, click the Inquiry flyout and then the Distance icon.

DOS: Choose Assist⇨Inquiry⇨Distance.

How to Use It

Pick two points; AutoCAD tells you the distance between them.

More Stuff

In a 3D drawing, AutoCAD calculates the true 3D distance between your points. To read the results, you may need to switch to the text screen using the F1 key (DOS) or F2 key (Windows).

DIVIDE

Divides an object into even segments, placing a point or block of your choice at each division point.

Windows: From the Draw toolbar, click the Point flyout and then the Divide icon.

DOS: Choose Draw⇨Point⇨Divide.

How to Use It

Select an object and tell AutoCAD how many segments you want to divide it into.

More Stuff

You can select the block option and name a block within your drawing. Choose whether to align the block with the orientation of your object and type in the number of segments you want. AutoCAD divides the object using the block instead of points.

Refer to DDPTYPE to control how point objects appear.

DONUT

Draws donuts, with or without holes.

Windows: From the Draw toolbar, click the Circle flyout and then the Donut icon.

DOS: Choose Draw⇨Circle⇨Donut.

How to Use It

AutoCAD asks you for inside and outside diameters. If the inside diameter is 0, the donut (once known as a doughnut, but no longer) has no hole. Then you specify the center point.

More Stuff

The fill mode determines whether your donut is filled in (choco-late) or not (vanilla). The DDRMODES command allows you to set the fill mode.

'DRAGMODE

Set the display for dragged objects.

Windows and DOS: Type **dragmode** at the command line.

How to Use It

Dragging means that when you move or modify an object by dragging, you see a copy of the object that moves as you move your mouse. There are three options:

On   Allows dragging, but you need to type **drag** within the command to see the dotted copy of the object.

Off   Disables the copy completely. You never see it.

Auto Always shows the copy.

More Stuff

The value of dragmode being on is that you can visualize what your object will look like in its new location or condition. How-ever, it can slow down your system and sometimes is annoying in a complex drawing. So it's up to you.

DSVIEWER

Opens the Aerial View window for quick zooming and panning. Except see the end of this command for information on the secret DOS Aerial Viewer.

Windows: Choose Tools⇨Aerial View; or from the Standard toolbar, click the Tool Windows flyout and then the Aerial View icon.

How to Use It

AutoCAD opens the Aerial View window with your drawing cozily nestled inside. There are three menus items: View, Mode, and Options. However, you can do most of the stuff using the icons.

 Pan

> Drag the view box to the part of the drawing you want to see. You can also pan with the scroll bars. The large-screen drawing pans accordingly.

Zoom

> Click the first corner of the area you want to zoom to, drag to the second corner, and release the mouse button. This area then becomes the new view. The large-screen drawing zooms accordingly.

Zoom in

> This icon affects the image only in the Aerial View window.

Zoom out

> This icon affects the image only in the Aerial View window.

Global

> This icon affects the image only in the Aerial View window.

There's also a magnifier that shows a magnified view of your drawing in the Aerial View window.

- Choose Locator Magnification from the Options Menu of the Aerial View window. In the Magnification dialog box, you can either type in a magnification or use the + and – arrows to increase or decrease the magnification.

- Click OK.

- Click the Locator icon and, holding down the pick button on your mouse, drag the cursor to the place on your large-

More Stuff

 Some people like to keep the Aerial View window open a lot for whenever they want to zoom or pan. But since the Aerial View updates its window whenever you change your drawing or move from viewport to viewport, AutoCAD has to update two drawings rather than one. This can slow things down. So you can disable this updating by deselecting Auto Viewport in the Options menu. Then AutoCAD updates the view only when you click on the title bar of the Aerial View window. You can also deselect Dynamic Update in the Options menu so that AutoCAD doesn't update the Aerial View window each time you edit your main drawing.

EXTRA! EXTRA! Read all about it! DOS also has an Aerial View! But it's a deep, dark secret. You won't find it documented in the regular manuals. Not a word in on-line Help. The only thing is that you must have a VGA screen. If you do, and you chose `Accelerated Display Driver v1.0.0 ADI 4.2 - by Vibrant Graphics` when you configured AutoCAD, you'll have the Aerial View. (If you didn't choose that driver, use the CONFIG command to reconfigure — go figure.) Choose Tools⇨Aerial View to open the Aerial View window. Here's how it works.

The left button toggles the mode. Here are the options:

Dzoom   This is a dynamic zoom. Move your cursor around and watch your drawing zoom about! Don't get dizzy.

Zoom   Gives you a window. Click on two opposite corners. It's like ZOOM with the Window option.

Pan   Gives you a pan box. Move the cursor, click, and you pan the drawing.

Auto   Allows you to pan and zoom, like ZOOM with the Dynamic option.

The right button just toggles between Static, which means that you only affect the Aerial View Window, and Dynamic, which means you affect the large drawing view.

The Fit button fits the drawing into the Aerial View Window. It's like ZOOM with the Extents option. The All button is equivalent to ZOOM with the All option.

 Click the Control button to close the Aerial View window.

See the ZOOM and PAN commands.

 See "The View from Above: Aerial View in AutoCAD for Windows" in Chapter 9 of *AutoCAD For Dummies*.

DTEXT

Draws text line by line. The D stands for dynamic; you see the text on-screen as you type it in. (That might seem mundane to some of you, but us old fogies remember the old days of the plain-Jane TEXT command.)

Windows: From the Draw toolbar, click the Text flyout and then the Dynamic Text icon.

DOS: Choose Draw⇔Text⇔Dynamic Text.

How to Use It

The DTEXT command is suitable for one-line labels. Use MTEXT for paragraphs.

Pick a start point or provide a justification code or a style. The justification codes offer you many alignment choices for your text. Some of the most useful are

Align	Fits your letters between a start point and endpoint. The size of the letters is adjusted proportionately.
Fit	Fits your letters between a start point and endpoint, but you specify a height, which remains fixed.
Center	Centers the text around a point on the bottom of the letters.
Middle	Centers text both horizontally and vertically around a point.

Some of the others are TL (Top Left), MC (Middle Center), and BR (Bottom Right). You get the idea.

Once you decide on your style and justification, pick a start point and type. Press Enter to end a line. DTEXT continues to prompt you for new text. Press Enter again after the last line to complete the command.

The text you see on-screen moves to its proper justification only after you complete the command.

More Stuff

Refer to the STYLE command, which you use to define text styles.
See "The Same Old Line" in Chapter 10 of *AutoCAD For Dummies*.

DVIEW

Creates parallel projection and perspective views in 3D space.

Windows and DOS: Choose View⇨3D Dynamic View.

How to Use It

This is a weird one, but here goes. DVIEW is a way of viewing objects in 3D space, using the concept of a camera and a target. You decide where the camera is and what the target is, and AutoCAD shows you what you would see.

The first prompt is to select objects. Select as few as you can for the sake of speed. At the end of the command, you will see all the objects that would be seen by the view you have defined. You can also press Enter, and AutoCAD will supply a picture of a little house. You can use the house model to set the angles and distances and then see your picture after you exit DVIEW.

First, type **ca** to place and point your camera. AutoCAD starts you from the center of the drawing. Try moving the cursor to rotate the imaginary camera. First, you'll be moving up and down, which technically means changing the angle from the XY plane. It's sort of like rolling your eyes up and down. Click the Return (right) button of your mouse when you like what you see. An alternative is to type an angle at the command line. An angle of 0 degrees is looking straight out. An angle of 90 degrees looks down from above. The Toggle angle in option toggles between locking the camera at the specified angle and unlocking it so that you can use the mouse to set it.

Now AutoCAD prompts for the angle relative to the X axis. Again you can use the mouse and click the Return button to set the angle, or type in an angle at the command line. In this case, 0 degrees means that you are looking along the X axis toward 0,0. This angle can go from 180 degrees to –180 degrees (which would both mean the same thing, looking along the X axis out towards infinity — sounds enlightening!).

If you just want a parallel projection view, and you picked only one object, press Enter to see the view. You're done.

If there are several objects involved, you may want to set the target. This action creates your line of sight. Type **ta**. The prompts here are the same as for the camera option. You can press Enter and see a parallel projection view.

If you want to see a perspective view (where objects that are farther away look smaller), use the Distance option. A slider bar appears that you can use to set the distance between the camera and your objects. Drag on the slider bar, move your mouse (watch what happens to the slider bar), or type in a number.

The POints option just shows you your camera and target points. You can use this to type in new points.

DVIEW has its own pan and zoom (and so the regular PAN and ZOOM commands can't be used transparently in this command). If you use the OFF option to turn off perspective viewing, zoom moves you in to the center of the drawing, using another slider bar. If perspective viewing is on, zooming in has an effect like going from a wide-angle lens to a normal lens to a telephoto lens.

The CLip option creates invisible walls that obscure what is in front of a front-clipping plane and what is behind a back-clipping plane. Pick either Back or Front and use the slider bar to drag the clipping plane. Or you can pick both Back and Front.

The Hide option removes hidden lines (lines that you wouldn't see from the chosen viewing angle) for the selected objects.

Keep on using options until you're finished defining the view. (There's an Undo option, of course.) Then press Enter to complete the command and see your view.

DXFIN

Imports a drawing interchange file (DXF). A DXF file is a translation of a drawing into a text file, which is an amazing accomplishment. Because many CAD programs accept DXF files, you use it to transfer a drawing from one CAD program to another. (Of course, you would *never* use any CAD program other than AutoCAD, would you?)

Windows: Type **dxfin** at the command line.

DOS: Choose File⇨Import⇨DXF.

How to Use It

AutoCAD opens the Select DXF File dialog box, which is like a typical File⇨Open dialog box. Browse through drives, directories, and files and then click the file you want, or click Type It and type in the filename and path on the command line. Click OK.

More Stuff

If you are in a drawing when you use DXFIN, and it already has layer definitions, text styles, and so on, AutoCAD will import only the objects, without their properties, to avoid conflicts. If you want the whole shebang (that is, objects and properties), open a new drawing using File⇨New and select the No Prototype option in the dialog box.

DXFOUT

Creates a DXF file from the current drawing. (See DXFIN for an explanation of DXF files.)

Windows: Type **dxfout** at the command line.

DOS: Choose File⇨Export⇨DXF.

How to Use It

The Create DXF File dialog box opens. Type in a filename. It will have a *.DXF* extension. Click OK. AutoCAD prompts you for the precision of floating-point numbers, that is, how many decimal places you want after the decimal point. The default is six, which is enough for most of us.

If you just press Enter, AutoCAD creates the DXF file. You have an option to type **o** for objects and select only certain objects in your drawing.

EDGESURF

Draws a 3D polygon mesh surface.

Windows: From the Surfaces toolbar, click the Edge Surface icon.

DOS: Choose Draw⇨Surfaces⇨Edge Surface.

How to Use It

First, you need four touching lines, arcs, or polylines that together create a closed path. To create the surface, all you do is select a point on each of the four edges, in any order. AutoCAD creates a mesh surface.

More Stuff

The surface created by EDGESURF approximates something called a Coons surface patch. Just think of a small corn patch where raccoons come to feed.

ELEV

Sets elevation (height above the "ground" XY plane) and thickness of new objects.

How to Use It

At the New current elevation prompt, type in a distance, or press Enter if you want to keep the current distance (which is kindly provided to you after the prompt). When AutoCAD prompts for a thickness, type in a number.

More Stuff

A negative thickness will extrude objects along the negative Z axis.

The EXTRUDE command gives thickness to existing objects.

ELLIPSE

Draws an ellipse.

Windows: From the Draw toolbar, click the Ellipse flyout.

DOS: Choose Draw⇨Ellipse.

How to Use It

The default is to specify the first endpoint of the first axis. Specify a point. Then specify the other endpoint. AutoCAD asks you for the other axis distance, which is similar to a radius, from the midpoint of the first axis to the edge of the second axis. Specify a point.

You can select Center at the first prompt to draw an ellipse by specifying first its center, then the first axis endpoint, and finally the other axis distance.

Select Arc at the first prompt to draw an elliptical arc. Specify the two endpoints of the first axis and the axis distance. AutoCAD goes on to prompt you for a start angle and end angle of the arc. There's also an option to specify the included angle, which is the number of degrees included in the arc starting from the start angle.

More Stuff

See "Ellipses (S. Grant?)" in Chapter 7 of *AutoCAD For Dummies*.

END

Saves your drawing and exits AutoCAD.

Windows and DOS: Type **end** at the command line.

How to Use It

AutoCAD just saves your drawing and throws you out — of the program, that is.

More Stuff

If you haven't already saved the drawing and given it a name (you should have saved it many times already!), AutoCAD opens the Create Drawing File dialog box so you can name your drawing.

See the SAVE and QSAVE commands.

ERASE

Erases objects.

 Windows: From the Modify toolbar, click the Erase icon.

DOS: Choose Modify⇨Erase.

How to Use It

It's really simple. Select objects. Press Enter to end the selection process, and AutoCAD makes 'em go away.

More Stuff

OOPS restores previously erased objects. U and UNDO undo previous commands and also restore your precious objects.

EXPLODE

Breaks up blocks and other compound objects into individual components.

 Windows: From the Modify toolbar, click the Explode flyout and then the Explode icon.

DOS: Choose Modify⇨Explode.

How to Use It

You just select the objects, and AutoCAD explodes them. For example, if you made a block of a square and a circle, you'll have your square and circle back as individual objects.

More Stuff

 You can explode not only blocks but polylines, multilines, solids, regions, bodies (sounds messy), and meshes.

See also the XPLODE command.

 See the section, "Exploding a block," in Chapter 15 of *AutoCAD For Dummies* for more.

EXPORT

Translates drawings or objects into other file formats.

Windows: Choose File⇨Export.

How to Use It

AutoCAD opens the Export Data dialog box. In the List Files of Type box, choose the format you want to create. In the File Name box, type the name of the file. Click OK. AutoCAD prompts you to select objects. AutoCAD then creates the file.

More Stuff

There are also individual commands to export to different formats: DXFOUT, ACISOUT, 3DSOUT, WMFOUT, BMPOUT, PSOUT, and STLOUT.

EXTEND

Extends a line, arc, polyline, or ray to meet another object.

Windows: From the Modify toolbar, click the Trim flyout and then the Extend icon.

DOS: Choose Modify⇨Extend.

How to Use It

AutoCAD first prompts you for the boundary edges and asks you to select objects. These are the edges you want to extend *to*. Then you select the object you want extended. AutoCAD repeats this second prompt so that you can extend more objects to the original boundary edge. Press Enter to end the command.

More Stuff

If your objects are 3D, this gets more complicated because what looks like an intersection of objects in 2D might not be in 3D.

EXTRUDE

Creates simple 3D objects by extruding (giving a thickness to) existing, closed, 2D objects.

Windows: From the Solids toolbar, click the Extrude icon.

DOS: Choose Draw⇨Solids⇨Extrude.

How to Use It

Select the objects you want to extrude, including closed polylines, circles, polygons, and so on. Don't pick objects that have crossing parts like a figure eight. The default is to then specify a height. If you enter a negative number, AutoCAD extrudes in the direction of the negative Z axis. Now AutoCAD asks for an extrusion taper angle. If you press Enter for the default, which is 0 degrees, you get a solid that rises perpendicular from the original object, because there is no tapering.

You can specify a taper angle between 0 and 90 degrees to taper in. A taper angle between 0 and –90 degrees tapers out.

More Stuff

After selecting your objects, you can select the Path option. You select an object to be the path. It can be curved. The path object should start from the plane of the 2D object you're extruding and continue out of its plane, that is, into the third dimension. That way, the object can be extruded along its path.

See the "Extruding Walls" section in Chapter 16 of *AutoCAD For Dummies* by Bud Smith.

'FILL

Sets the fill mode for multilines, solids, and polylines.

Windows and DOS: Type **fill** at the command line.

How to Use It

You have two choices. On means fillable objects (multilines, solids, and polylines) will be filled. Off means they won't.

More Stuff

Lots of filled objects in your drawing will slow down regeneration time. You could turn fill mode off until you've finished your drawing. Actually, it takes a while to print or plot filled objects, too, and it certainly takes more ink or toner!

You can also set the fill mode in a dialog box using DDRMODES.

FILLET

Rounds off (fillets) the edges of objects to make rounded corners.

 Windows: From the Modify toolbar, click the Feature flyout and then the Fillet icon.

DOS: Choose Construct⇨Fillet.

How to Use It

The simple way to use this command is to select your first object at the prompt and then select the second object. AutoCAD fillets them. AutoCAD extends or trims your objects as necessary. If one of your objects is an arc or a circle, there may be more than one possible way to fillet. AutoCAD creates a fillet with endpoints closest to the points you used to select the objects.

If you choose the Polyline option and select a polyline, AutoCAD fillets the polyline at every possible vertex.

Choose the Radius option to specify the radius of future fillets. For some reason, this ends the command, so use it again if you actually want to fillet something with the new radius.

There's a Trim option. Usually, AutoCAD trims your lines to make a neat fillet, but if you choose No Trim, AutoCAD makes the fillet and leaves the lines, too. A little messy, if you ask me.

More Stuff

You can also fillet 3D objects. If you select a 3D object, AutoCAD prompts you accordingly.

'FILTER

Creates a filtered list of objects to help you select objects based on their properties.

Windows: From the Standard toolbar, click the Select Objects flyout and then the Selection Filters icon.

DOS: Choose Assist⇨Selection Filters.

How to Use It

You can create a filter first and then use it on an editing command. Generally, you use it transparently, within a command. Start the command and, at the Select objects prompt, type **'filter.**

AutoCAD opens the Object Selection Filters dialog box. The top shows you current filter lists. Use the Select Filter section to create new filters. First, select an object from the list box. Then you can use the following operators to further define the filter.

Operator	Meaning
=	Equals
!=	Not equal to
>	Greater than
>=	Greater than or equal to
<	Less than
<=	Less than or equal to
*	Equal to any value

For example, you can define a filter that will find only text with a height greater than .25 units. You can choose more than one object. AutoCAD will find only objects that satisfy *all* the restrictions you have set.

Once you have what you want, click Add to List and then click Apply. This action will exit you back to your command. Use a big window to select your objects. AutoCAD will select only those objects in the window that satisfy the filter.

More Stuff

You can name filters for easier use next time you need them.

'GRID

Displays a grid of itty-bitty dots.

Windows & DOS: Type **grid** on the command line.

How to Use It

AutoCAD gives you the following options:

Grid spacing(x)	Type a number. The dots will appear however many number of units apart that you type. Type a number followed by **x** to set the grid equal to that number times the snap interval.
ON	Turns on the grid.
OFF	Turns off the grid (did you guess?).
Snap	Sets the grid spacing equal to the snap interval.
Aspect	This option is used to set the X spacing and Y spacing to different numbers.

More Stuff

The grid is used to get your bearings. It's a drawing aid. It's useful to set the grid to the snap setting so that you can see where the snap points are. On the other hand, sometimes it's very annoying to have all those dots on your drawing. If you don't like the grid, you don't have to grid and bear it–turn it off.

See the SNAP and DDRMODES commands.

GROUP

Creates a named group of objects.

Windows: From the Standard toolbar, click the Object Group icon.

DOS: Choose Assist⇨Group Objects.

How to Use It

AutoCAD opens the Object Grouping dialog box. On top is a list of existing groups.

To create a group, type a name in the G̲roup Name text box. You can provide a description of it in the D̲escription text box if you want. In the Create Group section, click S̲electable. This means that when you select one object in the group, you get 'em all, which is the point of creating a group. (But you might want to turn off the S̲electable feature if you need to work with only one object in the group.)

Then click N̲ew to create the group. AutoCAD will return you to your drawing. Select the objects for your group and press Enter to complete the selection process. Back at the ranch (the Object Grouping dialog box), y'all click OK to complete the command.

Using the group when you select objects is automatic. Select one object, and they all come along. However, you can also use the group name at the `Select objects` prompt.

More Stuff

The Change Group section allows you to edit groups. You can remove objects from and add them to the group, or change its selectable status, or rename it.

HATCH

See the BHATCH command to create hatch patterns using a dialog box.

HATCHEDIT

Edits a hatch.

Windows: From the Modify toolbar, click the Special Edit flyout and then the Edit Hatch icon.

DOS: Choose Modify⇨Edit Hatch.

How to Use It

AutoCAD prompts you to select a hatch object. When you do, the Hatchedit dialog box opens, which is the same as the Boundary Hatch dialog box you get with the BHATCH command. Make the changes that you want and click A̲pply.

See the BHATCH command for details on using the dialog box.

HIDE

Hides lines of a 3D surface or solid object that would naturally be hidden from the 3D view you are using.

 Windows: From the Render toolbar, click the Hide icon.

DOS: Choose Tools⇨Hide.

How to Use It

Before using this command, you need a 3D object. And you need to use VPOINT or DVIEW to create a 3D view of your object. When you choose this command, AutoCAD goes ahead and hides lines that should be hidden. On a slow computer with a large 3D object, it may take a bit of time.

More Stuff

You create 3D surfaces with the 3D command. Some other commands that create surfaces are 3DMESH, PFACE, RULESURF, TABSURF, REVSURF, and EDGESURF. You create solids using BOX, WEDGE, CYLINDER, CONE, SPHERE, and TORUS. You can also use EXTRUDE and REVOLVE to create a solid.

HIDE doesn't hide objects on layers that are frozen or turned off.

'ID

Gives you the coordinates of a selected point.

 Windows: From the Object Properties toolbar, click the Inquiry flyout and then the Locate Point icon.

DOS: Choose Assist⇨Inquiry⇨Locate Point.

How to Use It

Just pick a point. It's a good idea to use an object snap. AutoCAD lists the point's coordinates.

IMPORT

Translates other file formats into AutoCAD drawings.

Windows: Choose File⇨Import.

DOS: File⇨Import, then choose the type of file to import.

How to Use It

AutoCAD opens the Import File dialog box. In the List Files of Type list box, select the format type of the file that you want to import. Select the filename from the File Name list box.

More Stuff

There are also individual commands for specific formats: the DXFIN, DXBIN, ACISIN, GIFIN, PCXIN, TIFFIN, WMFIN, and PSIN commands.

INSERT

See DDINSERT, which does the same thing as INSERT, but uses a dialog box.

INTERFERE

Creates a solid object from the volume where two or more solids overlap.

Windows: From the Solids toolbar, click the Interference icon.

DOS: Choose Draw⇨Solids⇨Interference.

How to Use It

AutoCAD prompts you for the first set of solids (after which you press Enter), then for the second set of solids. Usually, you'll just be selecting one solid for each set, but the point is that you can pick any number. AutoCAD checks the first set against the second set for overlapping. When you've finished selecting, press Enter and watch AutoCAD figure it out. AutoCAD will ask you whether it should create the interference solids. Type **y** to create them.

The next prompt begs your permission to highlight pairs of interfering solids. The idea here is that if you've selected lots of solids, it may be hard to see which are the interfering pairs. (I know, we could call them in-laws.) If there is more than one pair, AutoCAD will offer you the opportunity to see the next pair highlighted. Type **x** to end the command.

INTERSECT

Creates a region or solid from the overlapping area or volume of two or more regions or solids.

Windows: From the Modify toolbar, click the Explode flyout and then the Intersection icon.

DOS: Choose Construct⇨Intersection.

How to Use It

First, select either regions or solids. AutoCAD does the rest. What you're left with is only the area or volume that was in common among the selected objects. The rest goes bye-bye.

'ISOPLANE

Selects an isometric plane.

Windows and DOS: Type **isoplane** at the command line.

How to Use It

The default at the prompt is a toggle that rotates planes from left to top to right. You can also simply choose Left, Top, or Right. SNAP must be on and set to isometric.

More Stuff

Also, the DDRMODES command has more on isometric planes.

'*LAYER*

See the DDLMODES command to work with layers using a dialog
box.

LEADER

Creates a line used to connect annotation text with its object. The
leader usually has an arrow pointing to the object.

Windows: From the Dimensioning toolbar, click the Leader icon.

DOS: Choose Draw⇨Dimensioning⇨Leader.

How to Use It

AutoCAD prompts you for the start point, which is often at the
object that you want to annotate. Then AutoCAD keeps on
prompting you for points. Usually, you want to end with a
horizontal line on which to place your text. When you're finished
drawing lines, press Enter, and AutoCAD prompts you for an
Annotation. If you just want one line of text, type it in at the
command line and press Enter. This completes the command.

If you select Format at the first prompt to can choose to draw the
leader as a spline or choose other format options.

Press Enter at the Annotation prompt to get other options:

Mtext   Press Enter and specify two points that define the
            boundary of the text. Specify the height and
            rotations angle of the text boundary. AutoCAD
            then opens the Edit Mtext dialog box, and you type
            in your text. Click OK to complete the command.

Tolerance   Allows you to create a feature control frame with
            geometric tolerances. If you don't know what that
            is, you probably don't want to do this. But if you're
            interested, see the TOLERANCE command for
            details.

Copy   Copies an object and attaches it to the end of the
            leader. You get to select the object.

Block	Inserts a block at the end of the leader line, prompting you for an insertion point, scale, and rotation angle.
None	Use this option if you don't want to add any text to the leader.

More Stuff

Leader styles are controlled through the DDIM command.

LENGTHEN

Lengthens lines, arcs, open polylines, elliptical arcs, and open splines. Also changes the angle of arcs.

Windows: From the Modify toolbar, click the Resize flyout and then the Lengthen icon.

DOS: Choose Modify⇨Lengthen.

How to Use It

Select an object. AutoCAD lengthens a line from the endpoint closest to your selection point.

You have four ways to lengthen:

Delta	Specify the increase in length. Or, if you select the angle option, specify the increase in the angle.
Percent	Specify the increased length as a percentage of its current size. 100 means no change. Type 200 if you want to double the length of the object.
Total	Here you specify the total length (or included angle).
Dynamic	AutoCAD enters Dynamic Dragging mode, allowing you to drag the object to the desired length (or angle).

AutoCAD prompts you for more objects to lengthen (as if you have nothing else to do). Press Enter to get on to better things.

LIGHT

Creates lights for use in a rendered scene.

Windows: From the Render toolbar, click the Lights icon.

DOS: Choose Tools⇨Render⇨Lights.

How to Use It

This command opens the Lights dialog box. In the Lights list box is a list of all lights that have already been defined. Select a light and click the Modify button to modify a light. Modifying a light uses the same dialog box as creating a new one, so refer to the next few paragraphs. Select a light and click the Delete button to delete a light. Click the Select button to return to your drawing so you can select a light by clicking on it. That's if you know where it is but forgot its name.

On the right side of the dialog box is the Ambient Light section. Ambient light is background, overall light that covers all the surfaces in your drawing. Use the slider bar to adjust the Intensity, or type in a number from 0 (no light) to 1 (full brightness). Too low a number will make your drawing appear like a dark room or a romantic night scene. Too high a number will make your drawing look like an over-exposed photograph. Try 0.3 to start with.

In the Color section, choose the ambient's light color. You can use the Red, Green, and Blue slider bars, or click Use Color Wheel. Maximum red, green, and blue produce white light. (Light colors don't mix like paint colors.)

Now create some lights. (Makes you feel all-powerful, doesn't it?) Next to the New button is a drop-down list of three types of light. Select one of them and click New to create a new light of that type.

Point Light

Choosing Point Light opens the New Point Light dialog box. Point light is sort of like a light bulb. It emits light that radiates out in all directions, and it attenuates, which means the light gets fainter as it gets farther from its source. First, type a name for your light in the Light Name text box (you can use up to eight characters). If you're going to be creating different kinds of lights, it's a good idea to give the lights names that tell you what kind of light it is. For example, PL1 for the first point light. (I'm sure you can be more creative than that, but you get the idea.)

Next, set the Attenuation (that's how a light fades with distance). You can choose None, Inverse Linear, or Inverse Square. When selecting attenuation, remember that the brightness of inverse square drops off much more quickly than that of inverse linear.

Now set the Intensity of the light, using the slider bar or the text box. It can be any real number. However, there's a default that is based on the attenuation setting. Defaults are usually good settings to start with, and then you can experiment.

The following table displays the default intensity setting that corresponds with each attenuation setting.

Attenuation Setting	*Default Intensity*
None	1
Inverse Linear	One-half the extents distance from the lower-left to the upper-right corner
Inverse Square	One-half the square of the extents distance from the lower-left to the upper-right corner

So if you've chosen inverse linear attenuation, and your drawing extends from 0,0 to 120,90, then the extents distance is 150, and the default intensity will be 75.

To set the position of your light, click the Show button to see the current location. AutoCAD automatically places the light at the center of the current viewport. (Point lights radiate light equally in all directions, so there is no target.) You may wish to write down the location coordinates. Click OK. Now click Modify. This returns you to your drawing. AutoCAD has placed a point light block in your drawing so you can see where it is. You can pick a point or type in coordinates. However, don't forget that you usually don't want your light to be "on the ground," so you will want to include a Z coordinate.

Finally, select the light's color. This works just like the setting for Ambient Light in the Lights dialog box, discussed previously in this section. Click OK, and you return to the Lights dialog box.

Distant Light

Choose Distant Light from the drop-down box in the Lights dialog box and click New to get to the New Distant Light dialog box. Distant light produces parallel light beams in one direction that do not attenuate. It's supposed to be sort of like the sun. (You *are* getting all-powerful here, aren't you?) Type in a name for your distant light in the Name text box. The intensity can range from 0 (off) to 1 (full intensity). The color is set in the same way as for Ambient Light in the Lights dialog box, explained earlier.

You set the location of a distant light by using the astronomical terms *azimuth* and *altitude,* or by using the Light Source Vector system. Azimuth means the degrees from North. You can go from –180 to 180, both of which are south. Altitude goes from 0 (ground level) to 90 (straight overhead). Actually, in the text box, you can type a number between 0 and –90. You can also use the slider bar. The results of all this are shown in the Light Source Vector section, which defines the light source using X,Y,Z coordinates. Conversely, if you type coordinates in the Light Source Vector section, the Azimuth and Altitude numbers will change accordingly.

All of this is supposed to create a direction for your distant light. This may be more clear if you click Modify in the Light Source Vector section. AutoCAD returns you to your drawing and prompts you for a light direction to and a light direction from. You can pick points, but it will be more accurate to type them in. Remember that the sun usually comes from above the horizon, so you'll want to pay attention to the Z coordinate. (You don't want to totally change the laws of nature.)

When you're done, click OK to return to the Lights dialog box.

Spotlight

Choose Spotlight from the drop-down list in the Lights dialog box and click New, and you're ready to create a new spotlight. A spotlight produces light in a cone shape, radiating in a specific direction. The New Spotlight dialog box is very similar to the New Point Light dialog box, discussed earlier in this section. Here are the features that differ:

Position	There is not only a location but also a target.
Hotspot and Falloff	Spotlights have a hotspot, that is, the brightest cone of light. The default is 44 degrees. Falloff is the widest cone of light. The default is 45 degrees. Both can range from 0 to 160 degrees. If the hotspot and falloff angles are the same, the whole cone is bright. If the falloff is a few degrees larger than the hotspot, there is an area of softer light around the edge of the spotlight. You can get some cool effects this way.

Because spotlights have a location and a target, attenuation is calculated from the location to the object, rather than to the drawing's extents.

More Stuff

Use your lights with the SCENE and RENDER commands.

'LIMITS

Sets drawing boundaries.

Windows and DOS: Choose Data⇨Drawing Limits.

How to Use It

To specify the limits with X,Y coordinates, AutoCAD prompts you first for the lower-left corner. These coordinates will usually be **0,0**. Then type in coordinates for the upper-right corner.

You can also turn limits checking on. AutoCAD will reject points entered outside the limits. You can turn limits checking off, too.

More Stuff

AutoCAD uses the limits when you use the ZOOM command with the All option. Also, when you turn on the grid, AutoCAD uses the limits for the grid boundaries.

For more on limits, see the "Set Some Limits!" section in Chapter 5 of *AutoCAD For Dummies*.

LINE

Draws lines.

Windows: From the Draw toolbar, click the Line flyout and then the Line icon.

DOS: Choose Draw⇨Line.

How to Use It

This is surely the most commonly used command in AutoCAD. And it's easy! AutoCAD prompts From point, and you specify the start of your line. AutoCAD then prompts To point, and you specify the endpoint of your line. Often, you'll want to continue drawing connected lines, so AutoCAD continues to prompt you for points, and you continue to specify endpoints of new lines until you press Enter to end the command.

At any time, you can type **u** and press Enter to undo your last line segment. Also, if you've drawn more than one line, you can type **c** and AutoCAD will close your lines, that is, draw a line from the endpoint of your last line to the beginning of your first line.

If you end the command and then decide you want to continue drawing lines from the end of the last line (or last arc), press Enter at the `From point` prompt, and AutoCAD will pick up where you left off.

More Stuff

PLINE creates 2D polylines that can have width and can be filled. RAY creates a line that starts but *never* ends. (I just say that to get you interested. But go look it up, and you'll see that I'm right.) XLINE creates a line that never starts or ends but exists nevertheless (it's a riddle). MLINE creates multiple, parallel lines.

See "Lines (lines, everywhere a line . . .)" in Chapter 7 of *AutoCAD For Dummies.*

'LINETYPE

Creates, loads, and sets the current linetype.

Windows and DOS: Type **linetype** at the command line.

How to Use It

See the DDLTYPE command to load and set the current linetype. This section only covers creating linetypes.

To create a linetype, type **c** for the Create option. AutoCAD prompts you for a name. AutoCAD opens the Create or Append Linetype File dialog box. In the File Name list box, select a linetype library file (`ACAD.LIN` is the default), or you can type in a new name to create a new file. Click OK to close the dialog box. Then you can type in some descriptive text (up to 47 characters, so don't write a novel). Actually, it helps to make a representation of your linetype here, using the hyphen for dashes, periods for dots, and the spacebar for spaces (for example: – .. – ..).

At the Enter pattern prompt, type in the pattern definition in AutoCAD's secret code for linetypes. (There's an A at the beginning of the line. Ignore it. It's just part of the secret code.) Here's the key:

Positive numbers	Represent dashes — the higher the number, the longer the dash.
Zeros	Represent dots.

| Negative numbers | Represent spaces between the dashes and dots — the higher the number, the wider the space. |
| Commas | Go between the positive numbers, zeros, and negative numbers. |

The numbers for the dashes and spaces are in drawing units, so you might want to use decimals– for example, .5 for half a unit, .25 for a quarter of a unit, or whatever you want.

Press Enter to complete the command. To use your beautiful, new linetype, you have to load it. See the DDLTYPE command. (***Hint:*** your new linetype will be at the bottom of the list.)

More Stuff

AutoCAD stores linetypes in files with the extension *.LIN*. The standard linetypes that come with AutoCAD are in ACAD.LIN. Adding linetypes to ACAD.LIN means that you don't have to load a new linetype library file when you want to use the linetype.

LIST

Lists database information for the object or objects you select. This includes everything you ever wanted to know about the object and more, including its coordinates, size, layer, and type.

 Windows: From the Object Properties toolbar, click the Inquiry flyout and then the List icon.

DOS: Choose Assist⇨Inquiry⇨List.

How to Use It

I love this command. It's so satisfying to be able to find out all about the objects you've drawn. All you do is select objects, and AutoCAD tells all.

More Stuff

 You may need to switch to the text screen to see everything AutoCAD has spit out about your object. Press F1 (DOS) or F2 (Windows) or use the TEXTSCR command. Use F1, F2, or GRAPHSCR to get back to your drawing.

LOGFILEOFF

Stops recording the text window contents and closes the log file.

Windows: Choose Options⇨Preferences⇨Environment tab.

DOS: Choose Options⇨Log Files⇨Session Log.

How to Use It

In the Files section, clear the Log File button.

I explain how to use the log file under LOGFILEON.

LOGFILEON

Records and writes to a file the contents of the text window.

Windows: Choose Options⇨Preferences⇨Environment tab.

DOS: Choose Options⇨Log Files⇨Session Log.

How to Use It

In the Files section, choose Log File. AutoCAD records the contents of the text window each time you enter AutoCAD, unless you use LOGFILEOFF.

More Stuff

Each session is separated by a dashed line in the file. This file keeps on growing. So remember to sometimes get rid of the stuff you don't need. Your hard disk will thank you for it.

'LTSCALE

Sets the linetype scale, which is the length of the dashes and spaces relative to the drawing unit.

Windows and DOS: Choose Options⇨Linetypes⇨Global Linetype Scale.

How to Use It

AutoCAD prompts you for a new scale factor and gives you the current one for reference. Type in a new number. To make the scale smaller, type in a decimal. Press Enter to end the command. AutoCAD regenerates the drawing with the new scale factor.

More Stuff

See "Scaling, Scaling, over the Bounding Main . . ." in Chapter 5 of *AutoCAD For Dummies*.

MASSPROP

Calculates the mass of regions or solids.

Windows: From the Object Properties toolbar, click the Inquiry flyout and then the Mass Properties icon.

DOS: Choose Assist⇨Inquiry⇨Mass Properties.

How to Use It

AutoCAD prompts you to select objects. They need to be regions or solids. Regions are created by the REGION command, more or less for the purpose of analysis. AutoCAD struts its stuff on the text screen — and it may be a lot — and then asks whether you want to write the information to a file. If you type **y**, AutoCAD prompts you for a filename.

More Stuff

MASSPROP provides the following information for regions: area, perimeter, bounding box, centroid (the center of the region), moments of inertia, products of inertia, radii of gyration, and principal moments of inertia. For solids, the command also provides mass and volume. Obviously, if you have no idea what this stuff is, you won't be using this command.

MATLIB

Accesses a library of materials that can be imported and exported for use in rendering.

Windows: From the Render toolbar, click the Materials Library icon.

DOS: Choose Tools⇨Render⇨Materials Library.

How to Use It

AutoCAD opens the Materials Library dialog box. The Materials List contain materials currently in your drawing. Click Purge to delete all materials that are not attached to objects. Click Save to open the Library File dialog box and type in a name of a different materials library file, including its *.MLI* extension.

From the Library List, choose a material and then click Preview to see how the material looks on a sample sphere. Click Import to add the material to the Materials List. Export moves materials from the Materials List to the Library List. Click Delete to delete materials from either list. Click Open to open the Library File dialog box, allowing you to open another materials library file.

 ## More Stuff

See the RMAT command to attach materials to objects.

MEASURE

Puts points or blocks at specified intervals on an object (sort of like making a ruler).

 Windows: From the Draw toolbar, click the Point flyout and then the Measure icon.

DOS: Choose Draw⇨Point⇨Measure.

How to Use It

AutoCAD prompts you to select the object you want to measure. Select the object, picking a point nearest the end where you want AutoCAD to start measuring. Then specify a distance, called a segment length. MEASURE puts points along the object.

Or you can select the block option, and AutoCAD puts blocks along the object.

More Stuff

Use DDPTYPE to set the point type.

MINSERT

Inserts blocks into a rectangular array in one fell swoop.

Windows: From the Miscellaneous toolbar, click the Multiple Blocks icon.

DOS: Choose Draw⇨Insert⇨Multiple Blocks.

How to Use It

MINSERT prompts you for a block name. Type it in or press **?** to get a list. At the Insertion point prompt, specify a point. Next, type in an X scale factor (the default is 1), a Y scale factor, and a rotation angle. The rotation angle applies to the individual blocks and the entire array. Finally, AutoCAD prompts you for the number of rows and columns and the distance between them.

More Stuff

The problem with this command is that once you create the array, the members of the array cannot be changed or exploded. You can only edit the entire array.

See the DDINSERT and ARRAY commands; MINSERT is essentially a combination of these two commands.

MIRROR

Makes a mirror image of an object.

Windows: From the Modify toolbar, click the Copy flyout and then the Mirror icon.

DOS: Choose Construct⇨Mirror.

How to Use It

Select the object or objects you want to mirror. AutoCAD prompts you to specify points of the mirror line. If you want the line to be at a 90-degree angle, turn on ORTHO.

AutoCAD asks whether you want to delete the old objects, that is, the objects you selected. If you type **n**, you get both the original and the mirrored version of the object. If you type **y**, AutoCAD erases the original objects, and you get just the mirrored version.

More Stuff

If the objects you're mirroring contain text, you'll end up with the text reading right to left. You could tell your client to hold the drawing up to a mirror and read the text through the mirror, but you can also set the MIRRTEXT system variable to 0 to disable mirroring of text when you mirror an object. Type **mirrtext 0** on the command line and press Enter. It's a good thing to know.

MIRROR3D

Draws a mirror image in 3D space.

Windows: From the Modify toolbar, click the Copy flyout and then the 3D Mirror icon.

DOS: Choose Construct⇨3D Mirror.

How to Use It

First, select the objects you want to mirror. Then you define the plane around which the mirror copy will be created. Here are the ways you can define the plane:

3points	This is the default. Simply specify three points on the plane.
Object	Select a circle, an arc, or a 2D polyline to define the plane.
Last	Uses the last defined plane.
Zaxis	First, pick a point on the plane you are defining. Then pick a point on the Z axis of the plane, that is, a point on a line coming out perpendicular to the plane. (This is called a point *normal* to the plane.)
View	Pick a point on the viewing plane of the current viewport. AutoCAD uses a plane parallel to the viewing plane that goes through your point.
XY/YZ/ZX	Again, you pick a point on one of the listed planes. AutoCAD uses a plane parallel to that plane but passing through your point.

After you define your plane, AutoCAD asks you whether you want to delete the old objects, just as in the regular MIRROR command. Answer **y** or **n** and press Enter to complete the command.

MLEDIT

Edits the intersections between multiple parallel lines.

Windows: From the Modify toolbar, click the Special Edit flyout and then the Edit Multiline icon.

DOS: Choose Modify⇨Edit Multiline.

How to Use It

Click the image tile that displays the result you want. Some of the tiles are very similar, so you may have to try out some options before you get what you want.

AutoCAD prompts you to select the multilines. Sometimes it makes a difference which multiline you select first, because one will be trimmed, and the other will remain as is. AutoCAD wisely provides a **u** option to undo the results and try again.

When you are finished, AutoCAD continues to prompt you for more multilines. Press Enter to complete the command.

More Stuff

See MLINE to create multilines and MLSTYLE to manage multiline styles.

MLINE

Draws multiple parallel lines.

Windows: From the Draw toolbar, click the Polyline flyout and then the Multiline icon.

DOS: Choose Draw⇨Multiline.

How to Use It

Because multilines are so complicated, they are defined by styles. You usually create a style first and then draw your multiline. When you start MLINE, AutoCAD gives you the current justification, scale, and style and then prompts you for the first point. If you're happy with the settings, just pick a point. When AutoCAD prompts you for the next point, pick one. Continue on, picking points until you are finished and then press Enter to complete the command. The Close option will connect your last multiline segment with the first. Use the Undo option after any segment to delete that segment and try again.

However, things aren't so simple. So here are the options:

Justification   Top means that the start point you pick specifies the top line. The other, parallel lines are drawn below. Zero means that the start point you pick is the center of the multiline. The other parallel lines are drawn equally distant from the start point. Bottom means that your start point specifies the bottom line. The other lines are drawn above.

Scale   This scale is a factor of the multiline style definition. That means, if you type in a scale of 3, and the style says that the lines are to be 1 unit apart, the lines will now be 3 units apart. Type in a number.

Style   Type in a multiline style or press **?** to get a listing.

Once you've completed the options, you can start drawing multilines.

More Stuff

See MLEDIT to edit multilines and MLSTYLE to manage multiline styles.

For the Scale option, you can type negative values to flip the order of the lines. Typing **0** turns the multiline into a single line.

For more on multilines, see "Multilines (lines aplenty)" in Chapter 7 of *AutoCAD For Dummies*.

MLSTYLE

Manages styles for multilines.

Windows: From the Object Properties toolbar, click the Multiline Style icon; or choose Data➪Multiline Style.

DOS: Choose Data➪Multiline Style.

How to Use It

This command opens the Multiline Styles dialog box. The top section, called Multiline Style, manages the styles. If the style you want already exists, select it from the Current drop-down list box to make it current. Then click OK and go and make multilines.

Here's how you create a new style:

1. Click Add to add the style. (Ignore the invalid style message.)

2. Click the Element Properties button to open the Element Properties dialog box. Elements are the lines, and they are defined by their offset (distance) from the multiline start point, their color, and their linetype.

3. In the Offset text box, type in an offset amount. If you want a line right at the start point, your first offset will be **0**.

4. Click Add. The offset appears in the Elements box near the top of the Element Properties dialog box.

5. Click the offset there and choose Color. AutoCAD opens the Select Color dialog box, which also appears when you use the DDCOLOR command. (I'm sure you're reading this book from cover to cover and have already read about DDCOLOR.) Select the color you want or the BYLAYER or BYBLOCK options and click OK to return to the Element Properties dialog box.

6. Click the offset again in the Elements box and choose Linetype. AutoCAD opens the Select Linetype dialog box. You can find instructions for it under the DDLTYPE command. Select the linetype you want or the BYLAYER or BYBLOCK options and click OK. You're back to the Element Properties dialog box again.

7. Repeat steps 3 through 6 for other lines. Click OK when you're done with the Element Properties dialog box.

8. Back at the Multiline Styles dialog box, click Multiline Properties to open the Multiline Properties dialog box.

9. Click the Display joints check box if you want to show a short cross-line at the vertices of the multiline segments. It gives an effect somewhat like stained glass.

10. The Caps section controls how the start and end of the multiline are finished off, that is, how you put a cap on the multiline. Choose from Line, which is straight across; Outer arc, which makes a nice semicircle connecting the outer lines; Inner arcs, which makes nice semicircles connecting the inner elements; and Angle, where you can specify lines at an angle.

11. Go to the Fill section. Choose On to turn background fill on. This option is sort of like a diagonal hatch.

12. Click Color to select a color for the background fill. You get the Select Color dialog box again.

13. Click OK to return to the Multiline Styles dialog box. Notice that there's a picture of your multiline.

14. In the <u>N</u>ame text box, make up a name as pretty as your multiline. The name can have up to 31 characters.

15. Under <u>D</u>escription, type in a suitable description. This can be pretty long (255 characters) and can include spaces.

16. Click <u>S</u>ave to save the style in *ACAD.MLN*.

17. Click <u>L</u>oad, select the style from the list and then click OK. Don't forget this step or else you won't be able to use your new multiline style later. This works a bit differently from other loaded, named objects, such as linetypes.

18. Click OK again to complete the command. You're finally done!

Whew! That's a lot of steps. Are you sure you still want to draw multilines? But once you've created the style, drawing the multilines will be fairly simple (see the MLINE command).

More Stuff

When creating elements, use positive offset numbers to create lines above the middle of the multiline and negative offset numbers to create lines below.

In the Multiline Styles dialog box, use <u>R</u>ename to rename a multiline style.

For more on multilines, see "Multilines (lines aplenty)" in Chapter 7 of *AutoCAD For Dummies*.

MOVE

Moves objects.

Windows: From the Modify toolbar, click the Move icon.

DOS: Choose Modify⇨Move.

How to Use It

First, select your object or objects. AutoCAD prompts for a Base point or displacement. Pick a base point. When prompted for a second point, pick another point. AutoCAD moves your objects as indicated by the distance and direction between the two points.

More Stuff

You can use grips to move objects, too. See DDGRIPS.

MSPACE

Switches from paper space to model space.

Windows: Choose <u>V</u>iew⇨<u>T</u>iled Model Space or <u>F</u>loating Model Space.

On the status bar, double-click PAPER to toggle it to MODEL.

DOS: Choose View⇨Tiled Model Space or Floating Model Space.

How to Use It

Since you ordinarily draw in model space, the only reason you would switch to model space is if you have previously switched to paper space. You switched to paper space to create floating viewports containing different views of your model using the MVIEW command. (I know, floating viewports reminds you of being weightless in a spaceship and floating by a viewport, looking at some asteroid, but sooner or later, you're probably going to have to come down to Earth and deal with this stuff.)

More Stuff

If you use the command line for this command, you must first turn off the tilemode system variable. Type **tilemode 0** at the command line. Don't be alarmed if your drawing seems to disappear (see the MVIEW command).

See Chapter 14, "The Paper Space Chase," in *AutoCAD For Dummies* for more on using paper space.

MTEXT

Creates text in paragraph form.

Windows: From the Draw toolbar, click the Text flyout and then the Text icon.

DOS: Choose Draw⇨Text⇨Text.

How to Use It

At the first prompt, specify an insertion point for the text. Then AutoCAD prompts you for the other corner. Picking this second point creates a text boundary within which the text will flow. Now specify a height for the letters. If you have a DOS system, AutoCAD opens a text editor (the default is DOS's EDIT screen). If you have Windows, AutoCAD opens the Edit Mtext dialog box. Type your text and Click OK to complete the command.

The Edit MText dialog box has the following options:

Stack	This is for creating fractions where one character is on top of another. Type in the fraction, highlight it, and click the Stack button.
Import	This opens the Import Text File dialog box. When you import text, it appears in the text box.
Properties	This opens the MText Properties dialog box. I'll get to that in a minute (or however long it takes you to get to the end of this list).
Attributes	The options are:

	Overline	Puts a line over new or selected text.
	Underline	Underlines new or selected text.
	Font	Type in a font for new or selected text.
	Browse	Opens the Change Font dialog box where you can select a font file.

Color	Opens the Select Color dialog box where you can choose a color for your text.
Height	Sets the height for new or selected text.

Now back to the MText Properties dialog box. In the Contents section, you can set the Text Style, Text Height, and Direction (left to right for English text). In the Object section, you can select the Attachment point from a drop-down list. The attachment determines the point from where the text flows, as well as the text's justification. For example, any attachment option with "left" in its name is left justified; any option with "top" in it flows the text down from that top point. Finally, you may also specify the width and rotation angle of the text boundary in the Object section.

More Stuff

Although all the options described in the Mtext Properties dialog box can be done on the command line, you don't really want to do that. Instead, DOS users can create the Mtext using the default command line options and then use the MTPROP command to change the properties in a dialog box.

MTPROP

Changes Mtext properties.

Windows and DOS: Type **mtprop** on the command line.

How to Use It

AutoCAD prompts you to select an Mtext object, which is paragraph text created with the MTEXT command. The Mtext Properties dialog box opens. This is the same dialog box that opens when you click Properties in the Edit Mtext dialog box in the MTEXT command.

More Stuff

AutoCAD for Windows users can just use the MTEXT command to do this.

You can find more in the "Entering and Editing Paragraph Text" section in Chapter 10 of *AutoCAD For Dummies*.

MVIEW

Manages floating viewports. Floating viewports are created in paper space, and they are various views, viewpoints, and/or zooms of your drawing, placed in a border. The viewports themselves are actual objects that you can move, resize, and delete. Their purpose is to set up a final set of views of your objects for printing. They're usually used for 3D objects but can be used for 2D objects as well.

Windows and DOS: Choose View⇨Floating Viewports.

How to Use It

If you want one viewport, pick two points specifying the corners of the viewport. If you want two, three, or four viewports, select the 2, 3, or 4 option. If you select 2 or 3, AutoCAD gives you further options to specify how the viewports are configured. The Fit option is used if you want the viewports to fill the entire display. The ON and OFF options turn viewports on and off.

More Stuff

If you have saved viewport settings using VPORTS, you can restore them using MVIEW.

This command is used when tilemode is off. Use VPORTS when tilemode is on. See the MSPACE command for details.

MVSETUP

Sets specifications for floating viewports. MVSETUP is AutoCAD's attempt to help you create useful viewport layouts. Only for the brave-at-heart!

Windows and DOS: Choose View⇨Floating Viewports⇨MV Setup.

How to Use It

This command has more options than I can count, but who's counting. Here they are:

Align   Pans the view in the viewport to align it with a base
          point of another viewport. The suboptions are
          Angled, Horizontal, Vertical alignment, and Rotate
          view.

Create   Start with this option to create and delete viewports. If you press Enter, you get to create them. The suboptions are Single, Standard Engineering, and Array of viewports. Select the Delete suboption to delete a viewport. Try the Standard Engineering option to see a trial run of what the command does.

Scale   Adjusts the scale factor of the objects in the viewports. The scale factor is the ratio between the paper space size and the scale of the objects. The suboptions allow you to set the scale uniformly, for all viewports, or interactively, which means one at a time.

Options   The suboptions allow you to set a layer for the title block, reset limits after a title block has been in-serted, specify paper space units, such as inches or millimeters, and choose whether the title block should be an Xref or inserted into the drawing.

Title block   This option inserts a title block and sets the drawing origin. When you set the title block, you can choose from a menu of standard sizes. You can choose one and get a default border or choose Add and enter a title block description, filename, and usable area (lower-left and upper-right corners). Selecting the Origin suboption allows you to relocate the origin point for the drawing.

AutoCAD, in its great wisdom, knows that this is difficult stuff and offers you Undo options at each level.

More Stuff

This command switches you to paper space and so must be done with tilemode off. See the MSPACE command for details.

See Chapter 14 in *AutoCAD For Dummies* for more on paper space viewports.

NEW

Creates a new drawing file.

Windows: From the Standard toolbar, click the New icon; or choose File|New.

DOS: Choose File⇨New.

How to Use It

AutoCAD opens the Create New Drawing dialog box. The first section relates to the prototype drawing. The default is ACAD.DWG (which you can edit to suit your taste). However, you can click Prototype to select another prototype or click No Prototype. If you choose another drawing, you can click Retain as Default so that the new drawing will be the default prototype.

In the New Drawing Name text box, type in a name for your new baby, er, drawing.

OFFSET

Creates new objects at a specified distance from an existing object.

Windows: From the Modify toolbar, click the Copy flyout then the Offset icon.

DOS: Choose Construct⇨Offset.

How to Use It

First, type the distance of the new object from the existing one. Then AutoCAD prompts you to select an object. When you do so, AutoCAD asks which side. Pick a point on the side of the object where you want the new copy to appear.

There's an option to pick a point through which the new object passes. This is a simple way to indicate both the offset distance and the side where the new object appears. Type **t** for the through option, select the object to offset, and pick the Through point.

Either way, AutoCAD continues to prompt you for more offset opportunities. It can't get enough. Press Enter to end the command.

OOPS

This cute little command, the only one with a sense of humor, restores erased objects.

 Windows: From the Miscellaneous toolbar, click the Oops! icon.

DOS: Choose Modify⇨Oops!

How to Use It

After you erase something, just use OOPS to get it back.

 ### *More Stuff*

 Use OOPS after BLOCK or WBLOCK, because those commands erase the objects you use to make a block.

U and UNDO can also be used to reverse the effect of an ERASE command.

OPEN

Opens an existing drawing.

 Windows: From the Standard toolbar, click the Open icon; or choose File⇨Open.

DOS: Choose File⇨Open.

How to Use It

 If you have AutoCAD for Windows, OPEN displays the Select File dialog box. This is like any File⇨Open dialog box with the nice addition of a Preview box that shows you what a drawing looks like when you select it from the File Name list box.

Press Find File to open the Browse/Search dialog box. The browse tab displays small drawing images. The search tab allows you to specify a file type, date, or search pattern.

 If you have a DOS system, OPEN displays the Open Drawing dialog box, which is pretty much the same as the Select File dialog box in AutoCAD for Windows.

'ORTHO

Restricts the cursor to horizontal and vertical directions. Very helpful in creating nice straight lines.

Windows: On the status bar, double-click Ortho.

DOS: Choose Assist⇨ORTHO.

How to Use It

You just choose **on** or **off**.

More Stuff

If you are using a User Coordinate System or snap rotation, ORTHO will be set horizontal and vertical to those settings.

'OSNAP

See the DDOSNAP command to manage object snaps using a dialog box.

'PAN

Moves the drawing display so that you get to see something new and different.

Windows: From the Standard toolbar, click the Pan flyout and then the Pan Point icon; or choose View⇨Pan⇨Point.

DOS: Choose View⇨Pan⇨Point.

How to Use It

At the prompt, pick the first point and then the second point. AutoCAD moves the drawing according to the distance and angle between the two points.

More Stuff

In AutoCAD for Windows, you can also use the scroll bars to pan vertically and horizontally.

Edits polylines and 3D polygon meshes.

Windows: From the Modify toolbar, click the Special Edit flyout and then the Edit Polyline icon.

DOS: Choose Modify⇨Edit Polyline.

How to Use It

Select a 2D polyline. AutoCAD offers the following options:

Close/Open	If the polyline is closed, you can choose Open to remove the closing segment. If it's open, choose Close to close it.
Join	If other objects are attached to the polyline, you can join them into the Polyline Club with this option. Choose Join and select the attached objects. The objects never decline to join, unlike some people.
Width	Specify a width for the entire polyline.
Edit vertex	Offers you the following list of submenu options. PEDIT puts an X at the first vertex so that you know which vertex you're editing.

	Next	Moves the X to the next vertex. It stops at the last vertex.
	Previous	Moves the X marker to the previous vertex. If you've used Next to get to the last vertex, this is how you get back to the beginning.
	Break	Breaks the polyline into two pieces. However, this offers you a sub-submenu. (Are you following me here?) If you just type **go**, AutoCAD breaks the polyline. However, AutoCAD holds the current vertex, and if you use Next or Previous to specify the other end of the break and then use **go,** AutoCAD breaks the polyline between the two vertices, leaving a hole.
	Insert	Adds a new vertex after the vertex marked with the X. You pick a point for the location of the new vertex.

	Move	Moves the vertex with the X. (Did you notice the rhyme?) You specify the new location.
	Regen	Regenerates the polyline.
	Straighten	This option offers the same sub-submenu as Break and works the same way. Replaces the vertices with a straight line.
	Tangent	Marks a tangent direction to the vertex with the X, which can be used for curve fitting, that is, the Fit and Spline options. You specify a point or angle to indicate the direction of the tangent.
	Width	Edits the start and end widths for the segment after the marked vertex. Type in a starting and ending width. Use the Regen option to see the results.
	eXit	Exits the Edit vertex submenu and returns you to the original PEDIT prompt.
Fit		Turns the polyline into a smooth curve.
Spline		A spline is a mathematically constructed curve that uses the vertices of your polyline as the frame of the curve. There are different types of splines, which you can control using system variables. At any rate, just choose this option, and AutoCAD makes your spline.
Decurve		Undoes the results of the Fit and Spline options.
Ltype gen		Select ON to generate a linetype continuously through the vertices of the polyline. Select OFF to start each vertex with a dash. If you're using a continuous linetype, this option is meaningless.
Undo		Undoes operations one-by-one back to the beginning of your PEDIT session (which may seem like ages ago.)
eXit		Exits PEDIT.

More Stuff

If you select a 3D polyline curve (created with the 3DPOLY command), the prompts are slightly different, but not much. If you select a 3D polygon mesh, you also get similar prompts, but with more Edit vertex options because you can move the vertex in three dimensions, using the M and N dimensions.

How do you turn ordinary lines and arcs into a polyline? Use this command and select attached lines and arcs. AutoCAD informs you that this is not a polyline and asks whether you want to turn it into one. Type **y** and there you go!

PLAN

Shows the plan view of a User Coordinate System (UCS).

Windows and DOS: Choose View⇨3D Viewpoint Presents⇨ Plan View.

How to Use It

The plan view is the one looking down from the top, the regular, old 2D way of looking at things. Use the <u>C</u>urrent option or press Enter to get the plan view of the current UCS.

Use the <u>N</u>amed option (called Ucs on the command line) to restore a named UCS you have saved. Type in the name. If you forget it, type **?**, and AutoCAD lists name options for you.

The <u>W</u>orld option returns you to the World Coordinate System. If your current UCS was the same as the WCS, this option is the same as pressing Enter.

PLINE

Draws a 2D polyline, which is a connected series of lines and arcs.

 Windows: From the Draw toolbar, click the Polyline flyout and then the Polyline icon.

DOS: Choose Draw⇨Polyline.

How to Use It

AutoCAD prompts you for your start point. Specify a point. The next prompt offers the following options:

Endpoint of line   This is the default, and when you pick a point, you get a line.

Arc   Type **a** to switch into Arc mode. This option has its own submenu.

	Endpoint of arc	This is the default. Pick a point.
	Angle	Type in an included angle for the arc. A positive angle draws the arc counterclockwise. A negative angle goes clockwise. Then you get the rest of the standard options for drawing an arc (see the ARC command).
	Center	Specify a point for the center of the arc. Again, you then get the rest of the standard arc options.
	CLose	Closes your polyline with an arc.
	Direction	Pick a point to indicate a direction from the start point of the arc. Then pick an endpoint.
	Halfwidth	The halfwidth is the distance from the center of the polyline to its edge. Usually, you type in a distance. You can pick different starting and ending halfwidths for a tapered arc segment. I'm not sure how useful this is for drafting, but the results are pretty.
	Line	Returns PEDIT to line mode.
	Radius	Pick a point for the radius of the arc. AutoCAD continues to give you standard arc prompts so that you can finish the arc. (Don't delay finishing the arc, because it's going to start raining any day now.)
	Second pt	Complete the arc by specifying second points and endpoints.
	Undo	Undoes the last arc segment you created. You won't need this option.
	Width	Like halfwidth, but you specify the whole width instead of the halfwidth.
Close		Draws a line from the end to the start of the polyline, closing it.
Halfwidth		See the Arc submenu options.
Length		Picking a point specifies the length of the next line segment, which is drawn in the same direction as the previous one.

| Undo | See the Arc submenu options. |
| Width | See the Arc submenu options. |

More Stuff

The PEDIT command edits polylines.

For much more on polylines, see "Polylines (wanna crackerline?)" in Chapter 7 of *AutoCAD For Dummies*.

PLOT

Plots or prints a drawing.

Windows: From the Standard toolbar, click the Print icon; or choose File⇨Print.

DOS: Choose Draw⇨Print.

How to Use It

AutoCAD opens the Plot Configuration dialog box. It's a big one, with several sublevels of dialog boxes, too, but here goes.

Try a full preview (explained later in this section) first. If everything looks hunky-dory, click OK to plot. (You're very lucky!)

The Device and Default Information section shows you the current plotter or printer. Click the Device and Default Selection button to open the dialog box of the same name. That dialog box allows you to select your plotter or printer, save all of these complex plot configurations to a file so that you don't have to do it each time, and make some plotter/printer changes depending on the plotter or printer you have.

The Pen Parameters section allows you to set the parameters for plotters with multiple pens and other pen options. Click the Pen Assignments button to open a dialog box. Pen assignments are for plotters with more than one pen. The concept to understand here is that you base the assignment on an object's color. For each color you assign a pen, linetype, speed, and pen width. Click Optimization to set options that optimize pen motion in order to reduce plot time.

The Additional Parameters section allows you to specify what part of the drawing you want to print.

Display	Plots what is on-screen.
Extents	Plots the entire drawing. It's like ZOOM with the Extents option.
Limits	Plots the drawing as defined by the LIMITS command.
View	Plots a view you have saved using the DDVIEW or VIEW command.
Window	Plots any window you select. Click the Window button to return to the drawing to specify the two corners of the window you want to plot.

On the right side of the Additional Parameters section, you can choose Hide Lines, which hides lines in 3D objects that would normally be hidden from view. Choose Adjust Area Fill if you have filled objects. AutoCAD adjusts the pen width so that the fill doesn't go outside the boundaries. (Remember learning to color within the lines in kindergarten?) Click Plot to File to plot to a file instead of to a plotter. When you choose the Plot to File check box, the File Name button darkens, and you can click it to choose a filename other than the default, which is the name of your drawing with a *.PLT* extension.

In the Paper Size and Orientation section, you specify whether your drawing units represent inches or millimeters. The orientation icon shows whether you're in landscape or portrait mode. The Size button opens up the Paper Size dialog box, where you can choose from standard sizes of paper or type in your own size.

The next section is called Scale, Rotation, and Origin. The scale is the units plotted for each unit on the drawing. Type in the number of plotted units in the left box and the number of drawing units in the right box. For example, if you want to plot a drawing of a table that is 24" x 36", and you want it to fit on an 8 ¹/₂ by 11-inch piece of paper, using a 1=4 scale will result in a table that is 6" x 9" on paper. You can use inches and feet, such as, 1"=1'.

Click Scale to Fit to scale the drawing to fit the paper size you've selected.

If you're having trouble figuring out the scale, click the Scale to Fit check box and see what AutoCAD calculates. This will give you a ballpark figure to work with, and you can change the scale to something similar that fits standard scales.

Click the Rotation and Origin button to open the Plot Rotation and Origin dialog box. Here you pick the plot rotation and plot origin, which is usually 0,0.

Finally, the last section is Plot Preview. Choose Partial to see just a rectangle representing your precious drawing in a (hopefully) bigger rectangle representing the paper. Choose Full to get an accurate image of your drawing, including a Pan and Zoom button that works like 'ZOOM with the Dynamic option. Click End Preview.

Click OK. Load paper in the plotter. At the prompt, press Enter, and the plot starts.

More Stuff

If you've erased or moved objects resulting in a smaller drawing, do a ZOOM Extents before plotting so that AutoCAD knows the new size of your drawing.

See Chapter 13, "The Plot Thickens," of *AutoCAD For Dummies*, for a full chapter's worth on plotting.

POINT

Draws a point.

Windows: From the Draw toolbar, click the Point flyout and then the Point icon.

DOS: Choose Draw⇨Point⇨Point.

How to Use It

AutoCAD prompts you to specify a point (meaning a coordinate) and then draws a point (meaning a point object).

More Stuff

Use DDPTYPE to determine how points appear.

POLYGON

Draws a polygon, using polylines.

Windows: From the Draw toolbar, click the Polygon flyout and then the Polygon icon.

DOS: Choose Draw⇨Polygon⇨Polygon.

How to Use It

POLYGON asks you for the number of sides. You can type any number from 3 to 1,024. Next, you can specify the center. Now comes the interesting part. Your choices are:

Inscribed in circle	You specify a circle radius. The vertices of the polygon will be on the circle (so that the polygon will be inside the circle).
Circumscribed about circle	You specify a circle radius. The midpoints of each side of the polygon will lie on the circle (so that the polygon will be outside the circle).

There isn't any circle, however; it's just a way of defining the polygon.

Instead of specifying the center at the first prompt, you can type **e**, for edge, and then pick two points that define the endpoints of the first edge.

More Stuff

Because the polygon is a polyline, you can use PEDIT to edit it.

See "Polygons (so next time, lock the cage . . .)" in Chapter 7 of *AutoCAD For Dummies*.

PREFERENCES

Sets your preferences for various aspects of AutoCAD.

Windows and DOS: Choose Options⇨Preferences.

How to Use It

In Windows, this command displays the Preferences dialog box, which contains five tabs: S̲ystem, E̲nvironment, R̲ender, I̲nternational, and M̲isc.

S̲ystem	These options turn the menu and scroll bars on and off, turn on Automatic Save (a good idea), and — for those who like a pretty screen — control the colors and font used in dialog boxes. The default for Automatic Save is a ridiculous 120 minutes. Change it to 15 to 30 minutes — max.

Environment	Specify default directories and filenames for certain files that AutoCAD uses, and also configure memory paging.
Render	Set the directory for variables that are used by the RENDER command.
International	Set English or metric units of measurement and information for the prototype drawing.
Misc	Specify a text editor and font-mapping file for the MTEXT command, the size of the text window, and other miscellaneous stuff.

AutoCAD opens the Preferences dialog box, which isn't as pretty as in Windows but is a lot simpler. You can specify English or metric units of measurement and information about the prototype drawing.

PSPACE

Switches to paper space. This is a concept that allows you to create floating viewports to show various views of your drawing as well as to set up a title block and border and, in general, prepare a layout for plotting.

Windows: In the status bar, double-click MODEL; or choose View⇨Paper Space.

DOS: Choose View⇨Paper Space.

How to Use It

In paper space, the UCS icon in the lower-left corner of your screen changes to the triangular paper-space icon.

More Stuff

If you type this command at the command line, you have to set the TILEMODE system variable to 0 (off). Type **tilemode 0** and press Enter.

See the MVSETUP command for more information on paper space. See MVIEW to create those floating viewports.

See Chapter 14 of *AutoCAD For Dummies* for an excellent introduction to paper space and MVSETUP.

PURGE

Removes unused blocks, layers, dimension styles, text styles, multiline styles, and linetypes from the database of the drawing.

Windows and DOS: Choose Data⇨Purge.

How to Use It

You can choose a specific option to purge or choose the All option to get rid of everything. AutoCAD lists the names of unused layers, blocks, and so on. For each item that you want to purge, type **y** and then press Enter.

More Stuff

This command reduces the size of your drawing by removing blocks, layers, and so on, that you defined but never used.

QSAVE

Saves your drawing.

Windows: From the Standard toolbar, click the Save icon; or choose <u>F</u>ile⇨<u>S</u>ave.

DOS: Choose File⇨Save.

How to Use It

AutoCAD saves your drawing to your hard disk. If you haven't named your drawing, QSAVE opens the Save Drawing As dialog box so that you can type a name.

More Stuff

I'm not kidding with the Thumbs Up and Safe icons. Use this command a lot. *Not* using this command is *not* safe!

QTEXT

Turns off the display and plotting of text and attributes.

Windows and DOS: Choose Options⇨Display⇨Text Frame Only.

How to Use It

When you turn on QTEXT (it stands for quick text), text is displayed as just a rectangle around the text location. Then type **regen** to see the result.

More Stuff

Turning QTEXT on reduces the time AutoCAD takes to redraw and regenerate drawings with lots of text.

If you leave QTEXT on when you plot, all you'll get is rectangles, so don't forget to turn it off before you plot! (QTEXT might be useful for a draft plot, however.)

QUIT

Exits AutoCAD.

Windows and DOS: Choose File⇨Exit.

How to Use It

If you haven't made any changes to your drawing, AutoCAD throws you out unceremoniously. If you have made changes, AutoCAD opens the Drawing Modification dialog box to remind you to save your changes, if you want, before quitting.

More Stuff

See the END command.

RAY

Creates a line with a starting point that extends to infinity.

Windows: From the Draw toolbar, click the Line flyout and then the Ray icon.

DOS: Choose Draw⇨Ray.

How to Use It

At the From point prompt, pick a start point of the ray. AutoCAD prompts you for a Through point. Specify another point. The ray continues on, and on, and on . . . . AutoCAD continues to ask you for Through points, so you can make other rays starting from the same point. Press Enter to end the command.

More Stuff

Luckily, commands such as ZOOM Extents ignore rays; otherwise, you'd get some unusual results. Also, the PLOT command doesn't expect an infinite-size sheet of paper — it's all a mirage.

See "Rays and infinite lines (Buck Rogers, watch out!)" in Chapter 7 of *AutoCAD For Dummies*.

RCONFIG

Configures AutoCAD to Render on your computer system.

Windows and DOS: Choose Options⇨Render Configure.

How to Use It

First, AutoCAD lists your current rendering configuration. Press Enter to configure. Type **2** to configure the rendering device. You can render to a viewport, to the full screen, to a second monitor, or to a hard-copy device. Press Enter to return to the Configuration menu. Type **3** to configure the Render Window driver. Press Enter again to return to the Configuration menu. (The configuration is automatic for Windows.) Type **0** to return to your drawing. AutoCAD asks you whether you want to keep your configuration changes; type **y** to do so.

More Stuff

The options that you see depend on your system. For more information, see the DOS installation guide.

RECOVER

Tries to repair a damaged drawing.

Windows and DOS: Choose File⇨Management⇨Recover.

How to Use It

Use this command only after you receive some sort of error message, such as the famous AutoCAD FATAL ERROR message. (It's OK; I've gotten lots of error messages, and I'm still alive to write this book.)

First, try to reopen the drawing. The OPEN command can repair minor damage in a drawing. If that command doesn't work, AutoCAD may detect that the drawing is damaged; the program will ask you whether you want to proceed. Type **y**; AutoCAD attempts to repair the drawing.

If that procedure doesn't work, start a new drawing, and use the RECOVER command. AutoCAD opens the Recover Drawing File dialog box. Select the file from the list. AutoCAD starts recovering the drawing, displaying a report on-screen as it works.

More Stuff

Not every drawing can be recovered after a fatal error. If your drawings are important, get in the habit of making backup copies to floppy diskettes.

RECTANG

Draws a rectangle.

 Windows: From the Draw toolbar, click the Polygon flyout and then the Rectangle icon.

DOS: Choose Draw⇨Polygon⇨Rectangle.

How to Use It

This command is easy. AutoCAD prompts you for the two corners of the rectangle. You comply and — poof! — you have a rectangle.

 See "Rectangles (oh, what a tangled wreck . . .)" in Chapter 7 of *AutoCAD For Dummies*.

REDO

Redoes whatever the preceding U or UNDO command undid.

 Windows: From the Standard toolbar, click the Redo icon; or choose Edit⇨Redo.

DOS: Choose Assist⇨Redo.

How to Use It

When you use the command, AutoCAD puts back whatever you took out with the U or UNDO command (or vice versa).

More Stuff

You need to use this command *immediately* after using the U or UNDO command. Go straight to this command; do not pass Go; do not collect $200.

 See "The Way You Undo the Things You Do" in Chapter 6 of *AutoCAD For Dummies.*

REDRAW

Redisplays the drawing, removing blip marks and wayward pixels left behind by your editing.

 Windows: From the Standard toolbar, click the Redraw flyout and then the Redraw View icon; or choose View⇨Redraw View.

DOS: Choose View⇨Redraw View.

How to Use It

Just use the command; AutoCAD obeys.

More Stuff

If you're using viewports, REDRAW redraws only the current viewport. Use REDRAWALL to redraw all viewports.

REGEN

Regenerates the drawing, recomputes coordinates, and reindexes the database.

Windows and DOS: Type **regen** at the command line.

How to Use It

Type the command; AutoCAD obeys.

More Stuff

REGEN takes longer than REDRAW; it updates many changes that may have taken place since the last time you did a REGEN. Use REGENALL to regenerate all viewports.

REGENAUTO

Manages the way that AutoCAD regenerates drawings.

Windows and DOS: At the command line, type **regenauto**.

How to Use It

Type **on** or **off**. On means that AutoCAD regenerates automatically when needed — for example, during some zooms and pans. Sometimes, regeneration is time-consuming (you could use it as an opportunity for a coffee break), so you can set the command to off. Thereafter, each time AutoCAD needs to regen, it asks you whether it should proceed. You can type **y** or **n**, but if you say no, AutoCAD wimps out on you and cancels the command.

REGION

Creates a region object, which is a 2D closed area.

Windows: From the Draw toolbar, click the Polygon flyout and then the Region icon.

DOS: Choose Construct⇨Region.

How to Use It

AutoCAD prompts you to select objects. You can select closed polylines, lines, circles, ellipses, and splines. AutoCAD ignores internal objects as best it can and converts your objects to a region, deleting the original objects in the process.

More Stuff

AutoCAD can do certain things with regions that it can't with the original objects. For example, you can use the MASSPROP command to analyze certain properties, and you can hatch them.

 Finally, you can use INTERSECT, SUBTRACT, and UNION to play around with sets of regions (called *composite regions*).

See the BOUNDARY command, which also creates regions. See the BHATCH command if you want to hatch a region.

REINIT

Reinitializes input/output ports (such as COM1); digitizer; display (your screen); and ACAD.PGP, which holds command definitions.

Windows and DOS: Choose Tools⇨Reinitialize.

How to Use It

Use this command only if you changed your hardware configuration or the ACAD.PGP file during a drawing session. For example, if you exited AutoCAD temporarily by using the SHELL command, removed your mouse from COM1, and put a printer in its place to print something, you need to use this command after you return to your drawing and replace the mouse in COM1.

More Stuff

You won't use this command very often, unless you make changes in your computer setup.

RENAME

 See the DDRENAME command, which does the same thing by using a dialog box.

RENDER

Shades 3D solid or surface objects, using lights, scenes, and materials. Gives a semi-realistic appearance to your objects.

 Windows: From the Render toolbar, click the Render icon.

DOS: Choose Tools⇨Render⇨Render.

How to Use It

Before you render, you usually create lights with the LIGHT command and a scene with the SCENE command. You also may want to use RPREF to set rendering preferences. You can render without any preparation, however; RENDER will use the current view and a default distant light source.

This command opens the Render dialog box. The Rendering Type drop-down list includes AutoCAD Render and any other rendering applications that you have installed. (Autodesk sells other applications, such as AutoVision.) Select the one you want. I'll assume that you are using AutoCAD Render.

The Scene to Render box lists any scenes that you defined. The current view is listed as an option.

The Screen Palette section controls the color map. These options are explained under the RPREF command.

The Rendering Options section allows you to select Smooth Shading. This option smoothes the edges between polygon faces, resulting in a rounder object. (The option is explained further under the RPREF command.) Choose Apply Materials to use materials that you imported from the materials library and attached to objects (see the MATLIB and RMAT commands). The Smoothing Angle determines when edges are smoothed if you chose the Smooth Shading option. Angles greater than the smoothing angle are considered to be edges and are not smoothed. Click More Options (as if you wanted even more) to get to the AutoCAD Render Options dialog box. In this dialog box, you can choose two types of rendering: Phong, which results in higher-quality renderings and better highlights; or Gouraud, which results in faster but lower-quality renderings. (For a more detailed explanation, see the RPREF command.) Click OK to return to the Render dialog box.

The Destination section selects the location of the rendered image. If you want to see the results, the location must be either Viewport or (if you have Windows) Render Window.

If you have Windows, you can render to the viewport, but you have the additional option of rendering to the Render Window. This window has its own special menu and toolbar, which allow you to open an image file and save the rendered image to it. You also can copy the image to the Windows Clipboard.

Click Render Scene to render the selected scene. Click Render Objects to select objects to render. Rendering takes time; the less you select for rendering, the faster the process.

Redraw the screen to return to your original models.

More Stuff

The other commands related to rendering are LIGHT, MATLIB, RCONFIG, RENDSCR, RMAT, RPREF, SAVEIMG, SCENE, and STATS. It's no wonder that up until now, the rendering process was handled by a separate application.

RENDERUNLOAD

Unloads Render from your computer's memory.

Windows and DOS: Type **renderunload** at the command line.

How to Use It

AutoCAD takes care of this process for you. The purpose of unloading Render is to free up memory. The next time you use a Render command, Render is reloaded.

RENDSCR

Redisplays your last rendering.

DOS: Type **rendscr** at the command line.

How to Use It

This command applies only to DOS systems in which you used RCONFIG to render to a full screen (instead of a viewport). When you see the rendered image, you can press any key to return to your drawing and then use this command to return to your rendered image.

REVOLVE

Draws a solid by revolving a 2D object around an axis.

Windows: From the Solids toolbar, click the Revolve icon.

DOS: Choose Draw⇨Solids⇨Revolve.

How to Use It

First, you need an object to revolve. The object can be any closed polyline, polygon, circle, ellipse, closed spline, donut, or region. The object cannot have crossing or intersecting parts. Next, you need to decide what your axis will be. You may want to draw a line so that you'll be able to select it to specify the axis.

AutoCAD asks you to select objects. You can revolve only one object at a time, so select one object.

Next, you need to specify the axis, using the following options:

Start point of axis	This is the default. Specify a point; AutoCAD asks for the endpoint of the axis.
Object	Select an existing line for your axis.
X	This option revolves the object around the positive X axis.
Y	This option revolves the object around the positive Y axis.

For all options, AutoCAD then asks whether you want to revolve a full circle (360 degrees) or a specified angle. Your answer completes the command.

More Stuff

If several lines and arcs make up the shape that you want to revolve, you can use REGION to convert them to one object. Alternatively, see the tip under the PEDIT command for details on turning separate lines and arcs into a polyline.

REVSURF

Draws a surface by revolving a line, arc, circle, or polyline around an axis.

Windows: From the Surfaces toolbar, click the Revolved Surface icon.

DOS: Choose Draw⇨Surfaces⇨Revolved Surface.

How to Use It

First, you need a *path curve*, which means a line, arc, circle, or polyline. The path curve doesn't really have to curve; it can be made up of straight-line segments. Next, you need an object to be

your axis (a line or polyline). Create those first (that's the hard part) and then use the command. AutoCAD prompts you to select a path curve and then the axis of revolution.

Now you need to supply the start angle (the default is 0) and the included angle (the default is a full circle).

RMAT

Defines materials and attaches them to objects for the purpose of rendering them.

Windows: From the Render toolbar, click the Materials icon.

DOS: Choose Tools⇨Render⇨Materials.

How to Use It

Before using this command, use the MATLIB command to load materials from a materials library.

RMAT opens the Materials dialog box. On the left is a list of available materials, which always includes the *GLOBAL* default material. In the middle is a preview box for looking at your beautiful materials.

To create a new material, click New. The New Standard Material dialog box opens. Type a name for your material. On the left are four attributes: Color, Ambient, Reflection, and Roughness. Select these options one at a time. Also, for each option, complete the Value and Color settings in the center of the dialog box.

Color   Selecting a color for the color sounds funny, but this option sets the *diffuse color* — the base color that the object reflects. Value sets the intensity of the color. To set color, you must deselect the By ACI button.

Ambient   This option sets the color reflected from ambient light. (See the LIGHT command.) The default value for the ambient light is 1, which is a good guide to go by.

Reflection   A higher value would create a shiny effect.

Roughness   This option relates to the reflection value. You set only the value — no color. A higher roughness setting produces a bigger reflection highlight.

Now click the Preview button to see the results. You always see a sphere. Continue to fool around with the controls until you like what you see; then click OK to return to the Materials dialog box.

Click <u>M</u>odify if you want to change a material. This button opens a dialog box just like the New Standard Material dialog box.

Click D<u>u</u>plicate to make a copy of a material. The New Standard Material dialog box opens. Type a new name and make any changes you want. Duplicating a material is a shortcut way to create a similar material without having to define everything again.

Now comes the important part: attaching your new material to an object. Select your new material from the Materials list and then click <u>A</u>ttach. Back at your drawing you can select an object.

Suppose that you want to attach a material that you created a while ago and that you have forgotten its name but know you attached it to another object. Click the <u>S</u>elect button, and pick the object in your drawing. AutoCAD returns you to the Materials dialog box, with the material selected.

You also can attach materials by clicking ACI (AutoCAD Color Index), which opens the (take a deep breath) Attach by AutoCAD Color Index dialog box, where you select a material and an ACI color. Preview displays the selected material. <u>A</u>ttach attaches the selected material to the color. <u>D</u>etach detaches the selected material from its color. Click OK to return to the Materials dialog box.

Finally, you can attach materials by layer. Click B<u>y</u> Layer to open the Attach by Layer dialog box, which works the same way as the Attach by AutoCAD Color Index dialog box.

More Stuff

See the RENDER command.

ROTATE

Rotates objects around a point.

Windows: From the Modify toolbar, click the Rotate flyout and then the Rotate icon.

DOS: Choose Modify⇨Rotate.

How to Use It

The default way to rotate objects is the simplest. Select an object. Specify a base point around which the object will rotate. Type a rotation angle (this angle is relative to the object's current position). You also can pick a point to indicate the angle. Move the cursor, and the drag copy of the object moves.

You also can type **r** for the Reference option, which prompts you for a reference angle and a new angle. You can use this method to specify an absolute rotation and to align an object with other objects in your drawing.

ROTATE3D

Rotates objects in 3D space about an axis.

Windows: From the Modify toolbar, click the Rotate flyout and then the 3D Rotate icon.

DOS: Choose Construct⇨3D Rotate.

How to Use It

Before you start this command, you want to have in mind the axis for rotation. It may help to draw a line so that you can select it.

First, select the objects that you want to rotate. Next, the command offers you several options for defining the rotation axis:

2points	Specify two points on the axis.
Axis by object	Select a line, circle, arc, or 2D polyline segment. If you select a line or a straight polyline segment, the selected object becomes the axis. If you pick a circle, arc, or arc polyline segment, an imaginary line going through the object's center and exiting it perpendicularly becomes the axis.
Last	Uses the preceding axis of rotation.
View	Aligns the axis with the viewing direction and passing through a point that you select.
X, Y, or Z axis	Aligns the axis with the X, Y, or Z axis and passing through a point that you select.

After you define your axis (didn't I tell you that it would be easiest to draw a line and select it?), type the rotation angle, or use the Reference option to specify a reference angle and a new angle as you would for the ROTATE command.

RPREF

Sets preferences for rendering.

Windows: From the Render toolbar, click the Preferences icon.

DOS: Choose Tools⇨Render⇨Preferences.

How to Use It

This command opens the Rendering Preferences dialog box. The Rendering Type drop-down list includes AutoCAD Render and any other rendering applications that you have installed.

The Screen Palette section controls the way AutoCAD uses all the available colors when rendering to a viewport. A *color map* is a table that defines each color in terms of red, green, and blue intensity.

If you are using the viewport, my best suggestion regarding this nonsense is to simply try both of the first two options (Best Map/No Fold and Best Map/Fold) and view the results. You can make the change when you actually render in the Render dialog box. After you decide which option you like best, make the change in the Rendering Preferences dialog box.

The Rendering Procedure section defines how the command behaves. You can skip the dialog box and render immediately, render the entire scene, or prompt yourself to select objects. The last two options are available in the Render dialog box.

The Rendering Options section controls important aspects of the rendering process, but just sets defaults. You can change these options in the Render dialog box.

Smooth Shading	Smoothes out polygon mesh facets so that the surface appears to be continuous.
Merge	Allows you to combine images, such as an object appearing in front of a tree.
Apply Materials	Renders, using the materials that you defined and attached with the MATLIB and RMAT commands.
Smoothing Angle	Relates to the Smooth Shading option. The default is 45 degrees, which means that edges that are more than 45 degrees from each other are not smoothed. Edges less than 45 degrees from each other are smoothed.

In the same section, choose More Options to open the AutoCAD
Render Options dialog box. In the Render Quality section, choose
Gouraud or Phong. Phong calculates at each pixel and results in
more realistic highlights.

You have two Face Controls options. The rendering process
analyzes which faces are facing front and which are facing back.
When you draw a 3D face counterclockwise, RENDER counts it as
a front face and renders it. Back faces need not be rendered,
because they wouldn't be seen. When you choose the Discard
Back Faces option, RENDER does not calculate them, thereby
speeding the rendering process. Choosing the Back Face Normal
is Negative option reverses the faces AutoCAD considers to be back
faces. This option is for those of you who draw everything clockwise.
Click OK to return to the Rendering Preferences dialog box.

The next section controls the destination of your rendered image.
For DOS systems, Viewport is the easiest option. For Windows
systems, choose either Viewport or Render Window. Rendering
to the Render Window enables you to copy the image to the
Clipboard, print to the printer, and so on. The other options
require configuration with RCONFIG. This section also opens the
File Output Configuration dialog box, in which you can specify a
file type and other technical specifications.

The Lights section scales the blocks that AutoCAD inserts into
your drawing to indicate lights.

Click Information to find out about your rendering configuration.

When you finish with your preferences, click OK, and go render!

RULESURF

Draws a ruled surface mesh between two objects.

Windows: From the Surfaces toolbar, click the Ruled Surface
icon.

DOS: Choose Draw⇨Surfaces⇨Ruled Surface.

How to Use It

Before you use this command, you need to draw two objects that
will define the mesh. You can use points, lines, circles, arcs, or
polylines. Both objects can be open or closed. AutoCAD prompts
you to select the two defining curves (even though they can be
straight). Then AutoCAD creates the surface.

More Stuff

If the objects are open, such as lines, where you pick the objects matters. If the pick points are on the same side of the two objects, the ruled lines start from the side where you picked and go straight across. If the pick points are on opposite sides of the two objects, the ruled lines cross from one end of the first object to the other end of the second object, creating a self-intersecting mesh. (Well, you have to try it.)

SAVE

Saves the drawing.

Windows and DOS: Type **save** at the command line.

How to Use It

Actually, this command has pretty much been superseded by QSAVE, which is available in the Standard toolbar in Windows and under the File menu in both Windows and DOS.

SAVEAS

Saves a drawing under a new or different name.

Windows and DOS: Choose File⇨Save As.

How to Use It

This command opens the Save Drawing As dialog box. Type a name.

More Stuff

See "Creating the Primordial Prototype" in Chapter 5 of *AutoCAD For Dummies*.

SAVEASR12

Saves the drawing as an AutoCAD Release 12 drawing.

Windows: Type **saveasr12** at the command line.

DOS: Choose File⇨Export⇨Release 12 DWG.

How to Use It

AutoCAD opens the Save Release 12 Drawing As dialog box. Type a filename. Click OK.

More Stuff

Of course, any feature that exists only in Release 13 is lost when you convert a drawing to Release 12. AutoCAD writes a report in the command line, listing information that has been lost or changed. (How's that for service?)

When you type a name, it should be different from your Release 13 drawing's name; otherwise, you'll overwrite the drawing. This command, however, creates a *.BAK* file of the Release 13 drawing (which you can rename as a *.DWG* file) just for people who make this mistake.

SAVEIMG

Saves a rendered image to a file.

Windows and DOS: Choose Tools⇨Image⇨Save.

How to Use It

AutoCAD opens the Save Image dialog box. If you have rendered to a separate rendering window (as specified in the Destination box of the Render dialog box), the Save Image dialog box will have an Image Name and Directory box, in which you type the file to be saved and its path.

Next, for all situations, select the format of the file that you want to create. Your choices are TGA, TIFF, and GIF. Click Options if you want to save TGA or TIFF files in a compressed format.

If you rendered to a separate window, you will see a Portion box, where you can specify a portion of the image to save. Pick the lower-left and upper-right points. The result will be reflected in the Offset and Size boxes. Offset is the X and Y distance (in pixels) from the lower-left corner of the Portion box. Size is the X and Y pixels of the area that you selected. If you rendered to a viewport, you need to use this area to specify that you are saving part of a drawing. Specify Offset first. The numbers that appear in the boxes tell you the total pixels, so you need to work from there.

If you rendered to a viewport, select Active Viewport, Drawing Area, or Full Screen. Full Screen saves the menu areas and command line as well as the drawing.

In either case, a handy <u>R</u>eset button enables you to reset the offset and size values to the full screen or to the option you selected in the Portion area.

More Stuff

If you have Windows and rendered to a Render Window, you can choose File⇔Save from the Render Window's menu. This command saves the rendering in the BMP format.

SCALE

Changes the size of objects.

 Windows: From the Modify toolbar, click the Resize flyout and then the Scale icon.

DOS: Choose Modify⇔Scale.

How to Use It

AutoCAD prompts you to select objects. Then you specify a base point; the object will be scaled from that point. Next, type a scale factor. A factor of 2 doubles the size of the object; a factor of .25 reduces the object to one-quarter size.

You also can use the Reference option by typing **r** after you specify a base point. Specify a reference length and a new length.

SCENE

Creates, changes, and deletes *scenes*, which are like views but can have lighting effects.

 Windows: From the Render toolbar, click the Scenes icon.

DOS: Choose Tools⇔Render⇔Scenes.

How to Use It

Before using this command, you usually use DDVIEW to create a view and the LIGHT command to add lights to a drawing. The SCENE command puts a view and lights together and names them so that you can use them for rendering.

AutoCAD opens the Scenes dialog box, which simply lists defined scenes. The dialog box has three options: New, Modify, and Delete.

New   Opens the New Scene dialog box to create a new scene. Under Scene Name, type a new name. The Views section lists views. Select a view or *CURRENT* from the list. Under Lights, select as many lights as you want or *ALL*.

Modify   Select one of the scenes from the Scenes dialog box, and click Modify. The Modify Scene dialog box opens. You can change the scene name, view, and lighting.

Delete   Select one of the scenes from the Scenes dialog box, and click Delete. At the prompt, click OK to confirm the deletion.

More Stuff

Would you believe that you can have up to 500 lights in a scene? Talk about blinding!

SECTION

Creates a region from the intersection of a plane and solids. This region is the cross section of the solid.

Windows: From the Solids toolbar, click the Section icon.

DOS: Choose Draw⇨Solids⇨Section.

How to Use It

First, you need a solid to select. You also can have an object to select for the intersecting plane, or you can specify the plane during the command.

AutoCAD prompts you to select objects. If you select more than one solid, you get more than one region. Then choose options for defining the intersecting plane:

3points   Specify three points in the plane.

Object   Select a circle, ellipse, arc, 2D spline, or 2D polyline segment.

Zaxis   First, specify a point on the plane; then specify a point on the Z axis of the plane, which means a point exiting the plane perpendicularly. This is called a *normal*.

View	Specify a point in the view plane.
XY, YZ, ZX	These options align the sectioning plane with the XY, YZ, or ZX plane. You simply pick a point in the plane.

SELECT

Puts selected objects in the Previous selection set so that you can use the set with the next command.

 Windows: From the Standard toolbar, click the Select Objects flyout and then one of the icons.

DOS: Choose Assist⇨Select Objects.

How to Use It

You select objects with the SELECT command just as you do for any other command that asks you to select objects. Here, for the record, is the complete, exhaustive list of the ways you can select objects. After you select the objects, press Enter to complete the command; then you can type an editing command. Type **p** (for previous) to select all the objects.

AUto	This option is the default, so you probably are using it without knowing. The option simply means that pointing to an object selects it and that pointing to a blank space starts the first corner of a window, regular or crossing.
Add	This option, also the default, means that you can add objects to the selection set by selecting them, so that you get more and more objects.
ALL	Selects all objects in the drawing except ones on frozen or locked layers.
BOX	This option means that you select two diagonal points that define a box. If the first point you select is on the left and the second is on the right, this option is the same as Window. If you pick points from right to left, this option is the same as Crossing.

Crossing	You select two diagonal points that define a box or window, starting from the right and ending on the left. Any objects inside the box or crossing its perimeter are selected.
CPolygon	This option is like Crossing, but instead of picking two points, you pick a whole bunch of them, in a sort of roundabout direction, to create a polygon.
Fence	This option is like CPolygon, but open — a bunch of continuous lines that select any object they cross.
Group	Selects objects in a named group. You have to type the name. (See the GROUP command.)
Last	Selects the most recently created object.
Multiple	This option enables you to select objects without highlighting them during the selection process.
Previous	Selects the same objects that were selected in the last selection process. The SELECT command uses this option. The Previous option allows you to use several commands on the same set of objects. The Previous selection set gets lost if you delete objects or switch between paper and model space.
Remove	Use this option and everything you select is removed from the selection set instead of added. (This situation can get confusing.) Use the Add option when you finish removing and want to start adding.
SIngle	This option is for selecting only one object. AutoCAD doesn't prompt you to select any more objects. Because you can simply press Enter to obtain the same result, I'm not so hot on this option.
Undo	Cancels the most recent selection.
Window	You pick two points, from left to right; everything that is completely inside the box defined by those points is selected.
WPolygon	This option is the same as CPolygon, except that only objects completely inside the polygon are selected.

More Stuff

"Using the SELECT command" in Chapter 8 of *AutoCAD For Dummies* discusses this command in detail.

SETVAR

Sets values for system variables.

Windows and DOS: Choose Options⇨System Variables⇨Set.

How to Use It

System variables store all sorts of information about your drawing and about AutoCAD in general. Usually, you can use a regular command. When you use DDIM to create a dimension style, for example, you affect a whole slew of system variables that relate to dimensions.

Occasionally, you may need to change a system variable directly. If you know the variable's name, you don't even need the SETVAR command. Type the variable name and press Enter; then type the new value and press Enter to end the command.

You can get a list of all the variables by typing **?** at the first prompt.

More Stuff

See Part III of this book for a list of system variables not affected by regular commands.

SHADE

Creates a shaded image 3D object. Shading is much simpler than rendering.

Windows: From the Render toolbar, click the Shade icon.

DOS: Type **shade** at the command line.

How to Use It

When you use this command, AutoCAD shades everything in the current viewport, based on one light source.

More Stuff

If your screen shows fewer than 256 colors, SHADE does not include a lighting effect.

See "Shading" in Chapter 16 of *AutoCAD For Dummies*.

SHELL

Temporarily exits AutoCAD so that you can type commands at the DOS prompt.

Windows and DOS: Type **shell** at the command line.

How to Use It

AutoCAD offers you the DOS prompt for your pleasure. If you want to use only one command, enter it; afterward, AutoCAD pulls you back inside.

If you want to use more than one command, press Enter at the DOS prompt. You'll notice that the prompt contains an extra angle bracket (>>). Enter the commands. Then type **exit** to return to AutoCAD.

More Stuff

Do not use CHKDSK (especially with the /f option), run programs that require disk swapping, fiddle around with I/O ports, or load TSR (terminate and stay resident) programs while using SHELL. And absolutely do not delete locked files (extensions ending with *K* or temporary files (extension *.AC$* or *.$A*). CRASHSHSH!!!

SKETCH

Draws freehand line segments.

Windows: From the Miscellaneous toolbar, click the Sketch icon.

DOS: Type **sketch** at the command line.

How to Use It

This command is for you artists out there. When you start the command, AutoCAD prompts you for a *record increment* — the length of the line segments. The smaller the increment, the smoother the line. SKETCH draws temporary lines and adds them permanently when you exit. This command gives you a little menu that contains the following options:

Pen   Typing **p** raises and lowers the imaginary sketching pen. When the pen is lowered, you can sketch. Raise the pen to stop sketching.

eXit	Exits sketch mode and gives you a report on how many lines you sketched.
Quit	Erases all the temporary lines. You'll use this option a lot, because it's darn hard to get anything to look good with this command.
Record	Makes the temporary lines permanent and gives you a report on the number of lines recorded.
Erase	Erases any portion of a temporary line and raises the pen (if it is down).
Connect	Lowers the pen to continue sketching from the end of the last sketched line.
. (period)	Lowers the pen, draws a straight line from the end of the last sketched line to your current position, and raises the pen again. (You have to see this to understand it.)

More Stuff

You won't use this command often, but it's fun. You can use the command when you want to draw squiggly lines — in a map, for example. (Remember Etch-a-Sketch?)

See "Freehand sketches (free — free, at last!)" in Chapter 7 of *AutoCAD For Dummies*.

SLICE

Slices a solid with a plane. You can retain one or both sides of the sliced solid.

 Windows: From the Solids toolbar, click the Slice icon.

DOS: Choose Draw➪Solids➪Slice.

How to Use It

First, you need a solid object to slice. You also may want to have some object that you can select to define the slicing plane.

Select the solid. Then specify the plane by using one of the following methods:

3points	Specify three points in the plane.
Object	Select a circle, ellipse, arc, 2D spline, or 2D polyline segment.

Zaxis	First, specify a point in the plane; then specify a point on the Z axis of the plane, which means a point that exits the plane perpendicularly. This is called a *normal*.
View	Specify a point in the view plane.
XY, YZ, ZX	Aligns the sectioning plane with the XY, YZ, or ZX plane. You just pick a point in the plane.

AutoCAD then prompts you for a point on the desired side of the plane. If you pick a point, the part of the solid on that side of the plane is retained. The rest of the solid goes poof! Type **b** to keep both sides.

SNAP

Snaps the cursor to set intervals. This command is used for drawing to exact points.

Windows and DOS: Choose Options⇨Drawing Aids.

On most systems, you can use F9 to turn SNAP on and off. You also can press Ctrl+B.

Double-click SNAP in the status bar.

How to Use It

The shortcut methods in the preceding section only turn snap on or off, using the current value for snap spacing. To change the snap spacing, rotation, and style, use the DDRMODES command or SNAP command at the command line. For snap spacing, just type a number. Typing **.25**, for example, makes the cursor jump to every quarter-unit.

Aspect is used when you want the X and Y spacing to be different.

Rotation rotates the crosshairs and snap points from a base point. Specify the base point and rotation angle.

Style allows you to change to isometric mode. (See the ISOPLANE command.)

SOLID

Draws filled polygons.

Windows: From the Draw toolbar, click the Polygon flyout and then the Solid icon.

DOS: Choose Draw⇨Polygon⇨2D Solid.

How to Use It

First, use the FILL command to turn fill on. SOLID prompts you to specify two points. Now comes the tricky part. At the prompt for the third point, pick a point diagonally opposite the second point that you picked (this is *not* ring-around-a-rosy). If you want a triangle, press Enter at the prompt for a fourth point.

If you want more than three sides, pick a fourth point diagonally opposite from your first point. Again, you can end here by pressing Enter, but AutoCAD keeps prompting you for third and fourth points, so you can expand your polygon in new and unusual shapes.

More Stuff

Picking points around a rosy — that is, around the perimeter of your polygon — results in the famous AutoCAD bow tie that all of us have created too many times in the past. Try it, and join the family of frustrated AutoCAD users!

SPELL

Checks the spelling of text.

Windows: From the Standard toolbar, click the Spelling icon.

DOS: Choose Tools⇨Spelling.

How to Use It

Select the text that you want to spell check. The text can be text created with TEXT, DTEXT, or MTEXT. AutoCAD opens the Check Spelling dialog box. Following are the options:

Ignore   Leaves that occurrence of the word alone and goes on to the next.

Ignore All	Ignores all occurrences of the word.
Change	Changes that occurrence of the word with whatever is in the Suggestions box.
Change All	Changes all occurrences of the word to whatever is in the Suggestions box.
Add	Adds the word to the current dictionary.

You also can change dictionaries.

More Stuff

See "Checking It Out" in Chapter 10 of *AutoCAD For Dummies*.

SPHERE

Draws a 3D solid sphere.

Windows: From the Solids toolbar, click the Sphere icon.

DOS: Choose Draw⇨Solids⇨Sphere.

How to Use It

If you're looking for a smooth entry into 3D, you're in the right place. AutoCAD makes drawing spheres easy.

First, specify a 3D point for the center of the sphere (X,Y,Z coordinates). Then specify a length for the radius or type **d** to specify a diameter.

SPLINE

Draws a spline curve. A spline uses a series of points as a frame to create a smooth curve.

Windows: From the Draw toolbar, click the Polyline flyout and then the Spline icon.

DOS: Choose Draw⇨Spline.

How to Use It

Specify two to seven points to define the polyline. Press Enter when you finish picking points. Although the prompt doesn't tell you, you can type **undo** after any point to remove it (another example of AutoCAD's clear, user-friendly interface).

The SPLINE command now demands that you enter start and end tangent points to define the angle of the start and end of the spline. (No, I'm not going to give you a course in geometry here.) You can press Enter and have AutoCAD calculate default tangents.

You can type **c** to close the spline. You can choose the Fit Tolerance option and enter a value. A 0 tolerance means that the spline has to go through each point; a bigger number gives it more leeway, resulting in a less accurate but smoother curve.

More Stuff

At the first prompt, you also can choose the Object option. Then pick a 2D or 3D polyline on which you used the Spline option. SPLINE converts the polyline to a spline and deletes the polylines.

For your information, the technical name for what SPLINE draws is a quadratic or cubic Nonuniform rational B-spline (or NURBS) curve. Sounds NURBY to me.

SPLINEDIT

Edits splines.

 Windows: From the Modify toolbar, click the Special Edit flyout and then the Edit Spline icon.

DOS: Choose Modify⇨Edit Spline.

How to Use It

First, select the spline. Control points and any other controls (such as tangents and tolerance) are shown in the same color used for grips. Following is the menu:

Fit Data		This option may not appear if no controls for fitting the spline were specified. If the option appears and you choose it, you get a submenu that contains the following options:
	Add	Adds fit points to a spline. You select a fit point and then a new point. The new point goes between the selected point and the next point.
	Close	Closes the spline.
	Open	Opens a closed spline.

	Delete	Deletes a selected fit point.
	Move	Moves fit points. You get a sub-submenu (are you following me?) that allows you to move to the next or preceding point, select a point, exit the sub-submenu (whew!), or pick a new location for the fit point that you selected.
	Purge	Removes the spline's fit data from the drawing database.
	Tangents	Specifies new start and end tangents. (See the SPLINE command.)
	toLerance	Type **L** to get this option, which sets a new tolerance. (See the SPLINE command.)
	eXit	Leaves the submenu and returns to the original prompt.
Close		Same as Close in the submenu.
Open		Same as Open in the submenu.
Move Vertex		Oh no, another submenu. The Next and Previous options allow you to move from vertex to vertex. After you have it, pick the new location. Alternatively, you can choose Select Point to pick the vertex you want to move and then its new location. Of course, you also have the eXit option (thank goodness).
Refine		This command offers you suboptions so that you can add control points, elevate the spline's order (the words are so obscure that I can't even think of a joke about them, but they just mean allowing for more control points), and give more weight to certain control points, which is sort of like increasing their gravitational pull on the spline.
rEverse		Reverses the spline's direction.
Undo		Cancels the last editing operation. (You'll need this option often, I assure you.)
eXit		Ends the SPLINEDIT command.

STATS

Lists rendering information.

Windows: From the Render toolbar, click the Statistics icon.

DOS: Choose Tools⇨Render⇨Statistics.

How to Use It

This command provides the following information:

- Scene Name
- Last Rendering Type (the application used, such as AutoCAD Render)
- Rendering Time for the last rendering
- Total Faces processed during the last rendering
- Total Triangles processed during the last rendering

This command is just an opportunity for AutoCAD to brag about how complicated rendering really is. Click Save Statistics to File and type a filename if you want to save the information to a file. You can type an existing filename, and AutoCAD will append the information, giving you a running log of all your renderings.

STATUS

Lists the status of drawing statistics and modes.

Windows and DOS: Choose Data⇨Status.

How to Use It

This command simply lists the status of many of the commands you use for setting up your drawing.

STRETCH

Stretches objects.

 Windows: From the Modify toolbar, click the Resize flyout and then the Stretch icon.

DOS: Choose Modify⇨Stretch.

How to Use It

AutoCAD prompts you to select objects. You *must* use the crossing window or CPolygon method of selection. Any line, arc, or polyline that *crosses* the selection window is stretched by moving the endpoints that lie *inside* the window. Enclose the endpoints of the objects that you want stretched in the crossing window, and you'll come out OK.

Like the MOVE command, STRETCH asks you for a base point and a second point of displacement.

STYLE

Creates text styles.

Windows and DOS: Choose Data⇨Text Style.

How to Use It

AutoCAD prompts you for a text-style name. Type a name, or type **?** to get a list of current text styles.

When you type a name, AutoCAD opens the Select Font File dialog box. Select a font from the list. Click OK.

Now AutoCAD prompts you for a text height. If you type a height, that will be the height for text created with this style. Sometimes, however, you want to create a style that defines everything except the height so that you can vary it. If that's what you want, type **0.** When you enter text with such a style, AutoCAD prompts you for a height, and you can type whatever you want.

Now specify a width factor. A value of 1 is normal. A larger number gives you fat text; a smaller number (between 0 and 1) gives you skinny text.

For the obliquing angle, type an angle. Angles between 0 and 85 result in italics.

Now type **y** or **n** for Backwards, Upside-down, and Vertical. The Vertical option (like text going down the spine of a book) appears only for certain fonts that support it.

More Stuff

AutoCAD comes with one style, called STANDARD. This style is boring, so create your own.

You can use DDEMODES to set the current style. All the text commands also offer you an opportunity to change the style before you start writing your novel.

See "Text styles" in Chapter 10 of *AutoCAD For Dummies.*

SUBTRACT

Subtracts the area of one region from another or the volume of one solid from another.

Windows: From the Modify toolbar, click the Explode flyout and then the Subtract icon.

DOS: Choose Construct⇨Subtract.

How to Use It

First, select the regions or solids you want to subtract from; then select the objects you want to subtract. AutoCAD does the rest.

SYSWINDOWS

Arranges windows; equivalent to the Window menu in Windows applications. You can arrange windows in a cascade, or in horizontal or vertical tiles. You also can ask AutoCAD to arrange Windows icons automatically, for a neat and tidy screen.

TABLET

Calibrates a tablet with a paper drawing that you want to digitize.

Windows and DOS: Choose Options⇨Tablet.

How to Use It

To digitize a paper drawing, first tape the drawing neatly and securely to the digitizer tablet. Then mark three or more points on the paper — perhaps the corners. You can set the lower-left corner as 0,0. Then measure the other points, and write in their coordinates relative to 0,0. You'll need these coordinates later.

Use the CAL option to calibrate the tablet area with your drawing. Then use the ON option to turn the tablet on. On some systems, you can press Ctrl+T to toggle the tablet on and off. When you finish, turn the tablet off to return to regular drawing mode.

To calibrate the tablet area, type **CAL**; AutoCAD displays the prompt digitize point #1. With your digitizer (also called a *puck* or *stylus*), pick one of the points that you marked on the paper. AutoCAD prompts you for the point's coordinates. (I told you that you would need those coordinates.) AutoCAD keeps prompting you for points and their coordinates. You can enter as many points as you want.

Depending on how many points you entered, AutoCAD then may provide a very esoteric table that relates to various types of transformations, called Orthogonal, Affine, and Projective. You have to choose, so try Orthogonal; if you don't like the result, I refer you to AutoCAD's command reference documentation. (This information is not the stuff of a Quick Reference.)

If you use a digitizing tablet, you sometimes need to use the CFG options, which configure the menu and screen pointing areas (where you draw) of a large tablet. The menu should be attached to the tablet surface — either the one that AutoCAD provides or your own customized one. AutoCAD prompts you for the number of tablet menus you want. The menu is divided into areas; you type the number of areas that you are using. If you want to realign the tablet menu areas, type **y** at the next prompt. You need to digitize the points requested for each area. Then AutoCAD asks you how many columns and rows you want for each menu area. In this way, AutoCAD divides each menu area into little boxes, one for each command.

Finally, AutoCAD asks whether you want to respecify the screen pointing area. Type **y** if you do and digitize the points as requested.

TABSURF

Draws a 3D tabulated surface, based on a curve and a direction (called a *vector*).

Windows: From the Surfaces toolbar, click the Tabulated Surface icon.

DOS: Choose Draw⇨Surfaces⇨Tabulated Surface.

How to Use It

You need to select the *path curve*, which defines the shape of the surface, and a *direction vector*, which specifies the direction in which the shape will be extruded. You should draw these objects before using the command.

AutoCAD prompts you for a path curve and direction vector. You select objects for each of these items. The path curve can be a line, arc, circle, ellipse, polyline, or spline. The direction vector must be a line or an open polyline. AutoCAD creates the surface.

More Stuff

For the direction vector, AutoCAD ignores any intermediate meandering; it simply considers the beginning and end points.

The results of this command are somewhat like those of the EXTRUDE command, except that this command creates a surface and the EXTRUDE command creates a solid.

TBCONFIG

 Creates and customizes toolbars.

Windows: Choose Tools⇨Customize Toolbars.

How to Use It

AutoCAD opens the Toolbars dialog box. This dialog box controls three other dialog boxes that you display by clicking New, Customize, or Properties. You also can select a toolbar and delete it. The Show Tooltips button controls whether the tool name appears when you place the mouse on the tool. Unless you have memorized all the tools, keep this option checked! You can click Large Buttons if the standard ones are too itsy-bitsy for you, but of course, they'll take up much more of your screen.

Creating a new toolbar that contains the commands you use most and the ones that are hardest to get to is a great idea. Before you do so, use AutoCAD for a while, and keep a wish list of commands that you wish were more accessible. These commands will be the ones that you will put in your new toolbar. Also, before you create a new toolbar, decide which tools you want to place where. Then use the TBCONFIG command and click New. The New Toolbar dialog box opens. Type a toolbar name and menu group. (The menu group is ACAD, unless you have created a custom menu, in which case its name appears.) Then click OK. An empty toolbar of your own creation appears on-screen.

Now click Customize to add tools to your toolbar. Click Categories, and the tools for that category appear, helping you find the tool that you want. Drag the tool from the dialog box to your new toolbar. You also can copy a tool from another toolbar by holding down the Ctrl key while you drag the tool to the new toolbar. In addition, you can drag an icon to an existing toolbar.

More Stuff

There's more, lots more. You can use the Button Editor to design your own tool buttons; you can create flyouts, too. These features are not the stuff of a Quick Reference.

TEXT

Creates a line of text. (This command has been superseded, in my opinion, by DTEXT, so I refer you there.)

TIME

Lists date and time information for a drawing.

Windows and DOS: Choose Data⇨Time.

How to Use It

The TIME command displays when the drawing was created and last updated; it also tracks the total editing time minus plotting time (not including time when you worked but didn't save your changes). In addition, you can turn a timer on and off for more customized timing. (Maybe you don't want to charge a customer for correcting a mistake that was your fault.) To turn on the timer, use the ON option; to turn it off, use the OFF option. Reset brings the timer back to 0.

More Stuff

The timer is on by default, so AutoCAD is always timing you.

TOLERANCE

Creates geometric tolerances.

 Windows: From the Dimensioning toolbar, click the Tolerance icon.

DOS: Choose Draw⇨Dimensioning⇨Tolerance.

How to Use It

To use this command, you have to understand tolerances. (I'm not about to give you a lesson on the topic here.) AutoCAD creates *feature control frames*, which are little boxes that contain the tolerance information that you choose to put there. The frames are then placed next to your dimensions.

TOLERANCE first opens the Symbol dialog box. Click the type of tolerance symbol that you want. (AutoCAD's manual provides a list if you don't know which symbol to use.) Click OK.

Up pops the Geometric Tolerance dialog box, in which you build your feature control frame. This dialog box allows for up to two lines of symbols. You build a line from left to right, as follows:

Sym	This is the first column, containing the symbol you chose in the Symbol dialog box.
Tolerance 1	If you want to start with the diameter symbol, click the Dia box. Then type the tolerance value in the Value box. Click the MC box to open the Material Condition dialog box. These symbols define conditions that apply to materials that can vary in size. M is for maximum material condition, L is for At least material condition, and S means Regardless of feature size. Click the option you want, and then click OK to return to the Geometric Tolerance dialog box.
Tolerance 2	If you want a second tolerance, create it just as you did the first.
Datum 1	*Datum* refers to a theoretically exact geometrical entity from which you can verify the dimensions of your objects. First, type a reference letter that represents your first datum. Click MC if you want to insert a material condition. This process is the same one used in creating the tolerance.
Datum 2	Same procedure as Datum 1.
Datum 3	Same procedure as Datum 1.
Projected Tolerance Zone	Type a height, and click the Projected Tolerance Zone box to put in the Projected Tolerance Zone symbol.

The dialog box disappears, and AutoCAD prompts you for the tolerance location. Pick a point; AutoCAD inserts it.

TOOLBAR

Shows, hides, and moves toolbars.

Windows: Choose Tools⇨Toolbars; or click the Toolbar flyout and then any icon.

How to Use It

To show a toolbar, click the name of the toolbar that you want to show.

To hide a *floating* toolbar (one that floats somewhere in the drawing area and is not *docked* on the edges of the screen), click the Control-menu button in the upper-left corner. If the toolbar is docked, you can use a simple (and undocumented) method to hide it: First, float it (see the end of this section) and then click the Control-menu button.

The only things left to know are how to dock a floating toolbar and how to float a docked one. These terms may be making you seasick, but you'll soon see that setting up your drawing space for your ease and comfort is worthwhile.

To dock a floating toolbar, click the toolbar name, and then drag the toolbar to the top, bottom, left side, or right side of the screen. The toolbar changes to fit its new location.

To float a docked toolbar, click the gray border around its edge and then drag the toolbar to the drawing area.

More Stuff

See the TBCONFIG command for information on changing or creating a toolbar.

TORUS

Draws a 3D donut.

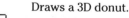

Windows: From the Solids toolbar, click the Torus icon.

DOS: Choose Draw⇨Solids⇨Torus.

How to Use It

First, specify the center with a 3D point. Then type a value for the radius of the torus, which means the outside radius. Next, type a value for the radius of the tube, which is half the width of the tube (not the distance from the center of the torus to the inside tube circumference.) At each radius prompt, you also can type **d** and then specify a diameter.

TRACE

 Draws lines that can have a width.

This command has been superseded by the PLINE command.

TRIM

Trims objects at an edge created by another object.

 Windows: From the Modify toolbar, click the Trim flyout and then the Trim icon.

DOS: Choose Modify⇨Trim.

How to Use It

First, select the cutting edge. (You can select more than one edge.) The object that you want to trim will be cut off where it intersects that edge (or those edges). You also can trim the object to where it *would* intersect the cutting edge if the cutting edge were extended (called an *implied intersection*).

Now select the object to be trimmed. Pay attention — you have to select the object on the part of it that you want to trim. If you have selected two edges and want the object to be trimmed between then, select the object between the edges. The result is like the BREAK command.

If the edge has only an implied intersection with your object, use the Edge option and then turn on the Extend option before selecting your object. That way, AutoCAD will know to calculate the implied intersection. Be sure to select the object on the side you want to trim.

More Stuff

Trimming in 3D is a bit more complicated, as you might expect. Select the cutting edge and then type **p** (for projection). You have three projection choices:

None   Trims objects that intersect with the cutting edge in true 3D (you know — real life on your computer screen).

Ucs   Projects on the XY plane of the current User Coordinate System (UCS).

View   Projects along the current view plane.

You can use the Edge option for 3D trimming as well.

U

Undoes the last operation.

 Windows: From the Standard toolbar, click the Undo icon; or choose Edit⇨Undo.

DOS: Choose Assist⇨Undo.

How to Use It

U is one of the nicest, sweetest commands around; you could hug it. Amazingly, you can use this command over and over; AutoCAD undoes every (well, almost every) command until you get to where you were at the beginning of the drawing session. Now *that's* a database.

More Stuff

 U cannot undo things such as plotting or saving your drawing.

See the UNDO command, which is a more robust version of U.

UCS

Manages the User Coordinate System (UCS).

Windows: From the Standard toolbar, click the UCS flyout. This command covers several of the icons in this flyout. Or choose View⇨Set UCS.

DOS: Choose View⇨Set UCS.

How to Use It

The simplest way is not necessarily the most intuitive way, but it may work for you. When you use the UCS command's 3point option, you first specify the origin, using X,Y,Z coordinates. (Feel free to leave the point 0,0,0, if that works for you.) Then specify a point on the positive X axis. Finally, specify a point on the positive Y axis. That's all you have to do — the Z axis is calculated automatically.

By the by, the default option is World, which gets you back to the default plan view. It's your panic button when you get confused from flying around the Earth so fast.

Often, you use a custom UCS because drawing a 3D object is easier if your axes are aligned with the object. Suppose that you're drawing a house. If you could fly over one side of the angled roof and draw from there, drawing would be a cinch — just a simple rectangle. Choose the OBject option and select the object. You can pick arcs, circles, lines, 2D polylines, solids, 3D faces, and a few other things (such as dtext and dimensions). When you have the basic alignment, you can use the other options to further customize the UCS to your liking.

Another nice option is View. Set up the view that you want, using DDVPOINT or VPOINT. When you see that this is the way to go, choose the View option of the UCS command. AutoCAD creates a new UCS based on your view.

After you create your UCS, don't forget to use the Save option. Type a name and press Enter. Typing **?** offers you a list of defined UCS names.

Following are the rest of the options:

Zaxis   Tilts the current X and Y axes in the direction of your new Z axis. You simply specify a point on the positive Z axis that you want.

X/Y/Z   Rotates the current UCS around the axis that you specified (X, Y, or Z). You then type an angle. If you're really adventurous, you can specify a negative angle.

Prev   Restores the preceding UCS. AutoCAD can step you back through the last 10 UCSes.

Restore   Makes a saved UCS the current UCS. Enter a name, or type **?** to get a list. You also can use the DDUCS command in a dialog box.

Del   Deletes a named UCS.

?   Lists defined UCSes, and provides their origin and X,Y,Z axes relative to the current UCS.

More Stuff

A UCS sets the direction of the X,Y,Z coordinates. Setting the viewpoint is a separate process, which you perform with DDVPOINT or VPOINT. If you restore a UCS and don't understand why you're looking at things from such a strange angle, use the PLAN command to return to the plan view of the UCS.

UCSICON

Manages the UCS icon itself (which usually appears in the lower-left corner of your screen). This command doesn't affect the UCS.

Windows and DOS: Choose Options⇨UCS⇨Icon.

How to Use It

The ON option displays the UCS icon; OFF turns it off. All shows the icon in all viewports instead of just the current one. Noorigin (sounds like Norwegian) shows the icon at the lower-left corner of your screen or viewport, no matter where the UCS origin is. Origin forces the icon to appear at the origin, if possible.

UNDO

Undoes commands.

Windows and DOS: Type **undo** at the command line.

How to Use It

This command is the big brother or sister (are commands masculine or feminine?) of the U command. Amazingly, AutoCAD retains a database of every action performed during a drawing session, so you can undo commands and return to the pristine state at which you started. Following are the options:

Number   This is the default. Type a number, and AutoCAD reverses the effect of that many commands. The difference between using this option and using U five times is simply that this option does not cause regeneration between each undoing. (Using U five times may or may not cause regeneration, depending on the commands.)

Auto   Undoes any operation performed with a menu used as one command.

Control   This option displays a submenu, which contains the options that control the way UNDO works. All gives you the full UNDO command. None turns off the U and UNDO commands. (Be careful — being able to undo commands is always nice.) One limits UNDO to reversing one command.

BEgin   This option groups a series of commands. Use this option when you're trying something new and exciting (but a little dangerous) and you want to be able to undo your work in one fell swoop.

End   Ends the group started by BEgin.

Mark   Places a mark at the current location. You then use the Back option to undo back to the mark.

Back   This option can be dangerous. You use Back to undo commands back to the most recent mark. But if you haven't created any marks, watch out. Luckily, AutoCAD displays this prompt: `This will undo everything. OK?` Quickly type **n** unless you want to undo everything that you've done today!

More Stuff

Obviously, some commands can't be undone. If you used the LIST command to get information about an object, AutoCAD won't get inside your head and remove the knowledge that you gained. (That's not on my list for a new feature for AutoCAD 14, either!)

UNION

Creates one combined region or solid from two or more regions or solids.

Windows: From the Modify toolbar, click the Explode flyout and then the Union icon.

DOS: Choose Construct⇨Union.

How to Use It

This command is how two regions or solids join in holy matrimony (very unexciting, I assure you). First, select the objects.

If the objects aren't regions or solids and can be converted, AutoCAD converts them. All you have to do is watch. (I told you, it's okay; nothing too risqué happens.)

'UNITS

See the DDUNITS command, which manages units from a dialog box.

UNLOCK

Unlocks locked files.

Windows: Choose File⇨Management⇨Unlock File.

DOS: Choose File⇨Management⇨Utilities. In the File Utilities dialog box, choose Unlock File.

How to Use It

Locked files are used in networked systems so that only one person can work on a file at a time. AutoCAD automatically locks a file when it is in use and unlocks it afterward. *You can destroy your file if you try to unlock it while it is in use. Never, ever unlock a file unless you're sure that no one else is using it.*

If you're sure that it's OK to use UNLOCK, go ahead. Select the file in the File(s) to Unlock dialog box and click OK. AutoCAD double-checks with you, giving you the name of the person who locked the file (so that you can mosey on over and ask why the file is locked). Then choose Yes to unlock the files or No to cancel the procedure.

More Stuff

If you aren't on a network, you can turn file locking off by using the CONFIG command.

'VIEW

See the DDVIEW command.

VIEWRES

Sets the resolution for circles and arcs, and controls Fast Zoom mode.

Windows & DOS: Type **viewres** at the command line.

How to Use It

AutoCAD first asks whether you want fast zooms. You almost always do.

Now comes the reason why you came to this command in the first place. AutoCAD asks you to enter a circle zoom percentage (1 to 20,000) and tells you the current setting. The higher the setting, the smoother your circles and arcs will be, and the slower AutoCAD's speed will be. Lower numbers speed things, but circles can look like polygons. Usually, you can get a setting that gives you smooth circles, and you won't notice the millisecond decrease in speed.

VPLAYER

Freezes and thaws layers within viewports.

Windows and DOS: Choose Data⇨Viewport Layer Controls.

How to Use It

First, TILEMODE must be off (0). Because you have to have TILEMODE on to create viewports, you'll probably have to deal with this situation. On Windows systems, you can click the TILE button in the status bar. On DOS systems, choose View⇨Tiled Model Space. You can't work with a layer that's frozen.

List	Lists frozen layers in a selected viewport. (This option appears as **?** in the command line.)
Freeze/Thaw	Choose one or the other. Type a layer name or several layer names, with commas between the names. The All suboption affects all viewports. The Current suboption affects only the current viewport. The Select suboption allows you to select the viewports that you want to affect. Press Enter to complete the command.

New Freeze   (This option is Newfrz in the command line.)
                    Use this option to create new layers that will be
                    frozen in all viewports. Type the names of the
                    new layers, with commas between them. Press
                    Enter to complete the command.

Default Visibility (This option is vpvisdflt — say that five times,
                    fast — in the command line.) This option
                    determines whether certain layers will be
                    frozen or thawed in newly created viewports.
                    Type a layer name, and then type **f** (for frozen)
                    or **t** (for thawed).

Reset   Resets layer visibility to the default setting.
                    Type a layer name, and use the Current, All, or
                    Select suboptions as for <u>F</u>reeze or <u>T</u>haw.

More Stuff

You can use the DDLMODES dialog box for many of these things.
Notice the Cur VP (stands for Current Viewport) and New VP
(stands for New Viewport) buttons in the dialog box.

VPOINT

Controls the 3D angle from which you view your drawing.

Windows and DOS: Choose View⇨3D Viewpoint⇨Tripod.

How to Use It

The VPOINT command does the same thing as the DDVPOINT
command, except that it offers a different conceptualization of 3D
space from which to define your viewpoint.

Imagine that you're Superman, flying around the Earth. In an
instant, you can see the Earth from any viewpoint that you
choose. Pick a longitude — let's say at Greenwich — to be your
left/right dividing line. The equator is the top/bottom dividing
line. This process is how you define viewpoints in 3D.

A compass and tripod appear. You pick your viewpoint on the
compass and see the results on the tripod, which is just X,Y,Z
axes moving in space.

The center of the compass is the North Pole, equivalent to plan view (the familiar 2D way of looking at things from the top). The inner circle is the equator. The outer ring is the South Pole. The whole Southern Hemisphere has been flattened out so that you can see it. Anywhere you click inside the inner circle results in a view from above. Anywhere you click between the inner and outer circles results in a view from below.

You also have to choose the corner of the Northern or Southern Hemisphere above which you are flying, cape streaming out behind you. You do this by paying attention to the crosshairs that go through the circles. Anything below the horizontal crosshair is a front view; anything above the horizontal crosshair is a back view. To the left of the vertical crosshair is a view from the left. To the right of the vertical crosshair is a view from the right.

These front, back, left, and right directions are meaningful in relationship to the plan view. As you're flying around the Earth, you really don't have a front, back, left, or right. But when you look at things from the top, you think that way — or else get very disoriented and come falling back to Earth like a meteor.

I hope that this explanation helps. Otherwise, create a model that doesn't look the same on all sides, start picking points, and see the results.

When you figure out where to click, just click; AutoCAD returns you to your drawing.

More Stuff

See the UCS command for information on creating a User Coordinate System based on your new view over Australia.

VPORTS

Creates tiled viewports.

Windows and DOS: Choose View⇨Tiled Viewports.

How to Use It

First, set the tilemode to 1. On Windows systems, double-click the TILE button in the status bar. On DOS systems, choose View⇨Tiled Model Space.

AutoCAD calls the number and layout of viewports *viewport configurations*. Options 2, 3, and 4 divide the screen into 2, 3, or 4 viewports (did you guess?). The 2 option offers horizontal and vertical suboptions. The 3 option offers you the possibility of putting the biggest viewport above, below, left, or right or having three equal horizontal or vertical viewports. The Layout option offers pictures of all these configurations; click the one you want and then click OK.

When you have your viewports, use the Save option and give the configuration a name. Typing **?** lists other saved configurations.

Use the Restore option to bring back saved configurations. (Bring back, Bring back, Oh bring back my viewports to me, to me. Do you think it'll make the Top 40?) Use the Delete option to delete configurations.

Join combines two adjacent viewports. Pick the *dominant* viewport first and then the secondary one. The new viewport will have the zoom, viewpoint, and other features of the dominant one (which simply means that you picked it first).

SIngle is your panic button for getting rid of all those unruly viewports and returning to one viewport, the default. The one viewport will show the view of the active viewport.

If you're working in 3D, now is the time to use the DDVPOINT or VPOINT command to do something interesting with your viewports. Click anywhere inside a viewport to make it active, and create different views in each viewport. Even if you're working in 2D, viewports can show different parts of your drawing at different zooms. The possibilities are endless!

More Stuff

See the section, "Viewports in model space," in Chapter 16 of *AutoCAD For Dummies* for more on the VPORTS command.

WBLOCK

Saves a block as a file on your hard disk. (WBLOCK stands for Write block.)

Windows: Type **wblock** at the command line.

DOS: Choose File⇨Export⇨Block.

How to Use It

AutoCAD opens the Create Drawing File dialog box. Type a name for the file and click OK. WBLOCK prompts you for a block name, which you can type. Often, you want the file and block to have the same name. (It helps when the copy has the same name as the original.) In that case, type an equal sign (=). Then press Enter. WBLOCK saves the block as a file on your hard disk so that you can use it in other drawings.

You also can create a block and save it as a file in one command. At the Block name prompt, press Enter; WBLOCK displays all the usual BLOCK prompts. In this case, the objects that you selected are deleted, just as with the BLOCK command. Use OOPS to restore the objects.

More Stuff

See the BLOCK and OOPS commands for more information.

See "Playing With Blocks," in Chapter 16 of *AutoCAD For Dummies* by Bud Smith, for a discussion on blocks.

WEDGE

Draws a 3D solid wedge.

 Windows: From the Solids toolbar, click the Wedge icon.

DOS: Choose Draw⇨Solids⇨Wedge.

How to Use It

At the prompt, specify a first corner for the base of your wedge. Then specify a diagonally opposite base corner. If the Z values of your points are different, AutoCAD uses the difference to create the height of the wedge. If the Z values are the same, AutoCAD prompts you for a height.

The cube option means a wedge with sides of equal length. You still specify the first point. Then type **c** (for cube) and type a length allowing you to define length, width, and height after specifying a first corner.

More Stuff

You can enter negative distances to draw the wedge in the direction of the negative axes.

XLINE

Draws an infinite line (used for construction lines).

 Windows: From the Draw toolbar, click the Line flyout and then the Construction Line icon.

DOS: Choose Draw⇨Construction Line.

How to Use It

AutoCAD prompts for a first point. Because this line theoretically is an infinite line, the point really just defines where the line will be. Pick a second through point. AutoCAD creates the xline.

You also can use horizontal and vertical options. You pick one point, and XLINE creates a horizontal or vertical xline. For the Angle option, you specify an angle — either by typing it or referencing it to a selected object and then typing an angle relative to that object. Then pick a through point.

You can draw an xline that bisects an angle vertex. Use the Bisect option; then pick an angle vertex, start point, and end point.

The Offset option creates an xline parallel to another object. Type an offset distance, select a line, and pick a point that indicates what side to offset. Alternatively, use the Through suboption to specify the offset distance by picking a through point.

XPLODE

Breaks blocks and other compound objects into individual components; gives you control of color, layer, and linetype.

Windows and DOS: Type **xplode** at the command line.

How to Use It

XPLODE prompts you to select objects. If you select more than one explodable object, the next prompt asks you whether you want to explode individually or globally. In either case, the suboptions are the same. If you select individual exploding, AutoCAD highlights objects one at a time so that you can make your decisions individually. Following are the options:

Explode   Same as the EXPLODE command.

All	Sets color, linetype, and layer of the individual objects after you explode them. You get the same suboptions as for Color, LAyer, and Ltype.
Color	Sets the color of the exploded objects. You can choose any of the standard AutoCAD colors, or you can choose BYBlock or BYLayer. Setting the color by block means that the objects will take on the color of the original block.
LAyer	Sets the layer of the exploded objects; otherwise, they would take on the current layer.
LType	Sets the linetype of the exploded objects. You can choose BYBlock, BYLayer, CONTinuous, or other loaded linetypes. Setting the linetype by block means that the objects take on the linetype of the original block.
Inherit from parent block	This is what happens to baby blocks when their parents die. But in AutoCAD language, it means that the color, linetype, and layer of the exploded objects will be the same as the exploded block if its layer is 0 and the linetype is BYBLOCK.

More Stuff

See "Creating and writing out blocks" in Chapter 15 of *AutoCAD For Dummies* for more on blocks and layers.

XREF

Manages references to external files. (*Xref* stands for external references in AutoSpeak.)

Windows: From the External Reference toolbar, click one of the icons. (This command covers all the icons.)

DOS: Choose File⇨External Reference.

How to Use It

Xrefs are external drawings that you insert into your drawing. You use Xrefs in much the same way that you use blocks. The main value of Xrefs is that each time you open or plot your drawing, the Xrefs are reloaded, so any changes in the external drawings are reflected in your drawing. Following are your options:

Attach	This option connects an external reference to a drawing.
?	When you type **?**, you can type in the name of a specific Xref or press Enter to get a list of all Xrefs.
Bind	Turns an Xref into a block and cuts the reference to the external drawing. AutoCAD asks you for the name of the Xref.
Detach	Erases the Xrefs and cuts the reference to the external drawing. The advantage of using this option instead of simply erasing the Xref is that you also get rid of the layers, colors, linetypes, and other elements of the Xref.
Path	If someone (not you, of course) had the nerve to rename or move the external drawing that you are referencing, your drawing won't be able to find it. Use this option to type the new path (including a new filename, if necessary) for the Xref.
Reload	If someone else changes the external drawing while you are working in your drawing, you can reload the Xref when that person is finished to see the changes.
Overlay	When you overlay a drawing, you get an image that is not attached to your drawing. This option is useful when you simply want to compare objects in different drawings.

For each option (except the path option), select or type the name of the file that you want to use.

More Stuff

See "Going External" in Chapter 15 of *AutoCAD For Dummies*.

XREFCLIP

Inserts a clipped portion of an Xref.

Windows: From the External Reference toolbar, click the Clip icon.

DOS: Choose File⇨External Reference⇨Clip.

How to Use It

This command is done in paper space, which AutoCAD prompts you to turn on.

AutoCAD prompts you for the Xref name. The next prompt is
Clip onto what layer? You need to type a new layer name —
one that doesn't already exist. The image covers the screen. Now
pick two diagonal corners to define a rectangular clip box.

You can specify a scale of paper-space units to model-space units.
First, type the paper-space units; then, type the model-space
units. Alternatively, accept the defaults of 1 for each prompt by
pressing Enter. Finally, AutoCAD returns you to your drawing so
that you can pick an insertion point.

'ZOOM

Magnifies or shrinks objects in your drawing.

Windows: From the Standard toolbar, click the Zoom flyout; or
choose View⇨Zoom.

DOS: Choose View⇨Zoom.

How to Use It

AutoCAD offers lots of zooming options. In Windows, each option
has a separate icon in the Zoom flyout.

Scale (X/XP)	This is the default. Typing a number scales the display relative to the drawing limits. If you type **3**, the display appears three times the size that you would see after using Zoom with the All option. This option can be confusing if you have another zoom value. So you can type **3x**, which scales the display relative to your current view. If you type **3xp**, AutoCAD scales the display relative to paper space units; use this format when in paper space.
All	You'll use this option a lot. AutoCAD zooms to the drawing limits or extents, whichever is greater. In a 3D view, this option is equivalent to ZOOM Extents.
Center	First, pick a center point for the new view; then specify a magnification or height. A height is a plain number that represents drawing units. Type **10**, for example, to get a display that is 10 drawing units high. To specify magnification, type a number followed by x — for example, **10x**, which magnifies the display by 10.

Dynamic	This option is a way of panning and zooming at the same time. The display zooms out, and a view box appears. This view box alternates between pan and zoom mode. The box starts out as a pan box, indicated by an X in the middle. Drag the box until you find the location in the drawing that you want; then click that location. You switch to zoom mode, which is indicated by an arrow at one edge. Move your mouse, and you'll see that the view box changes size instead of moving around the drawing. Resize the box until you have the window that you want to see. Press Enter to complete the command, or click to return to pan mode.
Extents	Displays the entire extents of the drawing.
Left	This option is just like Center, except that the point you select becomes the lower-left corner of the display.
Previous	Displays the preceding view. You can use this option up to 10 times before AutoCAD forgets.
Vmax	Zooms out as far as possible without regeneration.
Window	Pick two opposite corners of the display that you want to see.

More Stuff

Another option is Aerial View. (See the DSVIEWER command.)

ZOOM options that require a regen cannot be done transparently. Never fear — AutoCAD will let you know.

See Chapter 9 of *AutoCAD For Dummies*.

Part III

The System Variables

In this part of the book, you enter the exotic, arcane world of system variables. *System variables* are simply values that AutoCAD stores for all sorts of things. These variables allow you to fine-tune the way that AutoCAD works. Many system variables just provide information and, to tell you the truth, a lot of them are used only in LISP programs. Once upon a time, you had to use system variables frequently; nowadays, many of them are handled automatically by the choices that you make in dialog boxes. When you use the DDIM command to create a dimension style, you are working with system variables without knowing it (which is the best way, believe me).

Because so many system variables are handled automatically by regular commands, they are less important than they once were. Therefore, I have included only the system variables that are not accessible by regular commands. These variables are the ones that you may want to use directly. I've left out some additional system variables that only apply to customizing AutoCAD or using LISP program routines.

I have categorized the system variables by type to help you find them more easily.

You used to have to type **setvar**, then the name of the system variable, and then its value. AutoCAD now kindly allows you to simply type the name of the system variable in the command line, followed by its value. You can press Enter after the name of the system variable or just use a space. Press Enter after the value to complete the process. If the system variable just provides information, just press Enter after you type in the system variable name. Many system variables simply turn things on and off. A value of 0 means off; a value of 1 means on — usually!

TIP

Type **'HELP** at the SYSVAR name to see what the options are.

Most lists of system variables are not very useful, but on the rare occasions when you need to use a system variable, look here; I hope this list will speed you on your way. For more information, choose Help⇨Contents and then select System Variables.

3D

DISPSILH. Related to the ISOLINES system variable, which sets the number of lines on a 3D surface. DISPSILH turns on (1) and off (0) the display of silhouette curves of surface objects in wire-frame mode, so that no matter which viewpoint you use, you always see an isoline showing you the shape of the curve.

FACETRES. Affects the smoothness of 3D objects that are shaded or have hidden lines. You can set this variable from .01 to 10.

ISOLINES. The number of isolines per surface on an object; can range from 0 to 2047. The default is 4, which is pretty puny but may be okay in a large drawing to speed regeneration time.

SHADEDGE. Controls the way edges are shaded. Values are

0   Shades faces, but edges not highlighted

1   Shades faces and highlights edges

2   Doesn't shade faces, hides hidden lines, shows edges

3   Highlights edges only, with no lighting effect

Even though 1 probably is the most useful setting, 3 is the default.

SHADEDIF. Sets the percent of diffuse reflective light to ambient light. The default is 70. You may find 50 to be a useful value. Values can range from 0 to 100.

SURFTAB1. The number of tabulations used in the RULESURF and TABSURF commands. Also, for the REVSURF and EDGESURF commands, this variable sets the M (row) direction.

SURFTAB2. Sets the N (column) direction for the REVSURF and EDGESURF commands.

SURFU. The surface density in the M (row) direction. Applies to polyface meshes, such as the ones created by 3DMESH.

SURFV. The surface density in the N (column) direction. Applies to polyface meshes, such as the ones created by 3DMESH.

UCSFOLLOW. Determines whether AutoCAD returns you to plan view when you change the UCS. A value of 0 means that you do not return to plan view; 1 means that you do. The default is 0.

Attributes

ATTDIA. Determines whether you get a dialog box when you use the INSERT command to insert a block that contains attributes. A setting of 0 says that you don't get the dialog box; a setting of 1 says that you do.

ATTREQ. If you set to 0, AutoCAD uses default attribute values when you insert a block with attributes. If you set to 1, AutoCAD prompts you for values. The default is 1.

Dimensioning

DIMASO. Turns associative dimensioning on and off. If associative dimensioning is off, the parts of the dimension are separate objects and do not adjust when you change the dimensioned objects. The variable's values are ON and OFF.

DIMCLRD. Assigns color to dimension lines, arrowheads, and leader lines. DIMCLRD is for creating dimensions that have more than one color. You can type a color number or name, or BYBLOCK or BYLAYER.

DIMCLRE. Assigns a color to dimension extension lines. DIMCLRE is for creating dimensions that have more than one color. You can type a color number or name, or BYBLOCK or BYLAYER.

DIMCLRT. Assigns a color to dimension text. DIMCLRT is for creating dimensions that have more than one color. You can type a color number or name, or BYBLOCK or BYLAYER.

DIMLFAC. The global scale factor for linear dimensions. The default is 1. If you use this variable in paper space (which generally is where you want to use it) with the viewport option, AutoCAD calculates the scale factor for you, based on the zoom scale of the viewport. You must use the DIM command. Then type **dimlfac** and press Enter. Type **v** for viewport and press Enter. Select the viewport by which you want to scale. Type **exit** to leave the DIM command.

DIMSAH. Turns on and off the use of user-defined arrowheads. When the variable is off, normal arrowheads or the arrowhead defined by the DIMBLK variable used. When the variable is on, user-defined arrowhead blocks are used. You specify user-defined arrowheads with the DDIM command.

DIMSHO. When this variable is on, associative dimensions are recomputed continually as you drag an object. (Associative dimensions change automatically when you change the object.) If this feature slows your computer, turn DIMSHO off.

DIMSOXD. Suppresses dimension lines that otherwise would be outside extension lines. (DIMSOXD is not a baseball team.)

DIMTIX. Places text inside extension lines (if the variable is on).

Drawing Aids

EXPERT. This variable is for the experts among you who get annoyed when AutoCAD asks things such as `Block already defined. Redefine it?` ("Of course, I want to redefine it; why do you think I'm doing this?") A value of 0 is the normal setting. Values ranging from 1 to 5 suppress more and more prompts.

MAXACTVP. Specifies the maximum number of viewports that will be regenerated at one time. The default is 16.

PSLTSCALE. Controls the linetype scale in paper space. The value of this variable is to have the same linetype scale for objects shown at different zoom scales in different viewports in paper space. The variable creates a more uniform effect, which is the default setting of 1. A setting of 0 scales the linetypes to the space in which they were created.

TILEMODE. Turns on (1) and off (0) tiled viewport mode. Turning this mode off allows you to enter paper space. Using the PSPACE command from the menu or the status bar turns tilemode off automatically. You would use this variable when you use the PSPACE command at the command line.

VISRETAIN. Sets the visibility of layers in Xref files. A setting of 0 means that Xrefs take on the layer definition in the current drawing. A setting of 1 means that the layer settings in the Xref drawing take precedence.

WORLDVIEW. Determines whether the UCS changes to the WCS when you use DVIEW or VPOINT. A value of 0 means that the UCS remains unchanged; a value of 1 means that it switches to the WCS.

Edits

EXPLMODE. Determines whether EXPLODE explodes blocks that are nonuniformly scaled (NUS), which means that the X and Y scales are different. The default is to explode them (value of 1), but you can turn the feature off (0).

MIRRTEXT. When you are mirroring objects that include text, a value of 1 (the default) mirrors the text just like anything else. A value of 0 keeps the text looking normal, so that you don't need to look into a mirror to read it. This variable is a good one to know.

Information/Customization

Most of these variables provide information only. Many of the variables are *read-only*, which means that you can look at them and sigh, but you can't change anything.

ACADPREFIX. The directory path of the ACAD environment.

ACADVER. The AutoCAD version number.

AREA. The last area calculated by AREA, LIST, or DBLIST.

AUDITCTL. Determines the creation of an audit report file.

CDATE. Sets the date and time.

CMDACTIVE. Stores what kind of command is active.

CMDDIA. Turns dialog boxes on and off. If you set this variable to 0, you will not see dialog boxes. The default is 1.

CMDNAMES. The name of the active command.

DATE. The date and time in Julian format.

DBMOD. The drawing modification status.

DCTCUST. The custom spelling dictionary file.

DCTMAIN. The main spelling dictionary file.

DELOBJ. Determines whether objects used to create other objects are maintained in the drawing database. The default (1) retains these objects; a value of 0 deletes them.

DISTANCE. The distance calculated by the DIST command.

DWGNAME. The drawing name.

DWGPREFIX. The directory path for the drawing.

DWGTITLED. Indicates whether you've named your drawing.

DWGWRITE. How you opened the drawing: for reading only (just looking at) or for reading and writing (you can make changes).

EXTMAX. The upper-right corner of the drawing extents.

EXTMIN. The lower-left corner of the drawing extents.

FILEDIA. Turns on and off the display of dialog boxes that deal with files, such as the Open dialog box.

LASTANGLE. The end angle of the last arc that you drew.

LASTPOINT. The last point entered.

LIMMAX. The upper-right drawing limits.

LIMMIN. The lower-left drawing limits.

LOCALE. The ISO (International Standards Organization) language code of the current AutoCAD version.

LOGINNAME. The user's name (probably you). This is for networks that require a login name.

MAXSORT. Sets a maximum number of symbol or file names to be sorted by commands that list such things. The default is 200.

MENUECHO. Sets menu echo and display prompting.

MENUNAME. The current menu name.

PERIMETER. The last perimeter value calculated by AREA, LIST, or DBLIST.

PFACEVMAX. The maximum number of vertices per face.

PLATFORM. The computer platform that you are using (Windows, DOS, Macintosh, stage right, stage left, and so on).

PLOTID. Changes the default printer, based on the description you assigned when you configured AutoCAD.

PLOTTER. Changes the default printer, based on its assigned number, starting from 0.

RASTERPREVIEW. Determines whether drawing preview images are saved with the drawing and what type of images are saved.

SAVEFILE. Stores the filename that AutoCAD uses in auto-saving. Set the auto-save time by choosing Options⇨Preferences⇨ System tab (Windows) or Options⇨Auto Save Time (DOS).

SAVENAME. Stores the filename to which you save the drawing.

SCREENBOXES. The number of boxes in the screen menu area.

SCREENSIZE. The size, in pixels, of the current viewport.

SHPNAME. The default shape name.

TEMPPREFIX. Sets a directory name for temporary files.

TREEDEPTH. Configures the spatial index, which structures the database of objects.

TREEMAX. Limits the size of the spatial index, saving memory.

VIEWCTR. The center of the view of the current viewport.

VSMAX. The upper-right corner of the virtual screen.

VSMIN. The lower-left corner of the virtual screen.

WORLDUCS. Stores whether the UCS is the same as the World Coordinate System. A value of 0 means that the UCS is different; a value of 1 means that the UCS and the WCS are the same.

XREFCTL. Determines whether Xref log files (logs of Xref activity) are created. These files have the same name as a drawing and an *.XLG* extension. A value of 0 means that no log is created; a value of 1 means that it is. If you do lots of Xref work on a file, the log can get long, so you may want to delete it from time to time.

Object Creation

PELLIPSE. Determines whether the ELLIPSE command creates a true ellipse or a polyline representation of one. A value of 0 (the default) draws a true ellipse. A value of 1 creates a polyline representation of an ellipse. This concept of a polyline ellipse is a holdover from previous releases of AutoCAD.

SKPOLY. A value of 0 means that SKETCH creates lines; a value of 1 means that it creates polylines.

SPLFRAME. Sets spline-fit polyline display. If the value is 0, the frame that controls a spline or polygon mesh is not displayed; also, invisible edges of 3D faces and polyface meshes are not displayed. If the value is 1, you see the frame of a spline or polygon mesh, and invisible edges of 3D faces and polyface meshes.

SPLINESEGS. Sets the number of line segments that each spline generates. A higher number results in a curve that more precisely matches the frame.

SPLINETYPE. Determines type of spline curve created by PEDIT spline. Choose 5 for quadratic B-spline; 6 for cubic B-spline.

SURFTYPE. Sets the type of surface fitting used by the PEDIT Smooth option for 3D Polygon Meshes. Type **5** for a quadratic B-spline, **6** for a cubic B-spline, and **8** for a Bezier surface.

Text

FFLIMIT. Sets the maximum number of PostScript and TrueType fonts that can stay in memory. Values can range from 0 to 100. A value of 0 means no limit.

FONTALT. Sets an alternative font that AutoCAD will use if the font that you ask for cannot be found. (Little AutoCAD lost her fonts and didn't know where to find them.)

FONTMAP. A font-mapping file that lists substitutes for fonts. Each line lists an AutoCAD font, followed by a semicolon and the name (including path) of the substitute font. You need to create your own file — a plain ASCII text file. If you have DOS, you need to use this system variable to name the new file.

If you have Windows, choose Options➪Preferences; then click the Misc. tab in the Preferences dialog box. In the Font Mapping File section, type the filename you have created. This variable may be useful to import an AutoCAD drawing into Word for Windows and use a Windows font instead of the AutoCAD font.

TEXTQLTY. Sets the resolution of Bitstream, TrueType, and Adobe Type 1 fonts. You can set values ranging from 0 to 100. The default is 50, which is equivalent to 300 dots per inch (dpi). A value of 100 is equivalent to 600 dpi.

TEXTSIZE. Stores the default or last height for text styles without a fixed height.

TEXTSTYLE. The current text-style name.

Part IV

The Menus and Toolbars

This part guides you through the menus and toolbars. If you want to do something in AutoCAD but don't know the command name, try looking here. Menus and toolbars are usually organized by function; this part allows you to skim through the possibilities and find the command you need.

The menu items and toolbar ToolTips are not always the same as the command name, although they usually make more sense; the command names are often in unintelligible abbreviations. Luckily, when you choose a menu item or toolbar icon, the command name appears on the command line (well, most of the time).

Here's how you find the name of the command:

1. Choose a menu item or icon that looks useful.

2. At the next prompt, press Esc to cancel the command.

3. Look on the command line. You should see the name of the command. If the command name scrolls by too fast for you to see, press F1 (DOS) or F2 (Windows) to open the text screen. (Press F1 or F2 again to return to your drawing.)

4. Look up the command in Part II of this book.

A word about the ToolTips that are supposed to give you some tip about the function of the icon. Sometimes a tip such as the one AutoCAD gives you can be your worst enemy. The most you can say is that it's sometimes like a foul tip when the batter has two strikes: It keeps you in the game but doesn't get you much of anywhere. And those little pictures are not always very communicative of the icon's function either; sometimes a word is worth a thousand pictures. This section includes the ToolTip name next to each icon anyway, and occasionally an explanatory footnote when the ToolTip seems to do more harm than good. Also, a short explanation appears on the status bar when the ToolTip pops up that may provide the information you need.

One thing I have done is give you the name of each flyout. These flyout names don't show up on your screen, unfortunately, even though they are necessary to understanding the flyouts. Often Autodesk seems to assume that you know the names of the flyout, even though they are a well-kept secret. (How I discovered all their names is *my* secret!) I sometimes use the flyout names in Part II when I explain how to access a command, so if you're having trouble finding a command, look it up here.

AutoCAD for Windows Menus

The File menu

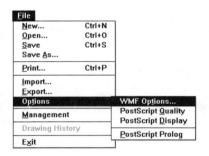
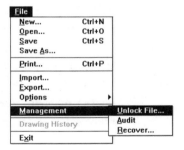

The Edit menu

The View menu

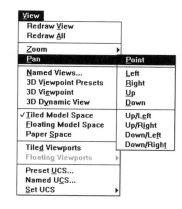

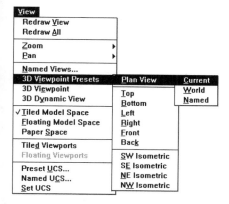

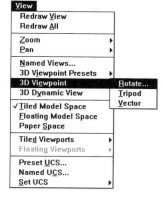

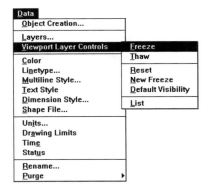

The Data menu

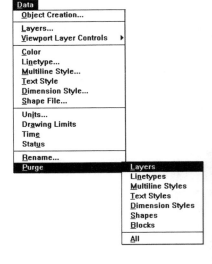

Viewport Layer Controls applies to layers in floating viewports. This is grayed out until you go into paper space and create floating viewports.

The Options menu

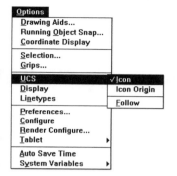

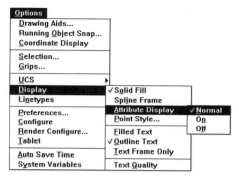

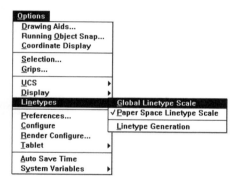

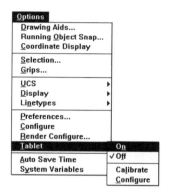

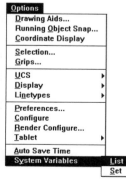

The Tools menu

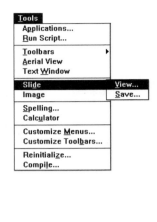

The Help menu

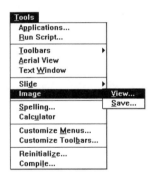

AutoCAD for Windows Toolbars

The Standard toolbar

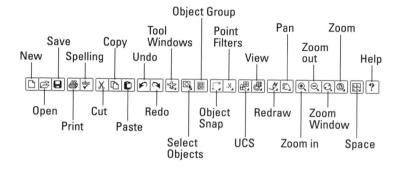

- As mentioned in the introduction to this part, Print is really the PLOT command.
- Cut, Copy, and Paste are the CUTCLIP, COPYCLIP, and PASTECLIP commands, respectively.

The Tool Windows flyout

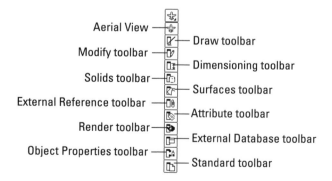

TIP For some reason the Aerial View icon hides a flyout that lists the toolbars. Click on the one you want to display. Since you're not likely to be able to figure out which icon is which toolbar, use Tools⇨Toolbars instead.

The Select Objects flyout

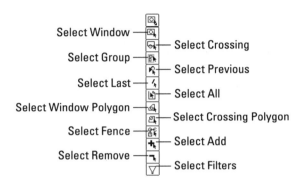

Select Window — Select Crossing
Select Group — Select Previous
Select Last — Select All
Select Window Polygon — Select Crossing Polygon
Select Fence — Select Add
Select Remove — Select Filters

The Object Snap flyout

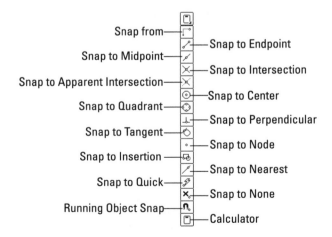

Snap from — Snap to Endpoint
Snap to Midpoint — Snap to Intersection
Snap to Apparent Intersection — Snap to Center
Snap to Quadrant — Snap to Perpendicular
Snap to Tangent — Snap to Node
Snap to Insertion — Snap to Nearest
Snap to Quick — Snap to None
Running Object Snap — Calculator

The Point Filters flyout

The UCS flyout

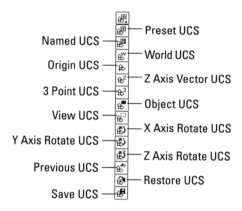

The View flyout

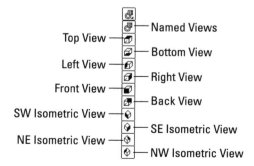

The Redraw flyout

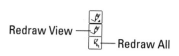

Redraw View

Redraw All

The Pan flyout

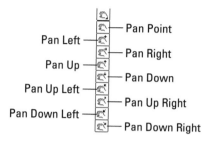

Pan Left

Pan Point

Pan Up

Pan Right

Pan Up Left

Pan Down

Pan Down Left

Pan Up Right

Pan Down Right

The Zoom flyout

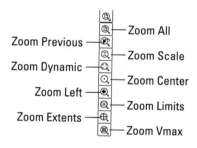

Zoom Previous

Zoom All

Zoom Dynamic

Zoom Scale

Zoom Left

Zoom Center

Zoom Extents

Zoom Limits

Zoom Vmax

The Space flyout

Floating Model Space

Tiled Model Space

Paper Space

The Object Properties toolbar

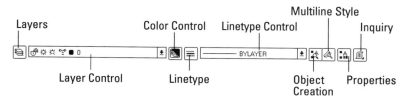

Multiline Style

Layers   Color Control   Linetype Control   Inquiry

Layer Control   Linetype   Object Creation   Properties

- Layers is equivalent to the DDLMODES command. Use this to create layers. Layer Control sets the current layer.
- Color Control is equivalent to DDCOLOR.
- Linetype is equivalent to the DDLTYPE command. Linetype Control just makes a linetype current.
- Object Creation is equivalent to the DDEMODES command. It sets properties such as layer, color, linetype, and so on, for new objects.
- Properties is equivalent to the DDMODIFY command.

The Inquiry flyout

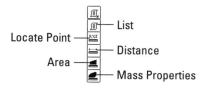

List

Locate Point

Distance

Area

Mass Properties

Locate Point is the same as the ID command.

The Draw toolbar

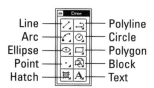

Line — Polyline
Arc — Circle
Ellipse — Polygon
Point — Block
Hatch — Text

The Line flyout

Line
Ray
Construction Line

Construction line is the same as an xline. See the XLINE command.

The Polyline flyout

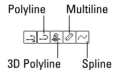

Polyline   Multiline
3D Polyline   Spline

The Arc flyout

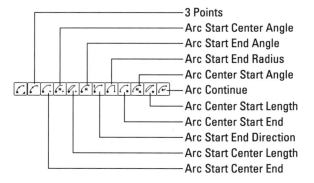

3 Points
Arc Start Center Angle
Arc Start End Angle
Arc Start End Radius
Arc Center Start Angle
Arc Continue
Arc Center Start Length
Arc Center Start End
Arc Start End Direction
Arc Start Center Length
Arc Start Center End

Somewhere along the line the word *arc* got left out of the 3 Point tool. It should say *Arc 3 Point* to be consistent with the options in the flyout. Luckily, the picture of the arc is pretty clear.

The Circle flyout

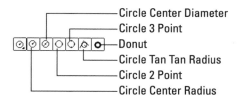

Circle Center Diameter
Circle 3 Point
Donut
Circle Tan Tan Radius
Circle 2 Point
Circle Center Radius

The Ellipse flyout

Ellipse Center

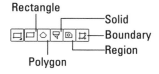

Ellipse Arc

Ellipse Axis End

The Polygon flyout

Rectangle

Solid

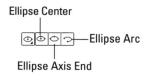

Boundary
Region

Polygon

The Point flyout

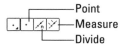

Point
Measure
Divide

The Block flyout

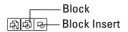

Block
Block Insert

The Hatch flyout

—— Hatch
—— PostScript Fill

The Text flyout

—— Text
—— Single Line Text
—— Dtext

The Modify toolbar

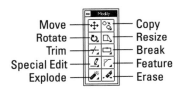

Move	Copy
Rotate	Resize
Trim	Break
Special Edit	Feature
Explode	Erase

The Copy flyout

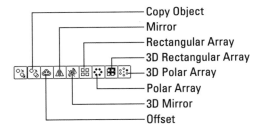

—— Copy Object
—— Mirror
—— Rectangular Array
—— 3D Rectangular Array
—— 3D Polar Array
—— Polar Array
—— 3D Mirror
—— Offset

The Rotate flyout

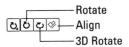

—— Rotate
—— Align
—— 3D Rotate

The Resize flyout

Stretch
Lengthen
Change
Scale

Point is equivalent to the CHANGE command with the point option. This could have been made just a wee bit clearer.

The Trim flyout

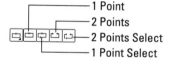

Trim
Extend

The Break flyout

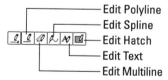

1 Point
2 Points
2 Points Select
1 Point Select

The Special Edit flyout

Edit Polyline
Edit Spline
Edit Hatch
Edit Text
Edit Multiline

The Feature flyout

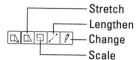

Chamfer
Fillet

The Explode flyout

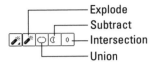

- Explode
- Subtract
- Intersection
- Union

The Dimensioning toolbar

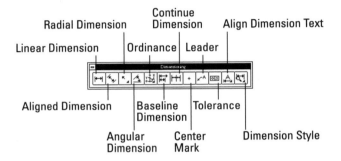

Radial Dimension
Continue Dimension
Align Dimension Text
Linear Dimension
Ordinance
Leader

Aligned Dimension
Baseline Dimension
Tolerance

Angular Dimension
Center Mark
Dimension Style

The Radial Dimension flyout

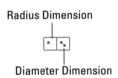

Radius Dimension

Diameter Dimension

The Ordinance flyout

- Automatic
- Y-Datum
- X-Datum

TIP

Automatic: Kill this one! This is actually equivalent to the DIMORDINATE command. Could you have guessed?

The Align Dimension Text flyout

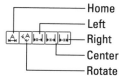

- Home
- Left
- Right
- Center
- Rotate

Home, Rotate, Left, Center, Right. These are equivalent to the DIMTEDIT command with its various options.

The Dimension Style flyout

- Dimension Styles
- Oblique Dimensions

The Solids toolbar

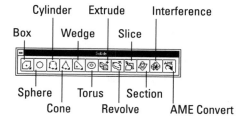

Cylinder Extrude Interference

Box Wedge Slice

Sphere Torus Section

Cone Revolve AME Convert

The Box flyout

- Center
- Corner

Here again, it's a little confusing to have a ToolTip that just says Center or Corner. Luckily, the icon pictures are fairly clear.

The Cylinder flyout

—Center
—Elliptical

The Cone flyout

—Center
—Elliptical

The Wedge flyout

—Center
—Corner

The Surfaces toolbar

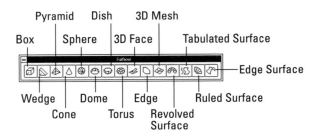

Pyramid Dish 3D Mesh
Box Sphere 3D Face Tabulated Surface
—Edge Surface
Wedge Dome Edge Ruled Surface
Cone Torus Revolved Surface

The External Reference toolbar

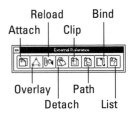

Reload Bind
Attach Clip
Overlay Path
Detach List

The Bind flyout

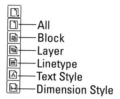

— All
— Block
— Layer
— Linetype
— Text Style
— Dimension Style

The Attribute toolbar

Define Attribute   Edit Attribute

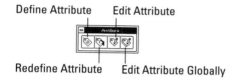

Redefine Attribute   Edit Attribute Globally

The Render toolbar

Render   Materials Library
Hide   Lights   Statistics

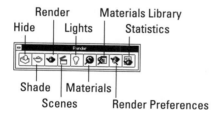

Shade | Materials
Scenes   Render Preferences

The Miscellaneous toolbar

Oops!
Mesh | Sketch

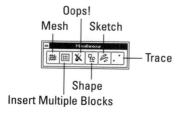

— Trace

Shape
Insert Multiple Blocks

AutoCAD for DOS Menus

The File menu

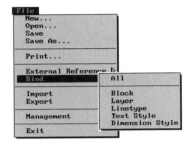

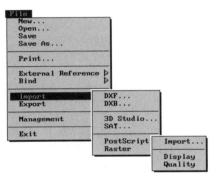

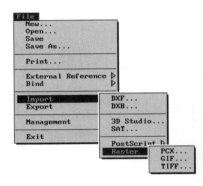

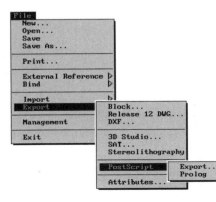

The Assist menu

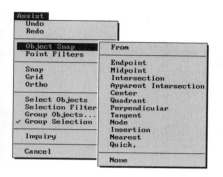

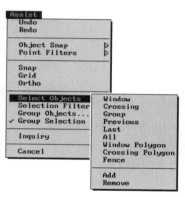

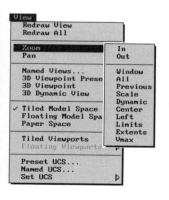

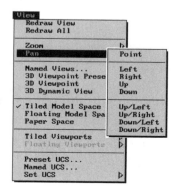

The View menu

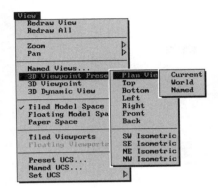

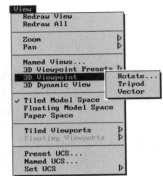

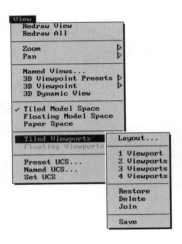

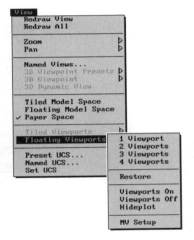

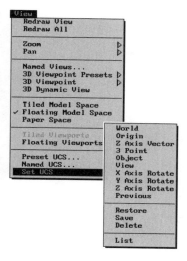

The Draw menu

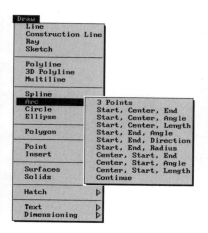

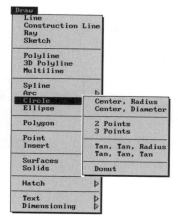

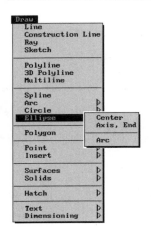

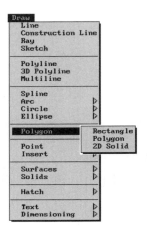

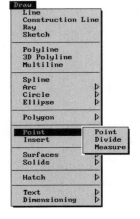

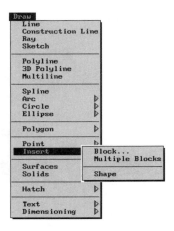

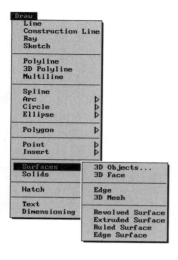

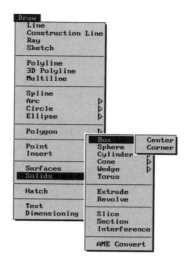

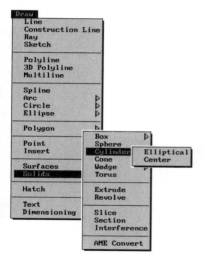

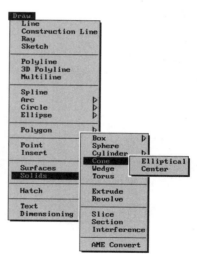

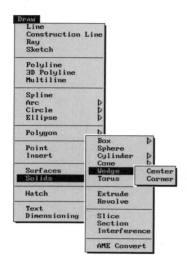

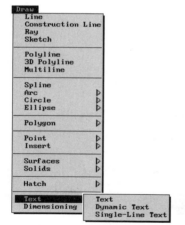

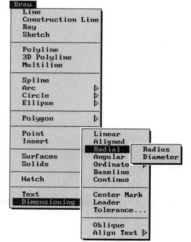

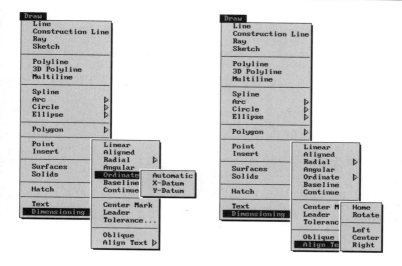

The Construct menu

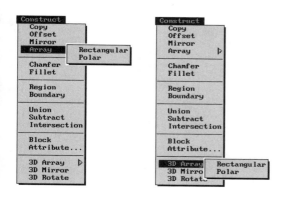

The Modify menu

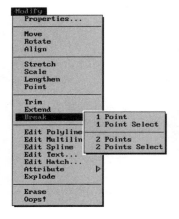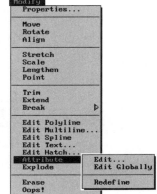

The Data menu

The Options menu

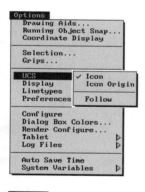

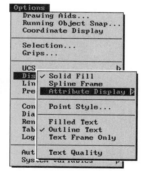

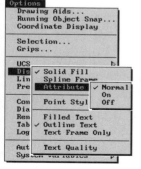

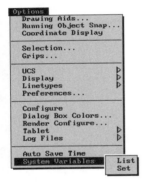

The Tools menu

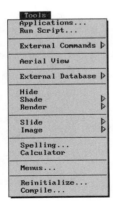

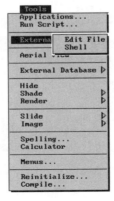

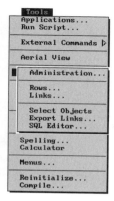

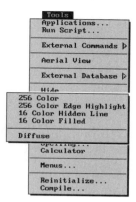

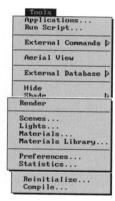

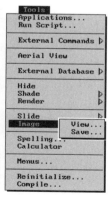

The Help menu

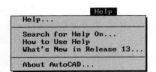

Part V

Glossary

No book on AutoCAD is complete without a glossary. The terms used in AutoCAD often are so obscure that understanding how to use the program becomes difficult, a concept I've called AutoSpeak in this book (after Newspeak in George Orwell's *1984*).

I hope that this glossary helps you; it includes some of the terms that always stumped me. If you can't find a term here, try the index and look up the page indicated. You may find that I defined the term in the main text.

ACAD environment variable. Tells AutoCAD where certain files that it needs are located — that is, their drive and directory.

ADI. AutoCAD Device Interface. A specification created by Autodesk, the creator of AutoCAD, that sets standards for drivers for printers, screens, plotters, and so on.

Aerial View. A window for zooming and panning. See the DSVIEWER command.

alias. A short name for an AutoCAD command. You can customize the ACAD.PGP file to create your own — for example, CI for CIRCLE and CO for COPY.

ambient light. Overall background light used for rendering. See the RENDER and LIGHT commands.

annotation. Text, dimensions, tolerances, symbols, or notes that explain a drawing.

aperture. The little box that appears when you use an object snap. The aperture is different from the pickbox (look under *P* for that one).

aspect ratio. The ratio of width to height on a computer screen. The aspect ratio is used for importing and exporting graphics.

associative. Applies to dimensions and hatches; means that these elements adjust themselves when you change the objects to which they're attached.

attribute. Text attached to a block that can be assigned a specific value each time that the block is inserted. All these values can be extracted and turned into a database, such as a bill of materials. See the DDATTDEF and ATTEXT commands.

AutoLISP. AutoCAD's version of the LISP programming language. You can use AutoLISP to write programs that control the way that AutoCAD functions.

B-spline. A curve defined by control points that you choose; also called a NURBS curve. See the SPLINE and SPLINEDIT commands. Also see the SPLINETYPE and SURFTYPE system variables.

Bezier curve. A type of B-spline curve. See the SURFTYPE system variable.

bind. To turn an external reference (Xref) into a regular block.

bitmap. A type of graphic defined by each pixel (rather than by vectors).

blips. Little markers on the screen that show where you specified a point. REDRAW gets rid of blips. See the BLIPMODE command.

block. One or more objects grouped to create a single object.

Boolean operation. Adding, subtracting, or overlapping solids or 2D regions.

boundary. A closed region or polyline. See the BOUNDARY command.

BYLAYER. Means that an object takes its color and linetype from its layer definition; you don't have to worry about the color and linetype. Many commands offer this option.

Cartesian coordinate system. A way of defining point locations using three perpendicular X,Y,Z axes.

chord. A line that connects two points on a circle or arc. See the ARC command.

clipping planes. Planes that cut off the field of view. See the DVIEW command.

color map. A table that defines color in terms of red, green, and blue (RGB) intensity. Anytime you use the color slider bars or color wheel, you're using the color map. See DDCOLOR.

command line. The place where you type AutoCAD commands, coordinates, or values.

control point. A point (usually, many points) that you specify to control where a spline curve curves.

coordinate filters. A way of extracting a coordinate point by filtering out one or two of the X, Y, or Z coordinates; also called point filters. See the section on filters in Part I.

digitizer. An electronic flat board that allows you to draw and execute commands with the tablet template. You use something called a puck, stylus, or digitizer, which is similar to a mouse but has crosshairs that provide for exact point specification.

DXF. Drawing Interchange Format; an ASCII file format that contains all the information of a drawing. DXF is used to import or export drawings between programs.

entity. Another word for an object (which is another word for anything in your drawing).

environment. The location of and settings for other files on which AutoCAD depends, such as ACAD.DWG (the prototype drawing).

explode. To break a block into its original objects. See the EXPLODE and XPLODE commands.

external reference (Xref). Another file that is referenced in your file, creating a link between the two. See the XREF command.

fence. A set of lines that you use to select objects. Anything that crosses the fence gets sent to jail for trespassing. See the SELECT command.

file locking. A means of preventing more than one person from working on a file at a time. File locking is appropriate for networks. Turn it off using the CONFIG command unless you're on a network.

fit points. Points that a curve must come close to or pass through. See the SPLINE and SPLINEDIT commands.

floating viewports. Bordered views of a drawing that show different viewpoints and/or zooms of your objects. Floating viewports, which are created in paper space with tilemode off, are objects that you can move, resize, and delete.

flyout. A bunch of hidden icons that fly out when you click the top icon. A flyout is just a secondary menu in disguise.

freeze. A mode for a layer that means that the layer is not displayed, regenerated, or plotted.

grid. A rectangular grid of regularly spaced dots that cover the screen. Grids help you get a feel for the unit size and assist you in drawing; if you don't like them, just grid and bear it. Otherwise, see the GRID and DDRMODES commands.

grips. Small squares that appear on objects when you select them. You can use grips to modify the objects directly. See the DDGRIPS command.

group. A named group of objects that you can select and modify as a group. See the GROUP command.

hatch. A pattern of lines used to fill a closed area to indicate shading or a type of material (bricks, grass, and so on).

hidden surfaces. Surfaces that would be hidden from a certain viewpoint. These surfaces are eliminated in the rendering process. See the RENDER command.

island. An enclosed area within a hatch area — for example, a small circle within a big circle. See the BHATCH command.

isolines. Lines that AutoCAD uses to show the curve of a surface. Isolines are like tessellation lines.

isometric drawing. A drawing that places the X,Y,Z axes 120 degrees from one another, used in 2D drawing to give the appearance of 3D objects.

linetype. A type of line. Linetype indicates whether the line is continuous or formed of dots, dashes, and spaces.

M direction. When AutoCAD draws 3D meshes, the M direction is set by the way that you define the first and second rows.

M size. When AutoCAD draws polygon meshes, the M size is the number of rows.

mass properties. Properties of an object that has volume, such as center of gravity.

materials. Materials are used in rendering. Materials are called by the names of real materials — such as steel, glass, and plastic — and are defined by their color, reflective qualities, and roughness (which affects highlights created by a light source). Materials are attached to objects. See the RMAT, MATLIB, and RENDER commands.

mesh (or mesh surface). A bunch of connected polygons that create faces and that together represent the surface of a curved object. By specifying the vertices of the polygons, you define the surface. A mesh has no mass or weight properties (unlike solids) but can be shaded and rendered. See the 3D, 3DMESH, PFACE, RULESURF, TABSURF, REVSURF, and EDGESURF commands.

model. A 2D or 3D drawing of a real object. AutoCAD has three 3D model types: wire frame, surface, and solid.

model space. The place where you create models, which means where you draw. Model space is different from paper space, in which you can lay out your drawing for plotting (if you want). See the MSPACE command.

node. The same as a point.

normal. A line that is perpendicular to a plane or surface; used to define a new plane in some editing commands. See the SLICE and SECTION commands.

Noun/Verb Selection. Selecting the object (noun) before the command (verb). See the DDSELECT command.

NURBS. Stands for nonuniform rational B-spline; a B-spline defined by a series of control points.

object. Anything that is considered to be one element in your drawing, such as a line, a circle, or a line of text. An object is the same as an element.

object snap. Called OSNAP in AutoSpeak; geometric points on an object that you can select automatically — for example, end-points, midpoints, and circle centers.

ortho mode. A setting that limits you to drawing horizontally or vertically.

orthogonal. Having perpendicular intersections.

paper space. A drawing mode used for laying out a drawing for plotting. In paper space, you create floating viewports with different views of your drawing. See the PSPACE, MVSETUP, and MVIEW commands.

parallel projection. A way of viewing a 3D object without showing perspective. See the DVIEW command.

pickbox. The little box that appears at the cursor when you see a `Select objects` prompt. You can change the size of the pickbox by using the DDSELECT command. (I never can remember which is which between the aperture — also called the target box — and the pickbox; I'm sure that it's just me.)

pixel. Short for picture element. Pixels are the teensy-weensy dots that make up the picture on your screen. Certain graphics programs allow you to change objects by changing them pixel by pixel.

plan view. The view of an object looking straight down from above. Plan view is the only accurate view for 2D objects but only one possible view for 3D objects.

polyline. A group of lines and arcs that are treated as one object. See the PLINE and PEDIT commands.

primitive. A basic 3D shape, such as a box, wedge, cone, cylinder, sphere, or torus. (When you have a desire to draw one of these shapes, it's called a primitive urge.)

prototype drawing. A drawing that contains certain settings (layers, styles, and so on) and that is used as the basis for new drawings.

raster image. An image created by converting math and/or digital information into a series of dots.

redraw. To refresh the screen, thereby getting rid of blip marks and stray remains of editing commands. Redrawing makes you feel like new!

reflection. The levels of highlights created by light on a surface. See the RMAT command.

region. A closed 2D area. See the REGION command.

resolution. The number of pixels that can be displayed on a computer screen, or the number of dots per inch printed on a printer. *Resolution* just means how clear the image is.

right-hand rule. A hokey but effective way to figure out which way is up (which way the Z axis goes). Hold the back of your right hand near the screen. Point your thumb in the direction of the positive X axis. Point your index finger up in the direction of the positive Y axis. Stick your middle finger straight out (not up; that's naughty!) at right angles to your index finger. That's the positive Z axis.

roughness. The spread of the highlight produced by a material's reflection. See the RMAT command.

ruled surface. A surface created between two curves or between a point and a curve. See the RULESURF command.

running object snap. An object snap that stays on until you turn it off. If you have a running endpoint object snap, every time you select an object, you'll be selecting the endpoint of the object. It's also a warning that if you run into an object, something might go snap. See the DDOSNAP command.

selection set. The group of objects that you have selected.

shape. A special kind of object that has been defined with certain customization codes and compiled into a compressed form. *Shape* usually refers to fonts; it doesn't mean any old regular shape that you draw on your screen.

snap. When snap is on, the cursor jumps to the nearest point defined by the snap spacing; you can't get to anything in between. See the SNAP command.

spline. A smooth curve passing through or near control points that you specify. AutoCAD uses a particular kind of spline called a NURBS (nonuniform rational B-spline) curve. (Sounds nurby to me.)

surface. A topological 2D area. You can create a surface by using surface commands, such as 3D, 3DMESH, TABSURF, RULESURF, and REVSURF.

system variable. Variables storing modes and values that affect the way that AutoCAD functions. Some system variables are read-only; many others, you can set. See Part III for an exhaustive (and exhausting) list.

tabulated surface. A kind of ruled surface defined by a curve and a line or polyline that indicates a direction.

temporary files. AutoCAD creates temporary files during a drawing session. These files usually are closed when you exit, but if your system crashes, they may be left on your hard disk (especially **.DWK* files if you have file locking on).

tessellation lines. Lines that help you visualize a curved surface. Tessellation lines are like isolines.

tiled model space. A drawing mode in which you can divide the drawing space into viewports that cannot be overlapped and that are arranged next to one another like floor tiles. See the tilemode system variable as well as the VPORTS command, which creates multiple tiled viewports.

tolerances. The amount of variance allowable in an object, shown after a dimension. Tolerances can be shown as limits tolerances or plus/minus tolerances.

ToolTip. The description of an icon when you put the cursor over a toolbar icon for a couple of seconds. ToolTips are supposed to be helpful.

transparent commands. Commands that can be used while you're in the middle of another command. Transparent commands appear with an apostrophe in front of the command name, because that's how you type them in the command line.

unit. Any distance that you use for measuring purposes. The unit is the basis of all coordinates. When you plot your drawing, you can set the unit equal to inches or millimeters. See the UNITS command.

User Coordinate System. A coordinate system that you define by specifying where (relative to the World Coordinate System) the origin is, as well as the direction of the X,Y,Z axes. See the UCS command.

vector. Any object that has direction and length, such as a line.

viewpoint. A location in 3D from which you can view your drawing.

viewport. A rectangular box that contains all or part of your drawing. There are two kinds of viewports: tiled and floating. Tiled viewports are used in model space with the TILEMODE system variable on. Floating viewports are used in paper space with the TILEMODE system variable off; these viewports are actual objects that you can edit. See the TILEMODE system variable; also see the VPORTS, MVIEW, MSPACE, and PSPACE commands.

virtual screen. An imaginary screen held in memory that allows AutoCAD to quickly translate complex coordinates held in the database into actual coordinates on your screen.

wire frame. A representation of a 3D object, using lines and arcs.

World Coordinate System. A coordinate system that is used as the basis for all other systems that you might define.

Index

IDG BOOKS WORLDWIDE REGISTRATION CARD

RETURN THIS REGISTRATION CARD FOR FREE CATALOG

Title of this book: AutoCAD For Dummies Quick Reference

My overall rating of this book: ❏ Very good [1] ❏ Good [2] ❏ Satisfactory [3] ❏ Fair [4] ❏ Poor [5]

How I first heard about this book:

❏ Found in bookstore; name: [6]

❏ Book review: [7]

❏ Advertisement: [8]

❏ Catalog: [9]

❏ Word of mouth; heard about book from friend, co-worker, etc.: [10] ❏ Other: [11]

What I liked most about this book:

What I would change, add, delete, etc., in future editions of this book:

Other comments:

Number of computer books I purchase in a year: ❏ 1 [12] ❏ 2-5 [13] ❏ 6-10 [14] ❏ More than 10 [15]

I would characterize my computer skills as: ❏ Beginner [16] ❏ Intermediate [17] ❏ Advanced [18] ❏ Professional [19]

I use ❏ DOS [20] ❏ Windows [21] ❏ OS/2 [22] ❏ Unix [23] ❏ Macintosh [24] ❏ Other: [25]

(please specify)

I would be interested in new books on the following subjects:
(please check all that apply, and use the spaces provided to identify specific software)

❏ Word processing: [26]

❏ Spreadsheets: [27]

❏ Data bases: [28]

❏ Desktop publishing: [29]

❏ File Utilities: [30]

❏ Money management: [31]

❏ Networking: [32]

❏ Programming languages: [33]

❏ Other: [34]

I use a PC at (please check all that apply): ❏ home [35] ❏ work [36] ❏ school [37] ❏ other: [38]

The disks I prefer to use are ❏ 5.25 [39] ❏ 3.5 [40] ❏ other: [41]

I have a CD ROM: ❏ yes [42] ❏ no [43]

I plan to buy or upgrade computer hardware this year: ❏ yes [44] ❏ no [45]

I plan to buy or upgrade computer software this year: ❏ yes [46] ❏ no [47]

Name: _____ Business title: [48]

Type of Business: [49]

Address (❏ home [50] ❏ work [51]/Company name: _____)

Street/Suite#

City [52]/State [53]/Zipcode [54]: _____ Country [55]

❏ **I liked this book!**
You may quote me by name in future IDG Books Worldwide promotional materials.

My daytime phone number is _____

IDG BOOKS

THE WORLD OF COMPUTER KNOWLEDGE

❏ YES!
Please keep me informed about IDG's World of Computer Knowledge. Send me the latest IDG Books catalog.